The Enlightened Journey of Eff C'effsky

Peter Weber '22

The Enlightened Journey of Eff C'effsky

by peter dueber

outskirts press
DENVER, COLORADO

This is a work of fiction. The events and characters described herein are imaginary and are not intended to refer to specific places or living persons. The opinions expressed in this manuscript are solely the opinions of the author and do not represent the opinions or thoughts of the publisher. The author has represented and warranted full ownership and/or legal right to publish all the materials in this book.

The Enlightened Journey of Eff C'effsky
All Rights Reserved.
Copyright © 2015 Peter Dueber
v4.0 r1.0

Cover Image: William Steidel www.steidelsart.com

This book may not be reproduced, transmitted, or stored in whole or in part by any means, including graphic, electronic, or mechanical without the express written consent of the publisher except in the case of brief quotations embodied in critical articles and reviews.

Outskirts Press, Inc.
http://www.outskirtspress.com

Hardback ISBN: 978-1-4327-8957-2
Paperback ISBN: 978-1-4787-5330-8

Outskirts Press and the "OP" logo are trademarks belonging to Outskirts Press, Inc.

PRINTED IN THE UNITED STATES OF AMERICA

We are all on a journey,
following various paths across
The Great Mountain of Life. Guidance is not
mandatory, but it is highly recommended over
the sometimes difficult terrains. Fortunately,
my Sherpas have also been my friends.
Thank you ~ Laurie, Sam, Teter,
Randy, Diane and Marilee.
I love you all.

Peter

Chapters

1. This Story Begins..................1
2. "Efffff"..................13
3. The Pageleaf..................20
4. Saturday Arrived..................38
5. In The Days That Followed..................55
6. "Toss Him On My Back!"..................60
7. As Dark As Halloween..................67
8. In The Realm Of Valrhun..................72
9. A Lady With Hair Of Burgundy..................87
10. "My Odyssey"..................91
11. Inside The Walls Of The Keep..................106
12. The Night Air Was Cool And Fresh..................128
13. "The Drunk!"..................139
14. In The Safety Of Their Own Room..................147
15. The Aroma Of Fresh Bread..................157
16. A Torch..................167
17. From Somewhere In The Hall..................176
18. A Troupe Of Six..................180
19. "I'm Not Going That Way,"..................185
20. The Battle Was Won..................194
21. The Eight Sided Room..................199
22. A Heavy Drizzle..................207
23. The Blocks Of Stone Echoed..................212

24. "This Door Be Bolted 224
25. God Bless Sister Margaret.......................... 230
26. "Greasy Little Devils".................................. 236
27. The Best That Quimby Could Do.............. 246
28. "No Suit Of Armour?"................................. 260
29. "Peevis? Right?" 265
30. "I Don't Understand," 274
31. Goblin Bodies.. 277
32. A Cloud Of Sadness 283
33. "And This Be Muk!".................................... 291
34. Nommie And Theodore............................. 298
35. "Bravo...Well Done!" 301
36. The Sign Read... 313
37. "We Must Be In Haste," 317
38. She Was Breathing................................... 320
39. Stepping Into The Unknown 325
40. Hurdling The Pile Of Stones..................... 331
41. The Length Of The Entryhall.................... 336
42. There Are Times In Life............................ 343
43. It Was A Peaceful Evening 349
44. Muk Awoke.. 357
45. A Heroes Celebration............................... 360

Prologue

Every child of the Realm has heard of the legend of Avery, the spry Halfling, and her heroic flight to freedom. It is an ancient tale celebrated in song and dance by all of the clans ~ HUMAN, DWARF, GNOME, FAERIE and ELF. In fact, if not for the bravery of this extraordinary young girl, who is to say that the five clans were ever to escape the Dark Years of imprisonment beneath the impregnable fortress walls of Darmund.

But there is an even grander tale to be told. Unheralded before now, it is an equally unlikely story, not of a particular battle or celebrated event, but an entire lifetime of courage, sacrifice and utter determination. It is a truly unique story of a young boy and his amazing, no, 'enlightened' journey ~ both to and from.

This is not a tale of fantasy, mind you, although it may well suggest itself to be one, given the fact that it begins well after it starts, and ends at the exact same place, only later.

However, not meaning to befuddle you ~ and hopefully, if this museful, spoony old man can keep the events in proper order ~ perhaps both of these stories will begin to make more sense if I start somewhere closer to one of the beginnings…

Chapter One

This Story Begins

…and ends on the same narrow, winding and bumpy road, but with much to understand between the then and the now. Through the thick, green hemlock, the fir and alders…lined with gorse and blackberry…it is a road that curls down to a wide, open gravel drive beneath a hill of green lawn. It is a well-kept lawn that almost reaches completely around an old, gray and weathered, four story building ~ 'The Rafferty Home For Boys'.

Lying on his back beside a faded rhododendron bush and hidden from view of the others playing atop the grassy knoll, there is a young boy. Alone and to himself, he is forming pictures with his outstretched hand against the late September sky. It is a rare and brief moment of peace.

Pronounced "healthy" that first and hapless day that he had been brought to the "Home", he has no memory of things before that time. His waking childhood memories never embrace the tender recollection of a mother or a father, although his heart and dreams forever whisper a vague reassurance and the enduring hope that he might be something more than the orphan he was.

But sometimes…sometimes late, late at night, when all the other boys were fast asleep and no one was connected to the surrounding energy, the young lad's head would fill with visions of a mother's loving face. Or a father's steadfast arms wrapped around him, swinging him around and around, then high into the air…stretching to give him the world…the birds, the clouds, the sky. But these passing visions, like his imaginary drawings in the sky, were sadly, always just beyond his reach. And, unfortunately, like most of his dreams, they quickly faded, replaced by the sudden and demanding reality of the "Home".

"There he is…" a voice shouted as a chorus of heavy feet stampeded across the lawn toward the lone boy. Did I mention that those were not at all happy times for the lad? That he was forever being bullied?

"Get Eff!"

"Get the Squirt!" came the cry of yet more voices.

Because he was small for his age, they had nicknamed him "Squirt", which he didn't mind really. It seemed that just about all the boys at the orphanage had a nickname. It was when they called him "Elfie" that he hated, which was on account of his ears…and the tiny points that stuck out on the top of them.

Abruptly, Eff was pulled back to reality and quickly

pushed himself up from the grass. With the others in hot pursuit, he ran pell-mell across the drive and through the open front doors of the orphanage ~ banging them closed behind him. This was the "Home" *he* was used to...never a lack of noise or bodies clawing for attention or dominance. A place where fighting was as common as oatmeal and toast was for the morning meal ~ even though officially, there were strict rules forbidding rough-housing or any such behavior. Actually, there were endless rules about proper behavior at the "Home", but only one ruler ~ Mr. Wittlesey!

At that very minute, both the front doors and the door to Mr. Wittlesey's office burst open at the same time.

"What is the meaning of all this racket?" shouted Mr. Wittlesey, a lean, wiry man with thinning hair and sharp critical eyes. He was not a tall man, but his commanding voice always made him sound much bigger than he was.

The only thing short about the Headmaster might have been his temper.

Eff had slipped unnoticed behind a post at the bottom of the stairwell, leaving the other boys standing stock still in the path of Mr. Wittlesey's wrath.

"McNaught...Blake...in my office!" he spat. "The rest of you wash your hands for supper......*quietly!*"

It was always the same with the Headmaster, who presided over the orphanage like a tyrant-general, dispensing responsibility and punishment without recourse. For, whenever a reprimand was called for, which seemed to the boys like a daily event, the first two faces he saw got a hundred long sentences to hand write…the rest of the malfeasants a stern warning. And eventually, later, it was payback time for the poor soul who had started the ruckus in the first place.

And so it was with a sense of pride that Eff "Squirt" C'effsky took his place at the dining table that night. He had taken his punishment while washing up in the lavatory, of course. His arms ached of fresh bruises, allowing his fork to barely reach his mouth, but he had gotten the whole lot of them in trouble without having been caught himself. Aches or not, the achievement was monumental and the grin on his face was as big as his accomplishment.

There was dew on the grass the following morning. Mr. Wittlesey had sent Frank, the orphanage's cook, to awaken Eff and send him down to the office. A quiet, tall and muscular man, Frank was well liked by all the boys.

His dark hair and black, bushy mustache was such a contrast to the white t-shirt, pants and apron that he always wore.

From his corner window, Eff could see the sun was just

rising and he found himself sitting up, half out of bed, staring out at the lawn. Drowsily thinking that the awakening had been a dream, he nearly had the covers back up to his chin before he spotted Frank's white kitchen apron waving behind him as he retreated back down the hall. Realizing that it hadn't been a dream, panic hit him like a glass of ice cold water. Hurriedly the lad dressed, slipped on his shoes without stopping to tie them and scurried from the dormitory and the warmth of his bed. An annoying clicking of shoelaces followed him down the hall, but he didn't dare to stop to tie them. Knowing that whatever he had done to warrant a demand to the "Office" at that early an hour, he also knew that to dawdle would only have made the reprimand ten times worse.

Swiftly, he descended the wide stairwell from the third story, passing the dark and empty classrooms on the second floor, down another flight of steps and finally, a little winded and with nervous stomach, Eff pushed open the office door and stood before Mr. Wittlesey's desk and his cold, beady eyes.

"Hmm!..." was the first reaction of the Headmaster as he looked Eff up and down. The boy could tell at once that Mr. Wittlesey was unhappy with his hurriedly dressed appearance, but thankful that he ignored commenting on it. Instead he pointed to a chair.

"Take a seat, Mr. C'effsky," he said, fingering through a

desk drawer behind him and pulling out a thin manila file. There was a long pause. The Headmaster was glancing at a single sheet of paper, which he quickly placed back into the file on the desk in front of him. "You are an interesting case," he said at long last, as if he were choosing just the right words to say. Eff was all eyes and ears. Other than his name typewritten on the index tab, Eff had no idea what secrets the file might hold. Until this very moment, he hadn't even been aware that he had a file. A file that now rested in front of the Headmaster, a file that Mr. Wittlesey was now thoughtfully drumming his fingers over. "Interesting…" he muttered to himself.

"Sir…?" Eff added to the growing stillness within the office. But the Headmaster remained silent. Lost in thought, he stood and walked around his desk to the office window. He was silhouetted against the early morning light, gazing out over the thick swamp trees that surrounded the rear of the orphanage.

"Eff…" he finally uttered, "most of the boys come to me with some sort of history ~ broken homes, parents' deaths, or sent here as just plain misfits! Some history. Some court papers. A birth date, for example," he added, as he continued to stare out into the trees. "You have been with us what…four years now?" he asked, turning to face the young boy.

"Yes sir!" Eff assured him, as if they had genuinely been

the best years of his life. To this, Mr. Wittlesey broke into a rare smile. There had been a few times over the past four years when the Headmaster actually seemed happy, times when he even had smiled and had said pleasant things to the boys in the hall. But Eff wasn't yet exactly sure that this was going to be one of those times.

"You are curiously short...er, small for your age...," mused Mr. Wittlesey, taking a chair from under the window and sliding it around the desk and placing himself directly across from the young boy.

Eff tried to moisten his dry mouth. Other than a hand to the backside, this was the closest he had ever been to the Headmaster. Was there a word that came after nervouser? Nervousest, maybe? His young mind began to race. He wasn't at all sure, but it seemed to him that Mr. Wittlesey was fishing for something, or perhaps waiting for him to confess to something. Eff had heard of x-ray machines, and now he thought he knew what it felt like to be in one.

"I know that you must have had some...'turbulent years'...before coming to stay with us." Mr. Wittlesey continued, his eyes coming to rest on the lad's untied shoes. "The doctor's report in the file indicates that you have absolutely no memory of your past."

Eff tried to choke out an answer to this, but nothing came out instead. And then Mr. Wittlesey was looking directly at him…or was it through him, with those tight, searching, beady eyes.

"You are intelligent…and have a quick wit…"

"Thank you, sir!" Eff managed to squeak out.

"…*AND*…" he added with emphasis, "a quick mouth at times too!"

"Yes, sir…I'm sorry, sir!" the boy apologized, hoping that he wasn't going to end up having to write sentences.

Mr. Wittlesey walked back around to his desk and dropped heavily into his chair and reached back into the file in front of him.

"We have no records from the state. No files on lost or abandoned children matching your description," he continued to say, reaching back into the file to grasp something small and solid. "You came to us with no family history or date of birth. We were left with such little information about you." Eff was certain that the whole time Mr. Wittlesey was explaining this, he was turning something over and over in his hand. Something wooden?

"You see…I was the one who entered your name and birth date on this certificate four years ago. Your first name came from the *only* piece of information we have about you," he explained. "And the man who found you was a friend of mine. His name was Stanislaw C'effsky." At this, the Headmaster smiled. "We served together in the Army, although he was a lot older than I was. It was he who discovered you asleep in his cart of fruit and vegetables. He delivered around here for years, he and his horse drawn cart. Of course, that was long before the warehouses and the delivery vans." With those last few words, Mr. Wittlesey's beady eyes actually seemed to soften. Perhaps he was reflecting upon a gentler time, thought Eff.

"Eventually, you ended up with the nuns at Saint Mary's. And of course, that led you to here. Four years ago today. Exactly!" Mr. Wittlesey slapped his hand on the desk when he emphasized the word 'exactly', and then considered the boy ever so carefully before continuing. "I make it a point to divulge certain information to all the boys who end up here, about *their* histories," he said matter-of-factly. "As a rule…" he paused, "…on their tenth birthday." He then frowned, but added, "At least what I think they need to know about their past. But that isn't the case here, is it? You know as much about yourself as I do. I'm sorry there isn't more…but you know…in a lot of ways this is better. It may not be abundantly clear to you just now, but your situation here is…much less painful. After all, most of the histories here aren't very…uh…pleasant."

Eff frowned as he considered the words "less painful".

"So…!" he said sharply, giving Eff a start, "any questions?"

"Uhh…no sir," he fibbed. He had a thousand questions swimming around in his mind, but he couldn't concentrate on just one. Then, suddenly remembering the file on the desk, Eff quickly added, "uhh…?"

"Yes?"

"Well sir…uhh…about that one piece of information," began Eff, nodding to the file and wishing *he* had x-ray vision.

"Yes, yes…I thought about that. And I think you will agree with me, that with 'things' the way 'things' can be around here ~ it might be better to leave this unmentioned and in the file. At least for now. For safekeeping…hmmm?" Eff nodded reluctantly, but he could see his point. Whatever secret was hiding in his file, while it remained in the file, was safe. Anything brought to the attention of the other boys, no matter how insignificant, would immediately be wrestled away and more likely than not, be torn, broken or completely destroyed within minutes.

"Well then!" said Mr. Wittlesey, clapping and rubbing his hands together. "That leaves us with today being your birthday…" looking down at the file and then back at Eff, "…I'm guessing, but I'd say…about your tenth!" And with that statement, he turned in his chair and quietly filed away the boy's brief, but entire life history.

When Mr. Wittlesey swiveled back around and found the boy still sitting in the chair before him, he wore a look of surprise on his face.

"You're still here?"

"Uhh...well...yes, sir," Eff stammered.

"Well," he said waving to the door, "you know how we treat birthdays here.

Birthdays are celebrations," he continued. "You have complete freedom to wander. Come and go as you please. Skip classes. Read in the library, or help in the kitchen. The day is yours to muddle away, anyway you like."

"Thank you, sir!" Eff exclaimed with true emotion and turned to leave the office. But as he reached the door, Mr. Wittlesey tossed out a couple of warnings.

"Don't touch Sister Margaret's puzzle without asking!"

"No sir!"

"And no further than the lawn!"

"Yes, sir...I mean of course not, sir!" Eff replied, turning to face him from the doorway for further instructions. But all Eff could see of Mr. Wittlesey was his coffee cup and a free hand waving him away like some pesky fly.

The birthday boy was out of the office and across the hall in a shot. He didn't dare return to the office to remind the Headmaster that this was actually his first birthday in four years. Eff was certain that this had been just a small oversight and besides, he was so thankful that he had escaped the office with *no* sentences to write and with his life intact, he ran back up the stairwell with a sudden bolt of happiness and exhilaration. Pulling hard on every corner handrail post, he squeaked across the polished wood and swung to the next step without touching a single landing. Continuing at that same winged pace, he flew past the classroom level and did not stop until his weary legs reached the third floor landing. Overjoyed and suddenly exhausted, Eff sat, resting on the next step with his arms still hugging the banister post.

The hallway was still and hushed in shadows. Only a faint murmur found its way from the boys' dormitory and that was a muffled sound caused by a restless dream. The peace and solitude of being alone both in space and thought was as pleasing as the scent of aged wood and polishing wax that gently mingled in the hallway. For the first time in recent memory, Eff felt content. Much too excited to go back to bed and with the bell for breakfast not expected for at least another hour, his mind began to wander. It did not get a chance to wander very far though, before his ears caught an unexpected sound. It was a not too distant rapping. Something likened to the tapping of an open door caught in a slight breeze.

And then he heard a sound that sent chills running up his spine. The sound came from somewhere above him. The sound was coming from the "Attic!"

Chapter Two

"Effff"

...the attic seemed to call like a phantom with a raspy voice. Immediately, a creepy feeling began to seize Eff's entire body. He jumped up quickly from his quiet pose when he realized what stair he had been resting on. In his entire life at the "Home", Eff had never once even touched the first step leading to the attic! And for good reason. Besides the attic being haunted, the steps were very narrow and creaky and, out of all the gloomy rooms and closets in the entire building, that particular stairwell always seemed to be hidden in a heavier shadow than the rest. Thus, the boys labeled the attic and the stairs leading up to it, "Fraid Hollow" and it was avoided at all costs.

But Eff, sensing the calm, silent hall, reminded himself that he didn't believe in ghosts ~ except, of course, for the 'Holy' one on Sundays. And after all, wasn't he officially a year older now and allowed the freedom to 'wander'? So whether it was the spirit of inner peace or the adventure-seeking ten-year-old within, or a combination of both ~ something prompted courage to fill his shoes and force his legs up the gloomy staircase. And, before he could force sense back down into his feet, Eff was standing on the narrow upper landing, peering into the perpetual shadows above him. Five steps later, and what seemed like an eternity to his now weakening knees, he was eye level with the door knob and about to take another step forward, when a sudden cold breeze brushed by, chilling him to the bone.

"Effffff," the attic seemed to groan, this time only louder. The door opened slightly and closed on its own with a tap, tap, tap. Another rush of cold and the door opened even further, revealing a cobwebbed interior, dancing in a swirl of air. With legs too weak to run and a shaky and much less confident inner voice reminding him that he was now 'ten', Eff stepped into the dark unknown.

Crouched and waiting for some ghostly specter to come flying at him, Eff was ready to claw at it, then turn and run. But the first thing to hit him wasn't a ghost or a someone…it was a something. It was something not commonly found within the orphanage walls at all. It was a deep and soothing quiet, which immediately put the lad's frightened insides to rest. Aside from its cool darkness, what he found there did not measure up to the attic's notoriety or the torture of the last few steps. It was nothing more than a large empty room, completely open from end to end. As his eyes grew accustomed to the dark, Eff noticed that the ceiling was covered with tiny splinters of light, like a clear midnight sky. Upon closer inspection, he realized that these specks of light were not at all stars. Because there was no insulation, he was gazing at hundreds of nails poking through the ceiling and down the walls. And the attic's dismal appearance was due to the dirty panes in the two small windows, one at each end, which allowed only a sliver of light to penetrate its shadowy interior. Otherwise, there were no angry spirits or evil witches to be found and nothing but open rafters and beams ~ with the exception of a few unclaimed boxes and bedding piled high against the window closest to the attic door.

Eff rearranged a few of the smaller boxes and wiped a bit of dirt off one of the panes of glass. He could look down upon the knoll and the grounds below. He had an excellent view of anything or anyone coming up the graveled road. In the quiet of the attic, he heard the song of a train in the distance. It was the six-forty-five. Eff put his nose to the window and peered out over the seemingly endless forest of swamp-trees that bordered the orphanage to the east. But even from his high perch, he couldn't see the train. He only felt the heavy rumble that told him it was there. The engine let out a long, mournful wail, a reminder that somewhere through that pathless swamp was a ticket to freedom, a free ride to the 'outside' world. But the train waited for no one. And soon, too soon, the train rumbled slowly out of earshot, once again leaving the young boy alone with his thoughts in the quiet of the attic.

⸺

As his tenth birthday was being realized, Eff made the most out of his special day. Twice he strolled into *his* classroom, once to sharpen a pencil and the second time to grab a piece of construction paper. Frank was going to show him how to make a kite out of paper, glue and a few planting sticks from the garden. Both times, Eff slowed to a crawl on his way out of the classroom, a superior smile etched on his face. It was no wonder at lunch then, that he was greeted with a very sad rendition of 'Happy Birthday'. Charlie Halstead gave it his best, singing loudly and off-key as usual. Tommy Jacobson sang it like a little girl, but nobody else gave it much enthusiasm. When lunch was over, even with the ice cream and cake treat, the boys were back to picking on him.

"Thanks for the cake and Ice cream, Elfie," offered 'Chief' Butch Blake, pinching down hard on the points of Eff's ears. The others all laughed as they cleared the plates from the table. Then, one by one, each of the boys lined up to push the 'Birthday Boy' through the paddle machine.

There were several traditions at Rafferty that seemed like a good idea. Roast on Sundays was one of the most popular.

Fish Fridays were only so-so in Eff's mind. If had been left up to him, he would have changed it to hot dogs two or three times a week. But, having been given the joy of having a whole day to yourself, only to end it on your hands and knees and squirming as quickly as one might, through the paddle machine, was horribly unfair. Sure, it was the only legal hitting allowed at the orphanage without a one way ticket to the 'Office'. But it almost made you regret the whole idea ~ to celebrate being another year older. Once through the human paddling machine was bad enough, but McNaught caught Eff by the belt of his pants and, lifting him easily, turned him around and proceeded to send him back through the line for a second time.

"Damn you!" Eff shouted, loud enough to wake the ghosts in the attic had there been any. He wriggled to get free, but the only escape he could see was the opening at the other end of the tunnel of legs.

"Hey!" Frank bellowed, sticking his head out from the kitchen. "You keep pounding on that kid and he'll end up so short you'll have to get down on your hands and knees to see him!" Suddenly, the boys all found something better to do. But, not five minutes later, in the hall, Freddy 'Freckles' Pohl caught up to Eff and gave him a congratulatory pat on the back. It seemed, at first, a genuine act, until Walter's foot came from out of nowhere, sending Eff sprawling to the floor. Both the older boys offered their sincerest apologies as they ran past him, laughing all the way up the stairs. It was no wonder then, that Eff eventually searched out the kitchen, a sort of neutral zone, where the other boys would never be found unless they were sent there as a punishment.

"Frank," Eff bemoaned, sitting upon his favorite stool, "Why do the other kids hate me?"

The cook didn't answer him at first. He just washed off a dozen potatoes, put them into a bowl and handed them to the boy, along with a peeler. But Eff could see that Frank had heard him. His face was squished up. This meant that Frank was contemplating just how to put his thoughts into words.

"First of all…," he said slowly, "hate is a rather strong word. To tell you the truth, I think they're just jealous."

"Jealous!" Eff hooted loudly, and then he found himself wondering if he knew what the word really meant. "But, Frank," said Eff, taking a turn at squishing up his face, "how could someone be jealous of a nobody?"

"Well, that's easy," laughed Frank, a response that both shocked and surprised Eff at the same time; for Frank was actually grinning at him ~ his dark eyes sparkled at the boy as he spoke. "You're different. You're smart. You're special," he concluded. Having spoken his thoughts, Frank turned his attention back to the task at hand.

Eff found Frank's answer remarkable. He not only felt better, but he began to imagine his future life as a professional potato peeler.

The days slowly wandered by, but the only difference between sunny September and pleasant October was that the days were getting shorter. Mr. Wittlesey had been very blunt this morning at breakfast, when he spoke about this year's 'Halloween Excursion'. They were to break up into groups of six and be chaperoned by an adult. And, in his opinion, door-to-door begging, even in costume, required cheery 'Trick or Treat's' and sincere and thoughtful 'Thank You's'. Any rule-breaking in the coming weeks would instantly result in being left behind. Eff always enjoyed the preparation for Halloween and the costume making. Although in his memory, the weather never seemed to co-operate with the event, always leaving him both wet and miserable. Nevertheless, he vowed silently to be on good behavior and to watch his language and to definitely stay out of trouble. His vows of obedience did not dissuade him from sneaking off to the attic when he found the chance, however. And for a while, at least, the dark shadows of 'Fraid Hollow', became the only place that Eff could truly call his own. The pile of boxes became his throne, the attic his castle, and the solitude his only means of enduring the 'Home'. That is, until, he came across the 'Pageleaf'!

Chapter Three

The Pageleaf

…was beginning to bother Eff, even in his sleep. He wrestled both night and day with the thought that the attic, perhaps, was haunted after all. What other explanation was possible for the chilling breeze that had whispered his name and the extremely odd way in which the 'Pageleaf' had found its way to him? It all started like this.

Monday morning found Sister Celeste filling in, which she did willingly and often, whenever a teacher was ill or just not available. She knew all the boys by name and, right now, she was using one of the boy's names like it was wearing her thin.

"Eff…" she huffed. "You simply cannot put numbers down at random! Each group has a meaning…an exact number!"

"I know, Sister, but what are they? Apples? Pencils? Socks?" Eff replied, becoming more confused as she was becoming more impatient.

Sister Celeste muttered something about the "Saints", reached for an empty chair and sat down next to the boy.

There were giggles and coughs and barely audible words like 'idiot' and 'stupid', but both Sister and Eff ignored them completely.

"All right," she began, starting over for the third time. "Let's pretend they're apples. Bobby has 8 apples and Jane has 5 apples. Together, how many apples do they have?"

"Fifteen!" a voice answered wrongly from the front of the room, which was followed by a shower of wadded paper, erasers and pencils.

"Quiet!" shouted Sister Celeste. Her usual patient self was visibly coming to an end. She focused her attention back to Eff and took a deep breath. She was doing her saintly best to remain calm, but found it increasingly difficult in awaiting his reply.

"Well," Eff began, clearly thinking the entire problem through. "First of all, it would depend on the type of apples and…"

"…And why is that?" she sighed.

"Well…" Eff began again, slowly, sensing the fatigue in her voice, but trying his best to focus on the original question. "Frank says that some apples are better for baking and some apples are better for eating." Sister bowed her head as if in prayer. Eff gave her a moment to question his thinking, but when she remained silent, it was his turn to exhale heavily before continuing.

"I just need to know what I am doing with them. I

mean, if I am baking, the answer would be ten. If I were reselling them in the street, the answer would be the best eight." To this last statement, the sniggering in the room turned to full laughter. "And...if I were handing them out to the clowns in this room, the answer would be all thirteen! Including the three bruised ones...*AND*, the two with worms!" he concluded loudly to a room that suddenly fell silent.

Sister Celeste pursed her lips and slowly, but deliberately, put the chair back in place. With one hand counting her rosary beads and the other clutching a piece of chalk, she began to attack the chalk board with a new list of words. Apparently, math was over for the day and they were now moving on to spelling.

Sister may have withdrawn to her spelling, but Eff remained focused on the math, sitting with his arms folded across his chest. Why couldn't anyone see that he was right? Who wants Bobby's or Jane's apples if they're worm-ridden? And no one even asked the most important question of all...How Much Did The Apples Cost?!!!

Eff had had enough. Sister was facing the chalkboard with her back to him and totally immersed in grinding away with the chalk, so Eff took a deep breath and pretended to be invisible. He had easily reached the doorway unnoticed and started his bolt for the stairs, when he bounced off a hard object and sat staring up from the floor.

"Too much of a hurry to watch where you are going?" came the all too familiar voice of Mr. Wittlesey.

"Gosh…I mean…sorry, sir!" Eff stammered.

"And…?"

"And?" questioned the boy.

"And you were going…?"

"Oh…uh…I was…ah…in a hurry to the bathroom," he lied, but suddenly thought maybe he really needed to.

"Well…it can wait!" Mr. Wittlesey replied, looking at his watch. "Take a seat, this won't take long," he added and strode to the front of the class.

Sister Celeste was more than pleased with his timing and retreated to the back of the room. Exhausted and battle worn, she sat down in the empty seat next to Eff, dashing all his plans for escape.

"Gentlemen…" Mr. Wittlesey began, waiting for everyone to come to a hush. "I have a special lesson in store for you today and I want you all to pay very close attention. What you are about to witness this morning is nothing short of amazing! It is clearly something that only happens once or twice in a lifetime."

It wasn't very often that the Headmaster interrupted a class. In fact, it was very rare. And it was fortunate for Eff that he didn't really have a bathroom emergency by the size of the book Mr. Wittlesey took out from under his arm.

"Therefore…today's lecture is on…" he exclaimed to

a large wave of moans and groans that swept across the classroom…"the rare and significant occurrence of the scientific phenomenon ~ 'the total eclipse of the sun'!"

The less than happy reaction to the word *lecture* deterred him not from painstakingly sketching the earth, moon and sun onto the chalkboard. After a short explanation but skilled detail, Mr. Wittlesey ended his lecture with a sigh of accomplishment. Checking his watch, he turned back to the class with a sly grin, which - dollars to donuts - suggested that a quiz was about to follow. But to the surprise of everyone, he excused the entire class to the front lawn for a firsthand demonstration.

Instantly, there was an ear-splitting screech of chairs across the floor, as a mob of boys stormed the doorway. Eff watched as the classroom emptied and the trampling of heavy feet exploded down the hall like an upended bucket of water. He continued to watch as Mr. Wittlesey crossed the hall to check on Sister Margaret and the McKirdy twins. Because of sore throats, they had been quarantined to the sick ward, two single beds and a lone chair, and thrust into Sister's care. Apparently, they had recovered well enough to join the others, as they skipped happily ahead of the Headmaster, dancing footsteps echoing throughout the stairwell.

Quickly, Eff ran to the end of the hall and peered over the railing.

Sister Celeste was on the first landing and her robes were just disappearing from view. Then swiftly, silently, two steps at a time, he snuck to the shadows of the attic landing and sat there as still as a cat. From his perch in the dark, he calmed his breathing and waited, listening until he heard Mr. Wittlesey's heavy shoes click across the metal grate at the front door, before flinging open the attic door and jumping headlong onto his throne of boxes. Below, he spied the older boys pushing and shoving each other atop the grassy knoll, as if to get a better view. Mr. Wittlesey stood at the foot of the drive looking quite pleased with himself. Frank stood beside him and the Headmaster, checking his watch every few seconds or so, turned to the cook and began to form the earth, moon and sun with his fist, mouthing the words…'the rare and significant occurrence ~ the total eclipse of the sun'.

No sooner had he mouthed the words than the bright sky slowly began to gray. At first, it seemed to Eff as if a cloud was passing by. But there were no clouds in the sky. Only seconds passed, but it was obvious that something strange was happening. An eerie quiet enveloped him, as if the birds and the wind and everything on the earth was holding its breath. The calm alone sent a chill through him. But what frightened Eff the most was looking down at the hillside of frozen faces and watching the shocked expressions as the boys stared wide-eyed into some unknown terror. Holding back a sudden urge to cry, he immediately regretted not going down with the others. Even standing next to Mr. Wittlesey now, strangely enough, seemed a comforting thought.

And still the sky grew darker. Only now, Eff could see the sun without squinting. He was looking directly at it now, his eyes unable to turn away as a big, dark scoop slowly began eating its way across the sun. Everyone's mouth was agape. Everything was still. And then it went dark. Pitch black dark. And it stayed that way for what seemed like forever. Eff felt a sudden and horrible revelation that Mr. Wittlesey had only told them part of some terrible tragedy that was to befall them. Maybe he had wanted them all together for a reason, to face the 'whatever it was' together.

Tears began to well up all on their own just as Eff's panic was caught up in a whirl of air. He could feel it as it curled all around him. It was fresh and sweet and reminded him of Sister Agnes' flower garden. The scent was heavy and, although it did not tickle, it made him want to laugh. Instantly, he was glad to be in the attic and not concerned at all with the darkness. He was also strangely aware of a presence, something *there* with him in the dark. And then the whirlwind spun over his head, softly mussing his hair, and in an instant… was gone.

A faint light shone outside the dirty pane like the earliest of mornings. A pale crescent was now visible, as scoop by scoop, the sun slowly grew until it was too bright to watch anymore. And then it was back on, full and bright, just as Mr. Wittlesey had said. 'But why hadn't he mentioned the swirling wind or the fragrance of flowers?' Eff thought. Had he omitted it on purpose? Maybe he had wanted to surprise them. Perhaps that was the reason for the sly grin that didn't end up as a test. A little reminder that Mr. Wittlesey knows all but doesn't tell all.

Eff's attention was suddenly recalled to the front lawn. Out on the knoll, the older boys were releasing whoops of joy, relieved that everything was now back to normal. The younger kids at the bottom of the drive, however, were all pressed against Mr. Wittlesey in different stages of shock. Sobbing, stone still, crying. It took both Mr. Wittlesey and Sister Margaret to calm them and herd the small group back into the building. Apparently, the others were all being allowed to play outside a while longer. Eff pressed his nose to the glass to be absolutely certain of the Headmaster's whereabouts, when his elbow nudged against something on the windowsill.

Surprised, he sat straight up, staring down at a rolled up paper where nothing had been just moments before. Tightly curled around the white paper was a much smaller piece of paper, all held together by an opalescent gold coloured ribbon. It was an old note by the looks of it, a parchment that definitely looked to be hundreds of years old.

Cautiously, Eff unrolled the note. It was hand written and some of the words on the page were spelled quite oddly, but more curious than that, it was addressed to him...

Greetings

Oh ennobled Eff

Uplift thys Pageleaf with thy own hand to allow it to bespeak the quilled thereon. In thys whilst thee become the embodiment of the ancient journal scribed by Pan...the first High King...messages that allow thee glimpses as through open windows upon a tyme yet as merely myth et phantasy. I beg thee most solemnly... keep mindful the slathers of kinsfolk whom for survivance of thys precious Pageleaf grandly died.

Eff...a traveling orb now doth beckon me. With haste now do I cherish unto thee, thyne heirdom...most deserved.

May it become for thee...with whisp of heart et whirl of spirit...a truly wonderous journey et adventure....forever a forest of wandering footpaths.

All fellowship et illume

What manner of speech was this? Eff thought. He reread the note again and again. What was this? What was an heirdom? It made no sense. Surely it was an elaborate hoax put there by one or more of the other boys. He shook his head ~ he found it impossible to believe that anyone would venture alone into the attic. *And* in the dark? One thing Eff knew with absolute certainty was that the scrolled note had definitely not been sitting on the sill just moments before. He was bewildered. How then was it possible for this thing to just ~ appear?

Eff rolled up the note with his name on it and slipped the ribbon back in place. He then tucked the note safely into a tight space under the unfinished window frame. Later, he would admire the handwriting and the opening salutation, rereading it a thousand fold. But at that moment, he was in total awe of the mysterious yet somehow familiar warmth that he felt emanating from the white sheet of paper.

Twice the size of the handwritten parchment, the Pageleaf was shiny white and blank on both sides. It looked like a thick piece of paper but felt like heavy cloth. And when he happened to fold it over, it slowly laid out flat again, as if it had a mind of its own. He folded it over a second time. This time creasing it hard in half, he folded it over again and slapped it hard on the window sill. In half the time it took Eff to fold it up, the Pageleaf unfolded itself with a 'snap' and landed flat on his lap without a crease or mark on it.

It took a moment to sink in, but it was becoming more and more apparent that this was not a hoax. An overwhelming feeling began to stir in his heart. The strange sense of antiquity that surrounded the Pageleaf was somehow growing in him. And although Eff had no clue as to the meaning of the 'enobled' part, there was no mistaking that the Pageleaf was meant for him.

A distant thunder of footsteps signaled that the boys were all ascending the stairs and filing back into the classroom. Eff gave a precautionary glance toward the handwritten note, but it was nearly invisible in the shadows and safe enough where it was. Gingerly folding the Pageleaf into quarters, he slipped it into his back pocket and quickly rejoined the others.

"Bathroom?" quizzed Mr. Wittlesey as the two nearly collided again.

"Yes sir," Eff fibbed, backing into the classroom around him. The Headmaster eyed him suspiciously, but must have had other things on his mind, because he shot down the stairs and straight back to his office.

Eff heaved a heavy sigh and quickly took up the last seat in the row closest to the window. With the seats and bodies in front of him blocking his view of Sister Celeste, Eff pulled out the Pageleaf for a closer inspection. Once out of his pocket and onto the desktop, it again unfolded itself. Curious, Eff thought. In the bright daylight, it didn't seem to be made of paper. But it didn't feel anything close to rubber either.

"That piece of paper won't do," announced Sister Celeste, surprising the lad half out of his wits and drawing his attention back to the classroom. Her black robes swishing by, she placed a large sheet of blank, white drawing paper over the top of his Pageleaf. Walter 'Stick' Lent followed right behind, handing out tiny boxes of brand new crayons and making faces at each of the boys in turn. It didn't take a brain to figure out that they were about to draw pictures of the 'rare and significant occurrence of the scientific phenomenon ~ the total eclipse of the sun'!

With everyone's attention focused on drawing and the paper in front of them, Eff closely re-examined the Pageleaf in the light. Yep, he determined, definitely blank on both sides. However, when he held it in his hands and his fingers touched what felt like the fabric side, the shiny side of the Pageleaf began to shimmer. It didn't move or vibrate, but there was a soft audible hum and definite glow. With the light, there magically appeared a map. Then to his amazement, colourful pictures suddenly sprang to life as if being absorbed into the Pageleaf from the very air around him.

"Holy Moses!" Eff shouted across a room deep in artistic thought. He looked up to see everyone in the room glaring at him, including Sister Celeste. Quickly, he covered the Pageleaf with his drawing paper and wildly started to colour; the earth, the moon, the sun, the stars and the purple spot way off to the edge of the paper ~ Purgatory ~ where he knew he was going to have to spend at least a weekend, because of all his recent lies.

Finally satisfied with his masterpiece and seeing that everyone else was once again focused on their drawings, Eff set the Pageleaf back out on his desktop. He held it tight again in both hands as before and again there was a flicker of light. He suddenly felt lightheaded, like he was falling through a thin, white veil of clouds. Then far below, he spied an aerial view of a massive castle. Only it wasn't a map ~ *or* a picture. It was *real*. Eff could almost reach out and touch the birds around him. He was close enough to count the feathers. Was it his imagination, or did he even feel a light breeze that carried them above the castle walls, high enough to peek into the sun rising up from behind the mountains in the horizon and safely over the deep, dark canyon that etched its way around the thinning forest surrounding the massive, stone fortress below?

"Geez Louise!" Eff said aloud, not even realizing it.

"Eff?" Sister Celeste asked, appearing out of nowhere and who now stood over his desk. "Is something wrong?"

"Uh…no, Ma'am," he replied, his mind desperately trying to 'will' the Pageleaf invisible. But his arms had frozen stiff and the blank piece of paper just hung there, stuck in his hands like glue.

"And what have we here?" she demanded as Eff turned crimson. She took the Pageleaf and inspected it, front and back. To his surprise, she immediately handed it back and seized his drawing instead.

"And this?" she quizzed, examining his drawing.

"Heaven and earth?" he offered feebly.

"This is a very nice use of colours, Eff," she commended, carrying it to the front of the room, where she placed it in the chalk tray for the rest of the class to admire.

"Five minutes please!" she announced to the rest of the room. "Please finish up your art work in five minutes, so that we have plenty of time to wash up for lunch."

Eff let out a huge sigh of relief. And then, for five whole minutes he sat, thinking. Then, suddenly, with just seconds remaining before the lunch bell, it hit him. Just as certain as if someone had walked up to him and punched him in the stomach. Now it all made perfect sense to him! The strange words that he had read over and over earlier that morning, finally came to him with meaning:

"......messages that allow thee glimpses,

As through open windows upon a tyme

Beknownst yet as merely myth et phantasy."

Now there was just one burning question in Eff's mind. He had this one idea in his head and he couldn't eat his peanut-butter and jelly sandwich fast enough...couldn't waste time, although his stomach wanted another sandwich...couldn't wait to get outside with the others for recess...couldn't wait to find Butch...couldn't wait to engage him in conversation ~ yes, even if it meant a fat lip.

"Good afternoon, Sister!" greeted Eff, racing by Sister Agnes and her flower bed on his way up to the knoll. He was on a mission to find 'Chief' Butch Blake. Chief was supposedly part Indian. He was also, in Eff's estimation, the 'biggest liar that was ever born'. But one thing was for certain: Butch had lived with three different families before coming to the Rafferty Home For Boys. And liar or not, he had firsthand knowledge about a lot of things in the 'outside' world. Eff did not. More importantly, Chief knew about television. He'd even seen one. And, right at that very moment, Eff was willing to trade a bloody anything for the answer to just one burning question.

"Butch!" Eff hollered across the lawn. "Er...I mean... Chief," he added quickly, hoping he hadn't offended the older boy. His pals were all sitting around him on the lawn, long blades of grass hanging from their mouths like cigarettes.

"Hey...it's the Squirt," Butch pointed out.

"Yeah...nice use of colours today, Elfie," added Tommy

Jacobson in a high voice, intended to sound like Sister Celeste. The boys all around him snickered.

"Are you even allowed on the knoll?" one of the McKirdy brothers asked. Eff knew they were twins, but he never could tell which was Pat or which one was Mike. Either way, he was determined not to let anyone keep him from standing his ground.

"Say, Chief…what is television like?" Eff blurted, before he lost his nerve or one of the boys decided to chase him back off the knoll.

"Are you crazy? Whaddya mean…what's it like?"

"I mean…what does it look like again? Ya know…the picture and all?"

"Geez, Eff…I dunno. It's just a box. A big box. With a screen…and a bunch of dials." Butch turned to his pals and added, "But don't ever touch the dials…it pisses off the adults!"

"No…I mean…the picture on the screen. Can you go back and see it again…say, the scary part or if the words go too fast and you can't keep up?"

"Words? What the hell are you talking about?" Butch replied, looking around to see if everyone was properly impressed with his profanity. "Television is like..," he continued, "it's like a movie, only not in the dark. Ya just watch it." But Chief thought over Eff's question for a moment. "Nah…I got up to go to the bathroom once and I had to bend my step-brother's arm in half before he started to tell me what I had missed. What a sissy, he probably would've told me too…if his arm hadn'ta decided to snap the wrong way."

"Oh…" was all Eff could find to say. Someone coughed and a very personal silence enveloped the hillside. Taking advantage of the sudden hush, Eff thought that maybe now was a *real* good time to retreat to the kitchen.

"Frank, do you believe in miracles?" Eff asked as he rounded the long table in the center of the kitchen and took his customary spot on the stool by the sink.

"Miracles? Sure…Easter Bunny…Tooth Fairy…" Frank was always quick with a joke. But, for a man that big and strong, he seemed mighty uncomfortable talking and looking at you at the same time. Mr. Wittlesey had once commented that Frank was "bashful." Perhaps that was why he was always looking down at his shoes.

"No…I mean like angels and things. Things that just pop out of nowhere!"

"Are we talking religion or magic?"

"Uh…I guess I'm not sure," Eff confessed. There was a long pause while the lad thought about it. One of the reasons that Eff liked sitting in the kitchen, besides hiding from the other boys, was because Frank never asked questions and never spoke unless he was spoken to. To Frank, Eff was a permanent fixture ~ like the stove or a stool.

"You can help yourself to an apple there, while you're trying to sort it all out," he finally offered.

"Do Bobby or Jane have anything to do with these apples?" Eff asked, remembering his duel that morning with Sister Celeste and immediately burst into laughter. Frank laughed too…but right then and there, he couldn't have told you why.

Chapter Four

Saturday Arrived

...windy and wet. A fine, light rain fell sideways nearly the entire day. Secretly, each of the boys celebrated the fact that they were not outside, mowing and trimming ~ the usual weekend chore. Their joy was short-lived however, because the 'rainy day' routine indoors was twice as boring as watching the falling rain.

"Eff, spell *poultry*," quizzed Mr. Wittlesey. They were in the second story classroom and the desks had all been moved aside. The game was to spell the word correctly and then you got to take a giant step toward the front of the room. The problem was that none of the boys were good at spelling anything but four letter words, and the game had been going on all morning.

"Isn't that two words?" Eff replied.

"No...*poultry*!"

"P-O-L-E...T-R-E-E, pole tree."

"No. Mr. Riley, you're next...*poultry*."

"What kind of a tree?" whispered Alex, as Eff walked dejectedly to the back of the line. Eff just shrugged his shoulders and continued out the door and up the stairs to the dormitory. Up there, Frank had placed a number of mattresses on the floor and was attempting to teach those interested the fine art of wrestling. For a while, Eff felt that he might have an easier time wrestling with someone than he did wrestling with words. But he was wrong. One of the McKirdy twins, Pat or Mike, he didn't know which one, accidently elbowed him right on the mouth. Immediately, the word passed around that there was blood and all the boys quickly huddled around - all wanting a look-see at his newly bloodied lip.

"He'll live!" assured Sister Margaret, who shooed them away and whisked Eff off to the sick room. She then left him with a cold compress on his split lip and had hurriedly retreated down to the laundry room, where, she said, "the piles had gotten out of hand".

Eff eased back into several pillows and brought the Pageleaf out from his back pocket. The attic had been his only 'reading room' up until now, but the soft patter of rain against the windows coupled with the warmth of the small room, coaxed him into believing that the Pageleaf was safe from prying eyes. All week long, he had been reading up on the history of the Realm and the dark fortress of Darmund. He peered out at the empty hallway, pulled up his knees and began to read.

Avery was exhausted by the time she came to the toughest part of her journey. To her, it seemed as if she had been crawling on her hands and knees for an eternity. But she knew the worst was yet to come. The dark and narrow tunnel only got tighter and the rocks larger and sharper and more uncaring as she slipped cautiously under another wall of stone. She didn't want to think about how much harder it was going to get. She tried to put it out of her mind and just inch ahead…for she still had such a long way to go. She reached into the darkness with her right arm, then her left. Her bare feet were scratched and sore, but she raised her body up as high as the tunnel would allow and let her aching toes push her ahead as far as they would stretch. The sense of being buried alive was overwhelming, but it was not as strong as the memory of her mother's love.

"Shoulders…hips…push," she reminded herself in a whisper as her mind drew upon the strength that was her mother. From the very moment her sickly mother had breathed her last breath, the Elders had asked her not to grieve. That was the day she drew upon ~ the very day that the Elders had whisked her away and introduced her to the 'Plan'. And they had been right; it was the only way to have kept her secret hidden. For the Clan, it was a spark of new hope. And, for Avery, the 'Plan' was the path to fulfilling a promise to her dying mother.

"Do this for me," her mother had pleaded, her eyes bright with the energy that had long since drained from her body. Avery squeezed her mother's hand and promised her with a kiss before she succumbed. Since that day, never once did she waver from her oath to her mother or the Elders.

But anger too had been a strong force in Avery's preparation for the 'Plan'. Having been abandoned at birth by her Elfin father and never winning back his acceptance, was yet another reason that pushed her ~ kept her focused and practicing season after season for this day. No one, child or adult, could match her speed or courage when it came to wedging themselves through the narrow dirt tunnels under the city of Darmund. No one had her agility or her speed and endurance at running either. Her tiny Halfling body made her the best possible choice. Over the years, many before her had died in the tunnels, the rest having been caught just outside the castle walls and butchered by the Darmund Guard. But she was smaller and quicker than those before her and she was determined to succeed where the others had not.

That hadn't kept away the restless dreams, however – crawling spaces so small that she wasn't able to move – of dirt walls crumbling down all around her. Again and again, she awoke in a panic ~ crying and gasping for breath. But that was before Thistle, granddaughter to the King and her best friend, had given her the 'Stone'. An 'Emerald Star', she had called it. Its clear green colour was comforting just to look at, but when she had placed it on Avery's forehead, the soothing calm had been instantaneous.

"Is it magic?" Avery had asked.

"Yes...it is your magic. The Stone only brings out what is already inside of you," Thistle had assured her. "You are the one!"

With eyes closed, Avery now imagined the cool Stone pressed against her skin. "Elbows, knees...," she reminded herself and pushed on. Thistle's encouragement echoed throughout the small crawling space..."You are the one."

Once again, she raised a knee, but this time it barely moved before her back hit hard against stone and her next toe-push failed to gain her an inch. There was no more room in which to move. There was no more air. The rock surrounding her was cold and dead to the touch. Tears now filled her eyes and a hapless chill seeped into her skin. The image of the 'Emerald Star' faded and her nightmares began to take shape; the walls collapsing, the panic, the screaming. But her mother would not have allowed such thoughts.

"Mother!" she cried out with what she felt might be her last breath, but this time her mother wasn't there to comfort her. Now, she finally realized, success or failure was all up to her.

Avery summoned what little energy she had left, rolled onto her back, raised her knees and pushed with all her strength.

"I am the one!" she cried out again and again at the darkness that surrounded her, but her muffled voice only sounded hopeless and hollow. Unwilling to accept defeat, she made one last effort. With fingers clawing and leg muscles straining, her backbone scraped over the rough surface until her head slammed against stone. The sharp pain swimming in her head was nothing compared to the knowledge that there was no more tunnel, only a wall of rock, cold and heartless. There wasn't any room to maneuver…to turn around in or go back. She was wedged in tight and there wasn't enough air to breath. She had come all this way only to die ~ no, worse than that ~ to fail.

"Remember…the very last thing asked of you will be to make your way out," Hargus, the Dwarven King had warned her numerous times. And then with a humorous wink, he had added, "Well, they aren't about to leave a door open for ya, now are they?"

"Meaningless words!" she spit at the memory. "Try getting your fat, Dwarven ass through here," she sobbed, using her anger to force one hand over her head, clawing the darkness in front of her. She scratched her nails against the large rock in frustration, with no result. But around the rock, to her surprise, she was able to pry loose what felt like dirt or mortar. Quickly she wedged her other arm through and, with renewed energy, her fingers rasped away frantically against the darkness until she heard a solid 'thump'!

In rushed cool air along with an unexpected light. Without anything to hold on to, Avery struggled to pull her shoulders and body free. She shivered as she righted herself and stretched her cramped, tired and bruised limbs. But it wasn't from exertion or cold that she trembled. As she stood, she faced yet another horror. It had taken her all night to inch her way to freedom. The 'Plan' had been to flee into the darkness. Instead, the faint light of dawn had found her first. Which meant that the merciless Darmund Guard would not be long in finding her!

∞

The lunch bell rang, pulling a reluctant Eff from the pages of a story so real, *he* was finding it difficult to breathe. His knees and arms ached as if he too had been crawling over stone, as he slowly descended the stairs to the cafeteria ~ all the while trying to comprehend what he had just read. He was in awe of Avery…the 'what-was-it'? Halfling girl? Eff wondered what half meant. But when he reached the cafeteria, no one was there.

"Hey, we've got a Newbie!" hollered Alex who ran in and quickly darted out of the room. Eff joined a wave of excited bodies pushing and shoving their way out the orphanage front door. Mr. Wittlesey and the spelling class were already outside, waiting and watching as Father Griffin's black Buick circled the driveway.

Eff joined the crowd and stretched on tiptoe in an attempt to see over the taller boys, as Father Griffin strolled around the back of the car and opened the rear door. Out slipped a small boy with sandy hair and puffy eyes. Eff attempted to squirm his way to the front. If he could get close enough, perhaps he could warn the Newbie about the first two rules. One: crying would never do at the 'Home', and two: never let anyone stare you down. But he never got the chance. If anything, Eff was shoved even further behind as the boys closed in around the Newbie. Father put a hand on the boy's shoulder and prodded him forward.

"Mr. Wittlesey," Father announced, "this is Samuel Clayton. Sam, this is your Headmaster and your new home!"

The Newbie ignored the stares from the other boys, but kept his chin up as he shook hands with Mr. Wittlesey. Eff liked Sam's courage. And, when Mr. Wittlesey walked Sam past the boys and over the threshold of the orphanage, Eff was absolutely sure that they were going to be best friends...Samuel Clayton had to have been *at least* two inches shorter than himself.

In the dining hall, over dinner, the new boy was barraged with questions.

He met each question with a wide-eyed stare, but he made no attempt to answer any of them.

Finally, over a Jell-O dessert, the prompting of information changed from funny to mean.

"Maybe he's deaf!" "Maybe he doesn't speak English." "I bet he's from the moon!" "Are you a Martian?" "He just looks stupid to me." Eff admired the new boy. None of the remarks seemed to bother him at all ~ until Tommy Jacobson shouted in his usual nasty, grating voice...

"Maybe he's so stupid, his parents didn't want him anymore!"

Sam's eyes darted to Tommy and his face muscles went tight with rage. Before Eff could stop himself, he had grabbed for a dinner roll and flung it at Tommy Jacobson's head. It was a good shot too. But unfortunately, it bounced off him and hit McNaught who thought Chief had thrown it, who retaliated against whichever one of the McKirdy twins was sitting across from him ~ and when the rolls were gone ~ it was Jell-O. The food war didn't end until they had gotten down to the last pea. Anything that wasn't already eaten ended up in the fray.

That night, everyone got paddled. Even the Newbie.

Mr. Wittlesey probably didn't even take that into account, he was so mad. The mess was so widespread and slippery that Frank vowed to never, ever, serve Jell-O again!

Eff was never so happy to finally crawl into bed. He gingerly pressed a finger to his still swollen lip, thinking upon a truly rotten day ~ for himself and the Newbie. And now that he thought of it ~ so had it been for Avery the Halfling girl. Eff once again wondered what 'Halfling' meant. He wondered what her secret was. He worried about what had happened to her.

Lying still for the longest time, Eff patiently waited, just gazing out the window. The rain clouds had diminished somewhat and a bright moon was peeking out from behind them every now and again. Soon the room was quiet. There was always a certain kind of *feel* to the room when it was fully asleep. Slowly, Eff grabbed up his blanket and silently crawled under his bed. He took the Pageleaf from under his mattress and waited for the soft light and story to 'happen'.

The sky was a pale orange and birdsong filled the air. The trees against the side of the mountain were dark silhouettes, but the branches in the growing light were turning a brighter green with every beat of her heart. Avery was running now. Careful not to step on loose rock or 'telling' dry twigs, she knew her only hope of not being caught would be her head start. She surprised a Rabbit and then a flock of Quail, but she didn't stop to consider the consequences. She couldn't. It was only a matter of time after all. Gully after gully, every mound, every hill…she knew her only hope was a straight line aimed directly toward the canyon rim.

The air that now filled her lungs was fresh and exhilarating and the thought that her journey was nearly over filled her with hope. But the prospect was quickly dashed by a piercing howl in the distance. The frightening sound signaled that the final race was on. Just one more dry-wash and the last stretch was all uphill.

Eff pulled his blanket up under his elbows, which were beginning to hurt. That's when he was startled by another pair of eyes under the bed with him.

"Holy crap, Sam!" blurted Eff. A groan came from somewhere in the room above him, but no one stirred. "What are you doing?" Eff said, dropping his voice to a whisper. But the Newbie just gave him a quizzical look and nodded to the Pageleaf. 'Crap,' thought Eff…he'd been caught. But, more importantly, had Avery been caught?

Eff realized that he had to make a very tough decision. He quickly decided.

"Okay, can you keep a secret?" Sam's response to that was a beaming smile. "Right, I forgot…you don't talk… you're probably from Mars," Eff reminded himself. To this, Sam turned his grin back to the Pageleaf.

'Okay," Eff began, turning the Pageleaf slightly, so that they both could see the picture from the bottom.

"Here's the thing ~ her name's Avery and she's been tunneling for days and has been running all morning. She's a Halfling and she has an awful secret and she's being chased and she thinks she's just about to die. Got it?"

Sam's eyes widened as he stared at the blank page. It was then that he realized that his one and only friend at the 'Home' was absolutely crazy.

⚭

Fortunately for Avery, the elite Darmund Guard weren't sprinters. But they were very muscular and athletic and were trained to wear armor pads and carry double bladed axes twice their size at a dead run for miles on end. She knew that they *always*, eventually, ran down their prey. But she wasn't worried about them. The blood-thirsty Ghoulm were her concern. How could they not be? A Ghoulm was a two-headed dog with razor sharp teeth and extra-long hind feet that literally allowed them to fly forward. One Ghoulm was nasty, but several, while still called a Ghoulm, would tear at you until there wasn't a trace. They were also remarkable hunters. It was said that a Ghoulm could track a single, fallen leaf in a wind storm. And they wouldn't have to work hard to find her, not after she had spent an eternity crawling through the underground hell of Darmund.

Avery pushed the thought of the Ghoulm from her mind and concentrated all her energy on the path in front of her. In the end, the distance between freedom and failure, might be inches…she was counting on that. Her heart sank when the next howling cry met her ears. There were more than four Ghoulm~ six maybe, and a chorus of angry voices shouting directions to one another. They weren't far behind, but it wasn't time yet. Just a little bit further, she told herself.

"There!" came a shout. And a command was given to drop the beasts' leashes. The snarling and snapping was instantaneous. Without looking back, Avery knew they were still in the gully, but she was only half way up the rise, so she banked left. Her only hope now was the tree line. She trusted that it would keep the dogs from quickly spotting her in the open and dragging her down from behind. A volley of arrows snapped through the trees, but she had heard the initial twang, even at that distance, and had zigzagged further into the thicket. The Ghoulm pack bore down on her. The snarling was deafening and Avery could almost feel their hideous breath on her skin. Not far behind her, from the right, came a jaw-clamping snarl and then a yelp. Out of the corner of her eye, she saw the shadow of a Ghoulm beast being pulled to the ground ~ its leash perhaps, had gotten caught in the underbrush. Luckily, she was almost to the top of the ridge now, but so were the beastly horrors stealthily moving up on either side of her. Just another few feet, she prayed, and she could then 'unfurl'.

Eff's heart was racing. He had never been so caught up in a story before.

It was so real it was frightening. He looked over at Sam and couldn't believe his eyes. The Newbie had his head resting on his outstretched arms and was soundly, peacefully asleep. How could he have fallen asleep? Especially when Avery was literally running for her life? Eff shook his head and read on. He did not realize it at the time, but he had just learned another mysterious secret about the Pageleaf. *He* was the only one allowed to see and read its magic.

The Ghoulm were smart and had fanned out to either

side of her, for the trees were thinner and further apart there. But now the Guard were right behind Avery. She could hear the 'Zing' of the sharp axes, as the brush and trees that stood in their way were being chopped aside like twigs. The archers were only a few yards behind the Guard, but fortunately for Avery, they were at a full run and weren't able to manage any shots through the thick branches. That was all quickly coming to an end. The ridge of the canyon was now in full view and the last few yards were void of anything but scrub.

It was time, Avery knew, and awkwardly her elbows began dancing away from her body with every pounding footfall. Her lungs felt like they were going to burst as she reached the crest, but at least she knew that she would make it over the edge before dying. Death or freedom? Would a Ghoulm grab her and plunge them both to their deaths? Would an arrow or an axe ride with her to the bottom of the canyon floor? She believed that either would be better than a lifetime of imprisonment. With two steps left, the tight skin beneath her arms had unfurled and, without any hesitation, she closed her eyes, stretched her arms out in front of her as far as she could reach and threw her body over the edge of the canyon rim.

There was a vicious snap that nipped at her heel, followed by a high-pitched whine as one of the Ghoulm lunged, missed and plummeted into the canyon depths. An axe went sailing by her as well, but that, too, missed. Avery arched her back, just as she had been taught, stretching her hands out in front of her, as if trying to reach the other side of the canyon. Then came the headlong dive.

"Arrows!" became the shout, and the Guard backed away from the perilous edge and allowed the archers to move up and take aim.

'This is it!' Avery thought, dropping like a heavy rock. The whipping wind caused tears to rain from her eyes and her mind desperately fought back her stomach's insistence that she was plunging into oblivion. She closed her eyes to the tears and concentrated on her training, all the hopes of those she left behind. Thistle's voice reminding her that she was 'the one'!...her loving mother's face...her father's look of shame when reaching to welcome his new born Halfling daughter. Everything and everybody in her whole life now depended on something as simple as an updraft.

Avery waited until she heard the 'twang' of the first bow before she arched her back and forced her arms straight out from her sides. The force of her fall and the air around her screamed against her body. For several long moments, she shook violently from head to toe, but her mother's voice was there to calm her.

"Close your eyes to the pressure," her mother had reminded her.

"Feel the cool on your skin," Thistle had said.

Even with her eyes shut, she sensed the dark flash, as a deadly cloud of arrows sailed harmlessly behind her. And then, magically, with a soft nudge, the updraft finally found her wings and lifted her high out over the deep chasm. With the warmth of the early morning sun on her back, she again heard an angry shout for 'Arrows'! But it was far too late for that. From that distance, she could just as well have been mistaken for a Hawk or an Eagle.

Then, in a far off distance behind her, she heard a voice cry…"Faerie! It has wings! It's a Faerie!" And she smiled.

Chapter Five

In The Days That Followed

...Eff and Sam were nearly inseparable. For Eff, it was a relief that the constant knuckle sandwich and shove in the hall had, for the most part, come to an end. Now the other boys were getting used to just pointing to the pair or throwing verbal abuse instead of spit-balls or erasers.

'Hey look!" someone would holler, "shorty and shorter." By the end of the week, the two had heard about every 'short' joke there was, but thankfully they were mostly left to themselves.

Since Sam's arrival, the Pageleaf too, had taken on a new meaning. Not just the unexplained reason why only Eff could see the pictures and words, where Sam could not. The *real* joy was that the story now exhilarated him. It was almost as if what he was watching was all true ~ alive ~ reaching out from the page itself, instilling in him a pride in sharing. It most definitely was an unexplored feeling and one that he had never experienced before. At first, Eff worried about letting Sam in on his 'secret', but immediately found that the opposite was true. Reading the

Pageleaf to someone other than himself was fun. No...not just fun, but rewarding. Eff was smiling to himself, when Sam interrupted his thoughts.

"Why do you think he wants me?" Sam asked faintly, coming close to tears.

"Just to talk about your week. Don't worry, it's nothing really," Eff promised.

"But what if I did something wrong?"

The two boys were sitting in the hallway just outside Mr. Wittlesey's office, waiting for Sam's "appointment". Newbie's almost always had a week to 'adjust' before being called back in by the Headmaster; but for Sam, the wait was beginning to wear very heavy. Eff noticed the fear that was mounting in the younger boy's constant fidgeting and decided to tell a story.

"I saw a castle the other day."

"Wow...a real one?"

"Not just one, but two," Eff said matter-of-factly. But it was a half-fib. Not the castle part, but that Eff had snuck away to the attic and had read the story on his own. He hadn't told Sam and, afterwards, he had felt bad about it. He smiled now, recalling its beauty in every detail.

"Valrhun is a beautiful port city of great influence and activity. It is a walled city divided into two parts by a meeting of three rivers. Two of the rivers, the Weld and the Wander, meet to the East, entering the city together. On one side of the river, an enormous stone wall extends clear up the mountainside, encircles the lofty towers of a spectacular palace and drops back down to the water's edge, forming a bridge ~ shaped like a giant hand ~ that reaches out over the entrance to the port. The city on the far side of the river is like the first in every way. The trees and flowering vines are all alike, in that they drape over the narrow cobbled streets that wind up past the shops and cottages, up the hillside to yet another magnificent palace. So identical are the two sides of the city, it is like looking into a mirror."

"Is it an Elf city or a Faerie city?" Sam asked.

"Why the hell are you two snooping around?" snapped McNaught, who had just stepped out of Mr. Wittlesey's office. Eff couldn't help but notice the reddish rims around his eyes.

"Sam has an appointment!" Eff defended a little too abruptly. And when he stood to say it, he was speaking directly into McNaught's shirt. The next thing he knew, he was sitting on his backside looking up.

"You're blabbing on about Elves and Faeries," spat the older boy, now towering over the shrinking Newbie, "when there are more important things to consider!" McNaught stomped off in a visible cloud of anger. Whatever the Headmaster had discussed with him was clearly still on his mind.

"What's this about?" It was Mr. Wittlesey's turn to tower over them. He stood in the doorway, hands on his hips, staring down at the two boys.

"Nothing," said Eff who quickly pushed himself up off the floor. The Headmaster looked suspiciously around the empty hall and motioned for Sam to follow him inside.

"Chin up!" whispered Eff.

"And how do you feel about your first week?" began the conversation, as the door slowly closed behind them.

A minute hadn't gone by and Eff could hear Sam's heavy sobs escaping from the tiny space beneath the door. Eff heard Mr. Wittlesey's inaudible mumbling as the Headmaster tried to console the young boy. Embarrassed, Eff suddenly felt like he needed to be somewhere else. But he wanted to be there for Sam when he came out, so he stayed where he sat and let his mind wander instead.

For Eff, it was another of those rare moments when he suddenly found himself truly alone. Like in the attic or the Church at the far end of the narrow, bumpy road, with its huge airy ceiling and surroundings. The calm he was now experiencing was like being wrapped in a warm blanket of clear thinking and deep silence. Perhaps, as he thought about it, it was what Father Griffin had explained as 'Grace'…when clarity and inspiration combined to help you feel 'something' that wasn't there before. And suddenly, for Eff, that 'something' was overwhelming. It was an answer to his inner struggles with the Pageleaf. It was in fact, the very *purpose* of the Pageleaf. It wasn't just the caring for and the learning from ~ it was the reading to ~ the friendship brought on by the *telling* of the stories that was changing his life forever. In one unforgettable, defining and yes, *frightening* moment, he knew he was meant to share the Pageleaf and its wonderful tales. And not just with likeable Sam, but with the rest of the disgusting, bullying lot as well. Eff could feel the moment of truth. It was also like a growing knot in his stomach. He didn't know how long he could keep it from the others and even worse - he had no idea whatsoever how to begin.

Chapter Six

"Toss Him On My Back!"

...McNaught called out from the top of the knoll. The rain was now coming down in huge drops from a blackened sky. It had been early afternoon when the boys had first gone out to play, but the black clouds made one wonder just what time it actually was. It was unusual weather for October. The rain felt warm, like taking a shower. Perhaps that was why the boys were drawn out to the knoll on such a wet day. But something unexplainable was in the air as well. It was something warmer than the rain, something better than fun. It was even stronger than a dare. For the very first time in Eff's memory, the boys were actually enjoying each other's company and playing *together*.

"Not me again!" protested Sam, but it was too late. Several of the boys had already lifted him off his feet and thrown him onto McNaught's back.

"One, two, three...GO!" they hollered in unison and two screaming bodies flew from the top of the hill and over a very worn and muddy slide into a pool of murky water at the bottom. Two more bodies flung themselves down the trail of ooze, becoming unrecognizable because of the layers of mud they wore. Eff followed, all rolled up like a cannon ball, but when he saw Walter, struggling to make his way to the top of the hill, he reached out and tripped him with an outstretched hand on the way by. Walter yelped as it toppled him and, with a finger held firmly to the glasses on the bridge of his nose, he slid all the way back down on his backside.

McNaught grabbed Sam up around the waist and, carrying him like a loaf of bread, began his trek back up the hill.

"Hey…that was fun!" Sam exclaimed, hanging out in midair with a muddy smile. But the oldest of the boys only grunted as McNaught climbed. The quick part was the sliding down. The increasingly harder part was finding your footing and scrambling your way back up.

Walter and Eff raced back up together, pushing and shoving each other. When they regained the top of the hill, they were met with an unexplained hush. For some reason, the screams and laughter had come to an abrupt halt. Standing in numbed silence like stone statues lurking in a cemetery, the mud brothers gazed at the improbable. Father Griffin's black car sat empty at the bottom of the drive and two people dressed in black had just walked through the front doors of the orphanage. One of them was definitely Father Griffin. The other silhouette looked surprisingly like ~ Sister Superior!

The boys hurriedly slipped and slid over the wet grass and huddled just outside the open doorway. A lone light in the hall and an empty silence greeted them. But, on this particular afternoon, there was nothing warm or welcoming at all about coming in out of the rain.

Their 'guests' were standing just under the archway to the dining hall. Father's arm was still raised, holding firmly to the umbrella as if the weatherman had called for rain indoors as well as out. The 'I wonder where everybody could be?' look on Sister Superior's face was almost laughable.

As if on cue, Mr. Wittlesey entered the hall from the kitchen and his expression was anything but humorous. He had often boasted in public that 'his boys' could be called upon at a moment's notice. He probably hadn't meant *visiting* on a moment's notice, but there they all stood.

First, there was Mr. Wittlesey's blank, open-mouthed response to Sister Superior's presence. This was followed by a jaw-dropping, horror-stricken reaction to the wall of mud standing in the doorway. The Headmaster blinked several times to refocus, but it still took him another moment longer to process the reality.

Meanwhile, the boys could do nothing more than cower. Their clothes were dripping wet and caked in ooze.

Their faces and hair splattered with mud and grass ~ not a single one of them recognizable, aside from maybe Walter, whose glasses were so muddy and fogged over, that he had to take them off just to see anything. But when he did, it wasn't a pretty sight.

Mr. Wittlesey began to fume. His face turned beet-red and spittle flew, even before the words did. It was probably a good thing that Father Griffin was there to hear the Headmaster's confession, because the words that followed the boys upstairs were of the worst kind; probably not mortal sins because they had been provoked, but they most definitely had been venial sins. He whacked heads and slapped butts most of the way up the two flights of steps to the showers, only stopping to wipe mud from his shoes and wipe his hands off on the bannister.

It was easy to guess the exact moment that the hot water gave out. A sudden flurry of naked bodies jumped from the shower stalls to the towel rack. Frank was waiting for them, his long, tattooed arms holding a stack of neatly folded pajamas. His face was troubled. He shook his head at the massive sculpture of dirty clothes left near the drain. He sighed when he was handed the wet, half-muddied towels and the boys quickly jumped, cold and mostly clean, into their pajamas. But Frank usually, almost always, sided with the boys ~ at least silently. It didn't take the boys long to realize that his troubled expression had little or nothing to do with the wet clothes or dirty towels.

"Trick or treating has been cancelled. And Mr. Wittlesey wanted you to know that your dinner has been sent to the needy in Africa," he sadly announced. "You are to go to bed immediately... without your supper!"

Frank looked more pained by the announcement than the boys did, if that was possible. He lowered his eyes and walked directly to the hall closet. Grabbing a pail and a mop, he headed back down the stairs.

Cold and friendless, the boys slowly barefooted their way across the hall to the dormitory. Showered but hungry, they crawled into their beds.

"I can't sleep without eating something," Walter moaned.

"Well we can't sleep if your stomach's going to keep making all that noise!" came a reply.

Moments later, Sister Margaret appeared in the doorway with a plate of bread, although probably *not* with Mr. Wittlesey's blessing. The thin slices were cut in half. Apparently, she had counted them out carefully so that each boy had a small bite to eat.

"But that's only half a piece of bread!" Sam protested, looking up from the plate in disbelief. He defiantly refused the meager offering.

Sister Margaret countered with silence. The gentle lines in her face doured a bit as she reacted to his outburst. She watched as tears began to stream down his face. She nodded in agreement, but continued on to the next bed, still holding forward the bread offering. When she finished navigating the room, she once again stood in the doorway. Looking back at Sam and then at the plate with the lone piece of bread, she retraced her steps and again leaned the plate forward.

This time the sobbing boy didn't hesitate. He quickly took the piece of bread and shoved it into his mouth. But the tears and the sobbing had opened a door of despair and sorrow, too deep and much too wide for him to hold back.

"It wasn't my fault it rained," he continued to cry. "It wasn't my fault that I got throwed down the mud slide. And it wasn't my fault that I got borned and nobody wanted me!" The last statement escaped his lips with a pitiful wail and his tiny body shook uncontrollably.

And...there it was. Just as plain as the chewed bread that spilt from his mouth, rolled down the woolen blanket and landed on the floor with a soft 'plop'. *They* were orphans...the unwanted. It was the same dreaded thought... the same nagging dream, but with the same waking truth. It was the unspoken shame that belonged to each and every boy in that room.

Sam buried his head in his pillow and continued to sob into the night. The rest of the boys, almost in unison, pulled the covers to their chins and quietly became lost in their own thoughts. Sister Margaret retreated to the hallway. Her footsteps could not be heard over the muted crying or the pelting rain that raked against the window. Sometime later, the hall light went out like a distant flame extinguished to an impossibly heavy darkness.

Chapter Seven

As Dark As Halloween

...were the days that followed 'The Most Embarrassed I've Ever Been' lecture that Mr. Wittlesey gave before every meal. Torrential rains fell daily too, another reminder that the mood around the Rafferty Home For Boys was sinking lower than the swamp behind it. But hope for an Indian Summer sprouted wings on the following weekend, when the rains stopped and the sun brought warmth and cheer to the few bright coloured leaves that refused to relinquish their grasp on Fall.

It was getting to be mid-afternoon and most of the boys were doing what they did every Saturday after trimming and raking the lawn. They spent their afternoons up on the knoll when the weather was nice, sitting under the shade tree just above the orphanage, telling stories and dirty jokes. Normally, it was a day to be hidden away in the attic, yet on that particular afternoon, Eff found himself on the other side of the window pane, sitting on the knoll with the others.

"...his mother yells up the stairs at him. Then Johnny

yells back, I am mom, I am!" Laughter rang from the top of the hill.

"That wasn't as funny as my story," jeered one of the other boys.

"Maybe not, but mine was a lot dirtier!" replied the first boy, raising his fists in challenge. A blink later, the two were locked together in a brief scuffle, while the rest of the boys looked on with mild interest.

"Any other stories?" McNaught hollered out over the ruckus.

"I got one," eagerly offered Charlie Halstead, "but I can't remember how it goes." Snickering followed him as he chose to sit back down. By then, the two ground tumblers had stopped their fighting, with the dirty storyteller grinning and the other checking to see if his teeth were still in place.

Eff was lying on the grass, propped up on elbows, watching the tugs and strains of combat, while his mind too, was fighting furiously over the reasons that he continued to keep the Pageleaf to himself. Sam was sitting next him as usual and was carefully considering the pained conflict that washed over his friend's troubled face.

"Eff has one," Sam stated aloud, to the shock of everyone present. The Newbie hardly ever spoke and he had certainly never addressed the boys as a group before. If they were shocked, Eff was mortified. He shot a glance at Sam that could have burned up the entire solar system.

"No, it's my turn," butted in one of the McKirdy brothers.

"Hey, let the Squirt tell his story," commanded McNaught, in such a tone that it left no doubt as to who was going next.

"Really, McNaught?" Eff answered, surprised by his sudden good favor. Nonetheless, Eff hesitated a long moment before he cautiously removed the Pageleaf from his back pocket.

But the very moment the Pageleaf unfolded and popped open on his lap, no fewer than a dozen hands grabbed for the page and pulled it from his embrace. Eff and Sam both lunged to get it back, but they were shoved hard to the ground. Pinned there, they watched helplessly as the page went from hand to hand to hand. When everyone realized that the page was blank, they began to lose interest, except for Tommy Jacobson. With an evil grin on his face, he tried his best to rip it in half, but when his attempt was thwarted, he began crumpling the page into a ball.

Eff was up off the ground in a flash, but before the two boys could come to blows, McNaught stepped between them and wrestled the page from Tommy's grasp. Eff bounced off McNaught's muscular frame and once again found himself sitting on his backside. But this time he felt totally defeated. He could not find the energy to even look up ~ not only for the embarrassment of the tears welling in his eyes, but also for fear that the Pageleaf had come to some harm. He sat dejected and began to cry.

McNaught looked the page over carefully. He couldn't see any reason for an ordinary piece of paper to have caused that much of an outburst. When he looked down, Sam was standing before him, less than half McNaught's size, with his hand out, patiently awaiting the return of the page. Ceremoniously, Sam wiped the Pageleaf off on his shirt and handed it to Eff, reassuring him it was still in one piece, and then he took up a seat beside him.

"You can read a story to me," he said, as if nobody else was out there on the knoll but the two of them.

"All right, shut up!" demanded McNaught. "Squirt here is the storyteller and I'm gonna listen and so is everybody else. Unless you wanna discuss it with me first!"

Silence descended over the knoll like a gentle hand. Eff's fingers tingled as he held tight to the Pageleaf, searching through his tears for a place to start.

'My Mirthday of Enlightenment has at long last arrived...'

These were the first handwritten words to *EVER* appear on the Pageleaf and Eff read them aloud slowly. His heart pounded with joy. It was at *THAT* very moment, that he knew, beyond any reasonable or unreasonable doubt, that the importance of the Pageleaf was in the telling of the story. He sensed that everything was changing. Even the pictures were brighter and more colourful than they had been before. It was as if something special was happening both within him and the story at the same time. He was becoming the Pageleaf.

And so, it is here, that the *REAL* story begins…

Chapter Eight

In The Realm Of Valrhun

…on the first moon of Somber, there was a prestigious gathering of lords and ladies throughout the land. It was a very significant celebration ~ the Mirthday of the crowned Prince. Although the day was unusually gray for that time of year, the Great Hall of Cragburne was filled with brilliant colour and merriment. Jugglers, mimes and life-sized puppets greeted a continual parade of splendidly dressed people as they ascended the marble staircase into the banquet hall. Here, cloth-covered tables laden with handcrafted cutlery, Elfanware plates and forged silver goblets hugged the perimeter of the room. Along the far wall, massive stone archways reached clear to the thickly beamed ceiling and each stone alcove was alive with candlelight. Bright tapestries and marble caricatures on stone ledges covered the walls of the hall, and the crimson glow of the blaze in the over-sized hearth bounced lively from the lofty ceiling, giving the chamber a rich, majestic feeling.

A handful of monks dressed in gray robes entered the hall, pulling a gnarly tree trunk on wheels to the centre of the room. The trunk, as if freshly fallen, lay flat on a wooden frame and was thrice the length of a single monk, and the limbs of the tree, although trimmed closely to the trunk, reached nearly as high. The monks moved busily about the tree in animation, as if in a rehearsed play. First, they removed their robes ~ revealing colourful and amusing costumes beneath. Then, with great fanfare of waving arms, a traveling cloth covering the trunk was slipped neatly off the tree, exposing a most curious contraption. Every inch of the trunk was ornately carved and each oddly shaped limb or burl was crafted into a musical instrument of one kind or another. The heavy, root end of the trunk sported three large kettledrums. In the centre of the tree, where one would expect leaves on limbs, sprouted a bouquet of brass horns. At the far end was a large harp made from two curved limbs pulled together by strings, with a similarly made but smaller lute beside that. Lastly, a brightly painted keyboard had been carved into its side, pipes and chimes sticking out here and there at odd angles.

Five of the monks pulled up hunker stools as a low drone began to vibrate from the tree-trunk contraption. The sixth member, the director, climbed atop the instrument and lay back into a smoothly carved out gnarl. High above the others, with his feet protruding out in front of him, he nodded, and the one, two, three movement of his big toe began the first tune ~ 'The Royal Song Of Valrhun'.

Instantly, the guests stood and a sea of wine goblets were raised high as jubilant voices echoed to the chorus:

"From which all Trav'lers come

Over mountain trail,

Or follow waters run

To the place that we all hail!"

Before the last note was allowed to fade into the rafters, a loud voice greeted the festive gathering.

"Welcome…and hearty greetings to you all…family and friends!" bellowed the voice. At the centre table stood a tall, strong man of middle age, his goblet raised. Knight-like in appearance, his dark beard and curly hair flowed together and came to rest on his shoulders. Woven into his crimson red tunic was a golden lion with wings and talons. "Four moons of Awgust have come and gone and this, the harvest moon, the first moon of Somber, has been one of plenty…"

"Yes, and the food awaits…my long-winded brother," came a voice to his left. Standing and raising his goblet was a man nearly identical to the first. Their build and dark hair were similar, the difference being that the winged lion of gold on the second of the two was set against a tunic of royal blue.

"As I was saying," the first brother began again, "to fellowship...to the Festival Of Harvest...to Pan Reuschal's Mirthday...," he added triumphantly, motioning to the young man sitting between them.

"And to the food...which is getting ever colder!" laughed the second brother, as the two reached down and hoisted the 'Mirthday Boy' to his feet.

"Salute!" shouted the three of them in unison as the banquet hall burst out in kind, "Salute!"

Immediately, the musicians began playing a lively jig and, at this, the large doors at either end of the hall suddenly swung open as a gaily clad kitchen staff marched in on cue. Kitchen stewards carrying large silver trays between them, presented tray after tray of roasted goose, duck and pheasant; while Kitchen maids easily handled the trays of exotic fruits, nuts and cheeses. It took two Manservants to roll a heavy cask of wine to each table; and a third Servant, a bonneted and smiling Ladlier, scooped tirelessly from cask to waiting goblet until every goblet again had its fill. To cheers and applause, a jugglier tossing rings, added knives and then empty plates from one of the tables. A serpent-charmer, with a thickly coiled snake wrapped multiple times around him, wove in and out of the festivities, with a brightly coloured parrot perched on his hat. Music resonated throughout, as did the brattle of plates being filled, the clanging of goblets in celebration and the din of festive conversation.

The lively entertainment and the exquisite meal carried on as did the laughter and conversation, but soon the procession of trays from the kitchen began to dwindle. The logs on the fire eventually became embers, but the music, on the other hand, grew increasingly louder and more dissonant. The drumming from the hollow tree deepened, vibrating over the stone and wood. And the instruments ~ all playing at once ~ seemed to be fighting one another to be heard. There was a sound of awed voices remarking in unison, as a Wood Faerie suddenly appeared overhead, in the form of transparent smoke; her voice high and hauntingly beautiful, as if adding another musical instrument to an already bizarre orchestration. Then several Sprites, all aglow, lent their unearthly harmonies to the crescendo of instruments. The loud, haunting song was still gaining pitch as a strange array of winged creatures, fireflies and smoke wisps joined in the lithesome dance of the Wood Faerie. Like harried notes on paper, together they fluttered over the musicians' heads. Faster, but gracefully and almost hypnotically, the dancers wove higher and higher into the air to a melody undoubtedly threaded with magic.

The cacophony of music was not the only sound in the hall. Some of the guests were almost shouting to be heard. Others, strangely enough, had fallen asleep. Some sat back in chairs, snoring with mouths agape, while others with heads on arms, rested peacefully upon the tables. No one seemed to notice the oddness of the moment. Loud voices, then laughter broke out from the far end of the hall as some major point of discussion traveled back and forth between the groups involved. The drumming and strumming of instruments reached a fervid pitch and with this, winged creatures all…drifted from above their wooden stage down to the table tops. All waking eyes fell upon the sensuous movements of the magical dancers, yet, even as the creatures danced, several more guests succumbed to a deep sleep. At the centre table, the first of the two brothers reached for his goblet and rose to toast the celebration just one more time. Unable to be heard, he dropped back down into his chair. Smiling, he toasted himself.

To the near side of the room, one of the two large chamber doors swung open and a small boy dressed completely in white stepped purposely into the noisy room. Carrying a neatly folded woolen robe, he stopped and stood in military fashion directly between the two brothers. For a long moment he waited, wide-eyed at the disturbing frenzy about him. The young aide coughed lightly to announce his presence, but he could not be heard above the commotion that filled the hall.

"Tis midday, my lord," offered the aide, but it went unanswered. "My lord, tis midday!" he repeated a little louder, but his words were swallowed up by a sudden uproar of voices. Not knowing what else to do, but sure of his charge, the boy reached out a small hand and nudged his master softly. Quickly he drew his hand back, as his unexpected touch startled the young man who had been on the verge of a troubled sleep.

"Emery?!" he muttered more like a question.

"Yes," the boy was quick to answer, then remembering his task. "Tis midday, my lord!" he said boldly while nearly dumping the robe into his master's lap. The confusion of sound around him was unnerving and he quickly added with a pleading voice, "May I go now, my lord?"

The young aide, fairly certain he saw a nod, gave a quick, courtly bow and rushed hurriedly back through the entryway, the large door closing solidly behind him.

Although he had been curious and had only *sipped* the wine, the young man found it hard to blink away his drowsiness. Suddenly conscious of the weight of the robe in his outstretched hands, he was immediately filled with an urgent sense of duty. Searching for strength, he forced himself to turn his back on the celebration and muddled his way unevenly to a stop before a solid wall on the far side of the hearth pit. There, in the corner lost in shadows, was a concealed doorway. Hesitating, he considered going back and offering words of gratitude. But, at the moment, with his head swimming, words of any meaning failed to come to him. 'Later,' he said to himself. 'Yes, later, I will write a poem of thanks.' Moving on, he pressed against the wall, forcing open a doorway, which he quickly stepped through. Turning, he closed the heavy door to the cool relief of silence and cold, damp stone.

"You appear weary, my lord," came a familiar voice. The words from the dim light of the passageway belonged to a tall, slender man with salted, once-black hair.

"Dreaming of this day has come with little sleep," confided the young man with a tired smile, "and I find it hard to shake the celebration from my head."

"Surely you remember my cautions that wine and party can but blunt the edge of a man's sword," scolded the old man.

"But I didn't…well…but a taste!"

"Exactly," muttered the old man, taking the robe, pulling it over the lad's head and fussing with the pleats. "Come!" he added rather sharply, leading him downward along a sloping passageway. A distant clamour of dishes could be heard from the kitchens, as they slipped unseen through a small archway to the rear of the buttery. Quickly they traveled down a tiny and very narrow stairway hidden behind a cupboard to the side of the pastry ovens. The stairway emptied into a seldom used walkway, built between the inner wall of the castle and the thicker, fortified outer wall. Loose dust rose up as the young man struggled to keep up with his Guardian, as he was led ever downward into the depths of the castle.

Bothered by the old man's abrupt behavior, the young man sought to soften his disposition. "You look...splendid," he remarked, referring to the elder man's fine ebony trousers and royal blue waistcoat, pressed without wrinkle and looking as if polished.

"It seemed to me that an occasion of this caliber was in need of proper attire," he responded coolly and without emotion.

"Really...Elan! You act as if you were attending a funeral," pointed out the lad as they stepped into a long, marble pillared room. Their footsteps echoed the fact that the room was empty and in a secluded part of the castle.

"I suppose it is a funeral of sorts," Elan answered with a sigh so heavy that the young man could not hide his amusement. The old man, surprised by the lad's reaction, turned and confronted him in feigned disbelief. "You laugh at me?"

"I'm sorry, Elan, but you really don't play 'sombre' very well," the lad continued to laugh.

"I don't?" he responded, trying his best not to break into a smile.

"No, you do not. And lately, you really haven't been yourself."

"I suspect not," Elan admitted, "But this coming of age ~ this Mirthday of yours ~ is not only ill-timed, but a reckless custom that should have been scotched..."

"My lord!" echoed a child's voice from somewhere behind them. Tiny footsteps were heard, as the young aide dressed in white appeared on the stairway above them, struggling to carry a pack much too heavy for him.

"Emery, my son," called out the old man, retracing his steps and reaching to unburden the child of the journey bag. "What would I do without your quick mind and fast little legs?" he praised the boy, who could not stand still with embarrassment. "Now swiftly, off with you," he commanded with a wave of his hand. "And forget every turn and twist from which you came!" he added to the backside of the boy, who raced back up the stairway and quickly disappeared into the shadows.

"I believe these are the exact items you instructed me to prepare," Elan said, quickly rummaging the bag's interior to be certain.

"Was I ever thus?" asked the young man, nodding to the fading echo of footsteps.

"Ha...you were twice the runt and always running away from something," Elan laughed, handing over the bag by the leather strap. Then he added with an inquisitive look, "...are we *certain* we are not running now?" The young man opened his mouth as if to speak.

"Yes, yes...I know," the old man waved the thought away with raised palms. "You are bound by tradition and honour to survey the Realm ...*and* all the lands in-between.

I understand this, but these are lands that you will only *someday* rule. We have diplomats and delegates and councils and endless time to…"

"Elan…"

The two stood for a long moment, looking intently at one another, neither giving ground on their convictions. It was the old man who was first to speak.

"I affixed a good number of gold coins to the lining of your robe and journey bag," Elan admitted. Then he added with a smile, "Just as a loan, mind you."

"Bless you, Elan…" began the young man, but he never got a chance to finish his thought, as the old man turned on his heel and resumed his trek down the marble-columned hall. The lad slung the bag over his shoulder and had to hurry to keep up. When he eventually caught up, Elan was holding back a large wall tapestry and motioning him to pass through a secret passageway to the lower and dampest regions of the castle.

Finally, they came to a stop and turned to face each other before a well-latched, thick wooden door. The old man, his face long and pensive, placed an aged hand upon the lad's shoulder.

"Today, you become a man…" Elan began, grabbing a tighter hold of the robe, "…but forgive me, my lord, I must tell you plainly how I dread this overfed idea of tradition. If only I had inherited your father's robe. I most assuredly would have put an end to this nonsense! Everything you need to know, you can learn within these walls."

"Elan, please..." the lad began, but the old man was not finished.

"It is my only wish to see you happy," he asserted, "but truly, it is much more than a sadness to see you go. To me, this very day...holds with it a great sense of loss...owns something unforeseen and foreboding. And here must I stand...your Guardian these many years...and watch you turn to your travels alone. Plainly...I fear your future without so much as an escort or a lackey to lighten your load..."

"And that is just the point," interrupted the young man. "Give me an escort and I call attention to myself. Give me a lackey, and if danger should take charge, whom might I trust yet find foolish enough to follow?"

"Me, for one!" vowed the old man.

"You?"

"Yes, me! Gladly would I go."

"Dear Elan. Do you not know how my heart wishes it?" replied the lad, looking sadly into the eyes of his childhood Guardian. "But this is *my* Mirthday, *my* journey, that unfolds with the passing of the next four moons. I am happy in this. I want to see the whole of the Realm for myself. Find adventure. But, most importantly, to take *my* impressions and measure *my* judgments about that which I stumble upon. I truly welcome the unknown and anything fate might bestow upon me."

"Ahh yes, your Mirthday. Your great-grandfather's sense of gallantry and adventure," the old man nodded in defeat. "Well, come on with you then," bowed Elan and motioned toward the reinforced door. "My Lord, the world awaits you!"

It took both of them to unlatch the heavy bolts and force open the door.

The old man was the first to peer out into the narrow alleyway, scanning the mist beyond. Together, they walked the short distance to the pier and the awaiting vessel.

A heavy curtain of fog lay over the harbour, murky and sullen. The only sound to be heard came from under the dock as the great river lapped at its edges. Elan gazed upon the past and sighed.

"As a child, do you remember my leaving open the Forest gates, allowing you to camp out on your own?"

"It seems much like this," reflected the lad, joining the memory.

"What would you say to it now? You and I could camp out in the Forest for a short while…then you could go out on your own."

"Elan, I cannot."

"What I mean to say…is that it would be closer to home…and then…"

"Elan, I am going. This midday. Now. This day means nothing, should I choose to stay."

"Yes…of course you must. You are no longer the little boy I used to chase after," the old man conceded. The two locked hands in a solid grasp.

"Thank you, my friend, for trying." The young man hesitated as if wanting to embrace the old man, but turned and stepped quickly up the loading platform and stood facing him from the deck of the boat. A nodded command was given and bemisted shadows moved swiftly over the river frigate. Once the moorings were lifted, the vessel jumped too and found its freedom in gliding with the current.

"Earlier, I was uncertain as to what to say," the lad called back, pointing up to the castle. "Please thank them and bid them both farewell."

"I will, that I promise. Just as you must promise to return!" insisted the old man. "Remember your training… and I will always remain proud of you!"

"Yes, Elan. I will remember everything," vowed the lad to the now hazy figure standing alone on the dock.

"I wish you a thousand Forests of wandering footpaths… all fellowship et illume," whispered the old man, as the boat disappeared into the fog.

The images on the Pageleaf faded, turning as gray as the fog. Eff looked up to McNaught in surprise.

"What?" McNaught was quick to ask.

"Forests of wandering footpaths!" exclaimed Eff.

"Huh?" was his only comment, but Eff didn't get a chance to explain.

"What kind of story was that?" demanded Tommy Jacobson.

"It's a wonderful story!" Sam defended.

"Yeah, let's hear more 'bout faeries dancing," Freddy insisted.

"Yeah, faeries dancing," called out the McKirdy twins, followed by catcalls and cheers from the others.

"Please Eff, read us some more," pleaded Sam.

"We're with ya, Eff," Walter agreed loudly, "but we don't like the boat stuff. It makes us all seasick!" To the delight of the others, Walter pretended to retch and then vomit all over the grassy knoll.

"Shut up! Creeps!" yelled McNaught over the outbursts of laughter, throwing an angry fist into the air. "Is there anything else?" he asked momentarily, nodding to the Pageleaf.

Eff pressed his hand to the page and the story continued.

Chapter Nine

A Lady With Hair Of Burgundy

...stood alone on a balcony high atop a castle tower. She was young and of the Forest and her hair looked striking against garments of light green. Wrapped about her shoulders was a long woolen cloak and, tight in her hand, she gripped a bow as tall as herself. A quiver of arrows was strapped about her and rested at her side like a sheathed sword. From the balcony's lofty perch, her warm Elfin eyes scanned the courtyard below and the Father Forest beyond. But the pale-yellow sky of day about to dawn revealed nothing significant.

She retreated to the inner chamber, for the morning chill was heavier than her cloak of wool. A circular stone fire pit was ablaze and its smoke rose high into the vaulted ceiling. The flickering of red and orange flames cast an eerie light upon the other figures inhabiting the tower chamber. These figures were motionless, with frozen stone features, both beautiful and grotesque: a room filled throughout with statues of warrior and beast alike.

Meanwhile, outside the open window and vast forest

beyond, the morning sun began to rise ~ reaching in streaks through the tallest of the trees. From one of these high branches lofted a snowy white owl. Its glistening wings extended, it soared majestically over the cold-misted meadow and alit unseen on the tower sill.

In the blink of an eye, something akin to a heavy fog appeared on the balcony ~ and then just as quickly, in a blinding flash, evaporated, leaving in its stead a robed figure of an old man. He was very tall and the top of his head was shiny and bald, but only down to just above the ears. From there, his thick, white hair flowed into a beard so long that it covered the front of him, nearly reaching the floor. Silently, he approached the young lady in green, his steps muffled by the long robes.

Startled from her dreams, she anxiously turned to face the old man. Yet it was not fear that pounded within her, but a heart that danced at his arrival.

"Reza..." she began to say, quickly bending to one knee. But before she had time to bow her head or finish her greeting, he gently took her arm and led her back to the warmth of the fire pit.

"Child, we haven't time...an adventure awaits!" he said excitedly.

"But I understand not."

"Things have been set in motion and we must be swift," was his only explanation. And, taking an ordinary iron poker from the pit and shaking it free of ashes, he placed it neatly in a slit between two heavy stones and the fire-pit suddenly slid back to reveal a circular stairwell that dropped into solid darkness.

"Illume!" he commanded and the depths lit up like sunlight.

"But Reza, you hath said he comes here!"

"Yes, but things are ever changing…even as we speak," he said in a gentle tone. "Come. Follow. I'll explain."

―――

"Together they quickly descended the stone stairway, the old man explaining as they went. It is something of great importance by the look on the face of the lady with the burgundy hair," Eff read.

"What is he saying?" demanded Walter.

"I can't hear him," Eff explained.

"What happened to the party?" asked McNaught.

"I'm sorry, I can only tell you what I see or read."

"Well, what do you see?"

"Nothing right now," Eff apologized, "the page is blank."

"Is this a story about pirates or ships or Robin Hood?" came a question Eff could not answer.

"Wait! Hold on. What the hell…!" McNaught uttered in disbelief.

It was the dinner bell, striking for the second time. The third chime rolled across the short, green grass of the knoll and resounded over the leafy countryside, just as the last of the stampeding boys pushed and shoved their way over the porch of the kitchen entrance, slamming the screen door behind them.

Chapter Ten

"My Odyssey"

"...has brought me safely through curious terrains and settlements without number. Places both prominent and peculiar have I seen, yet notable deeds go unreported.

Unto now a leaf drifting from any branch of Nature's boundless Forest am I, save that fate has timely chosen to tumble and fall beside me. So it is that a mystery masks this distant Realm in the sudden disappearance of its Princess. To go in earnest rescue would fulfill my very purpose, yet it seems that my anxious determination flows swifter than this vessel would fare. My objective is an ancient Dwarven monument known only as 'The Keep' and is said to grace the threshold of the Gathire Mountains.

As day shades into twilight, I sense this heavy, unfeeling presence about these cold canyon walls and shiver in my aloneness as I draw ever nearer the foothills of Gathire..."

A Dwarven flatboat, its cargo covered by a tattered canvas, glided in semidarkness over a still lake. Two stout Dwarves poled the boat in succession, as they had since the break of day. On either side of the broad lake, rocky escarpments rose high into the light of the blue sky, but the sun had recently fled the watery canyon, leaving the vessel in a stew of shadows and mist.

From the prow of the flatboat, a hooded figure watched every turn and stretch of the seemingly endless water. As darkness befell the canyon, not-too-distant lights shone through a haze gathering in the center of the lake. As the boat drew nearer, the thinning mist revealed the monstrous height of the Gathire Mountain Range. The canyon walls now seemed minute compared to the Gathires as peak after peak faded into the distance, the farthest of them covered in snow and all of them still basking in the sunlight.

A huge pinnacle came into view. Carved away by centuries of ice, it had once belonged to the mountain range but was now a single rock formation surrounded by water. High above, nestled in a mound of green turf, what looked like a mighty fortress of stone stood in command over the lake. The sun's orange glow reflected off the castle's outer walls like a beacon in the night.

The flatboat neared the base of the monolith where it was met by numerous rock formations jutting out of the water. Sharp and deadly, they stood silent guard over the port's entrance. Unexpectedly, the two Bargemen began to pole feverishly, directing the boat toward the rocks at an alarming speed. The boat, too, reacted, as the stillness of the water was ruffled by a sudden current. Grabbing a firm hold on the side of the barge to steady himself, the hooded figure was surprised when he discovered the cause. To the right of the massive rock base cascaded white water, rock over rock ~ an endless progression of pools and eddys ~ carved out of the mountainside. And, on the left, from an amazing height, a majestic waterfall pummeled the river in a heavy mist. Two water sources, both feeding the lake, came together in a very narrow channel infested with deadly rock outcroppings. Straight ahead, with very little room to spare, lay a silent and still port, unaffected by the water currents.

One of the Dwarves took to the slippery footings along the outside run of the deck ~ pushing the vessel, using an oar as a lever. His counterpart continued to pole from the rear. For an anxious moment, there came a scraping from somewhere beneath them, yet neither Dwarf uttered a word or showed any outward sign of concern. The hooded figure noted this with admiration and a sigh of relief, as moments later the flatboat glided safely into the harbour.

Laying the poles aside, the Bargemen took up the oars and began churning the deeper waters. The closer they drew to port, the more ominous the mountains became and the darker their shadows. A flock of Gray Tufts skimmed the top of the murky water and winged gracefully up the towering rock face. High above, they gently feathered down into their nests as their aerial ballet came to an end. Higher still and silhouetted against a brilliantly coloured sky, a long expanse of bridge stretched from the castled peak and spanned the harbour, attaching itself to the sheer cliffs of the mountainside above the port.

Directly ahead lay the dock. Distinguishable only because it was outlined in torchlight, it was covered with cartons and crates and grain bags piled high. Amid the flickering light and shadowy motions from the dock came a burst of shouts and the loud crack of a whip. A flurry of activity revealed expressionless, weatherworn faces that shuffled quickly from one mound of tonnage to the next. For the most part, the laborers were Dwarves, banded together into small groups. While one carried a lantern, the other two or three, depending on the load, strained to lift the cargo and transfer it to one of several horse drawn carts waiting on the far side of the dock.

The Bargemen were commended, thanked and paid. The hooded figure took a sure hold on the piling and pulled himself up to the wooden platform and solid footing once again. As he wove in and out through the busy lumbering of workers and their heavy loads, the Stranger noticed, in particular, a tall, shirtless, bald-headed man. The light from the flickering lanterns glistened off his muscular body ~ his voice lashing out in a heartless tone. The Stranger also noticed the man's right arm, the one threatening to lower the whip, upon which the emblem of the Vischan Empire was tattooed.

Suddenly there was a loud crash and work came to an immediate halt as a half dozen lantern bearers rushed to the sound. With lanterns held high, it was quickly determined that no one was seriously hurt. The dropped wooden crate, however, had partially collapsed. The contents ~ burlap bags bulging with potatoes and grain ~ seemed intact, but at least one bag of flour had shot out over the dock. Immediately, the burly overseer coiled his whip and his voice pierced the night in a fit of rage.

"Wait!" called out the Stranger, surprising everyone including the overseer who lowered his whip. The hooded figure knelt to inspect the splintered crate. It was badly crushed on one side and flour covered the dock where one of the bags had burst its seams. Taking a hand from his cloak pocket, the Stranger ran his hand over the broken wooden pieces and down each slat and brace.

"It will hold," he determined, nodding to those closest to him, as they raised the damaged crate slowly from the dock and placed it gently on the back of the nearest wagon.

"It'll never make the top," declared the driver, after

careful inspection. But his statement was answered only by the crack of the whip, snapping the still night air.

"Get a move on that cart!" And, turning to find the workers still standing idly about, the angry overseer lashed his whip repeatedly to a flurry of movement and a chorus of low mutterings. The driver, too, was grumbling and looking doubtful at the crumpled remains of his cargo.

"You lead the horse and I'll see to the crate," offered the Stranger, pulling the hood from his head to reveal the young man's dark hair and smooth, youthful face. The driver stared at the lad in hesitation, but only long enough to second-glance the supervisor's merciless expression. Mounting the buckboard, he nodded to the back of the wagon and quickly grabbed up the reins.

"Gee up!" he called out and the wagon lurched forward. The young man grasped hold of the rear of the wagon and swung himself up next to the broken crate. With one hand resting tightly on the end of the flour sack and both feet dangling over the back, the Stranger made himself comfortable amongst the clucking chickens and crates.

Once again, the night air filled with the brutal cry of command and the sounds of the flailing whip. As wagon and passenger slowly pulled away from the dock, the overseer's dark eyes and those of the young man met in an intense, unblinking stare. Instantly, the angry man's scowling expression washed from his face. His arm lowered and the whip dropped from his hand. Meanwhile, the horse and wagon cornered the first bend and continued its snake-like journey up the face of the steep mountain. Higher and higher they climbed until the dock was nothing more than a tiny stage set in flickering light and a handful of busy shadows. Silence was the only noticeable difference.

The wagon jostled for some time over bumps and ruts along the winding road. Suddenly, the horse's hooves struck hard stone and the metal-rimmed wheels protested loudly over the new surface. They had entered a tunnel and the clamorsome wagon and steady clop of the hooves plainly echoed the discovery.

The air inside the black tunnel was soothing, cool and damp. The young man leaned back and closed his eyes, listening to the horse's pace and the resounding rhythm of the cart. He pictured himself a blind man and let his imagination reach out into the cavern, touching the distance between the walls and the cart.

'It is wider than it seems,' he determined, when a disagreeable sound caught his ear. It was the distant cough of a horse and the distinct sound of another clopping of hooves and the grinding wheels of another wagon. Gradually, the two advanced upon one another. The young man knelt up to face the oncoming sound, scanning the gloomy emptiness. His own driver was slumped in disinterest as a similarly-driven horse and cart passed and then melted into the void behind them. A fresh breeze also greeted him, followed by a hint of light. The breeze, dry and full of the sweet scent of wildflowers, grew to a whistling, and, with each rattle of the wagon, the wind and the light became ever stronger. Like drawing nearer a keyhole in a dark room, the mouth of the other end of the tunnel became more defined as fingers of bright light reached in to touch those lost in darkness.

They emerged and found themselves bathed in the brilliancy of the sun, just as it was prepared to set between another range of mountains to the west. The horse's pace quickened with a slight decline in elevation and the road came to a 'Y'. The path south into the steep mountains was both wide and well-traveled and rolled hill over crest through fields of wildflowers, deep with colour, until they vanished into the foothills of the snow-crowned peaks beyond.

The horse was directed to the right of the divide, however, and soon strained to pull its load up a sharp rise. To the right towered a sheer, unstable wall of rock and to the left, a small, neatly masoned wall was all that protected a traveler from dropping into a seemingly bottomless chasm. The road continued its long upsweep around the mountain face before leveling onto a massive expanse of bridgework. It was of ancient Dwarven construction, with enormous blocks of stone, laid together so finely that a single grain of sand could not find a place to rest between them. The left span was caught in the rays of the setting sun and stood out like torchlight, flaming across the gorge, while the right barrier fell in its shadow, almost melting into the dark shapeless canyon below.

The well-lathered horse pulled up short of the bridgework. On a hill above the bridge was their destination, the outer walls of a castle, but the driver turned and motioned toward the west and the spectacular view behind them. The sun, a blazing red wedge, was setting behind a peak of white, and the entire sky was a procession of clouds imbued in the brilliant sunset. After a moment's pause, the driver sat up and craned his head to scan the far side of the narrow bridge. He then gave the reins a vigorous shake and the horse responded, as did the deep canyon, echoing the wagon's approach over the cobbled pavement.

At length, they passed under a stone arch that connected the castle's two outer walls. To the young man's surprise, the entryway had no protective doors or gates. Inside the outer wall, there were no high-reaching towers or domes ~ no royal palace. 'The Keep' was no grandiose structure at all, only a simple village surrounded by an ancient stone wall.

The wagon rattled over the uneven dirt pathway that ran down the center of the flat, treeless enclosure. Lining either side of the clearing were structures not much worthier than shacks with thatched coverings, most of which looked in need of repair. At the far end of the village, however, there was yet a greater wall, which supported two giant wooden doors. They were partially open and it appeared that a continuation of the settlement existed within. 'That would have been the fortress wall seen shining like a beacon from the lake,' thought the young man, for its height far exceeded that of the entrance to the village, and above the battlements, helmeted guards paced the parapets.

The wagon finally came to a stop before a large barn. A spacious opening in the second floor revealed a number of Dwarves lifting and stacking bales of hay and bags of grain.

"Appreciate the help," commended the driver, jumping down and eyeing the broken crate with uncertainty. "You got business…friends?"

"No, sir."

"You'll be looking for the Inn…just beyond 'The Keeps' gates to the left," directed the driver, pointing a work-worn finger in the direction of the inner bailey.

"I'm grateful," replied the young man, as he headed up the road in the pointed direction. "Uhh…sorry," he added, turning to see the man's unsuccessful attempts to tear away the splintered pieces of wood from the crate. "Just pry it open from the other end and it shouldn't be a bother."

The driver nodded in agreement, while the Stranger continued his stroll through the centre of the village. A young boy, part Elf, stopped to offer a smile and hurried on with an armload of unhusked corn toward the barn. Right behind and half the size was his sister, ears pointed straight out from under a hand-knitted hat pulled over her braided hair. Her arms were reaching out in front of her as far as they would go, two ears of corn her limit.

A gathering of women, both Dwarves and Halflings together, were washing clothes by the side of the waterhouse. They eyed the Stranger with side-glances, without actually looking directly at him. A Potter's wheel sat unattended on a patch of grass before one thinly planked shack and a 'Tailor' sign hung askew from another, yet no one was walking or shopping along the road.

The last building to the left of the enclosure was by far the sturdiest structure in the village. Two stories tall and constructed of solid beams and fully rounded logs, the wide porch and long building angled to face 'The Keeps' gated entrance. The only soldiers thus far encountered were those lazing about the porch. Rough and unkempt, they looked to be mercenaries rather than palace guards, yet they gave no acknowledgement of the Stranger when he passed.

Opposite this dwelling and forty paces in each direction to the point of actually leaning against the great wall, was a Dwarven camp. Oddly, it was a clump of shoddy lean-tos and shacks pieced together with rough stones, sticks and shakes. Running frantically throughout the hovel were a handful of riotous urchins who spotted the young man as a Stranger and ran toward him, eyes dancing with mischief.

"Who are you?" demanded the tallest of the Dwarven children.

"Who are you?" returned the Stranger.

"Byron," he answered suspiciously. "Cost's a gold piece to pass our Dwelling!" he added and the outrageous demand received a loud chorus of approval from his rag-tag army.

"I've something better!" offered the Stranger, dropping to one knee and reaching into his robe pocket.

"What's better than gold?" demanded Byron with a frown. But the Stranger only smiled. Then, holding both hands out in front of the children, he turned one hand over, palm up, revealing a hand full of tiny, bright red beans.

"Ha! Those are just beans," Byron was quick to observe, and the rest of the children began to laugh.

"Ahh…so they are," agreed the Stranger, "but when I rub this hand over the other and hold them back out to you, what do you see?"

Eager Dwarven eyes combed his outstretched hands, yet spied nothing more than the tiny, red beans. A moment later, there was a crackling sound and one of the beans jumped, then another. Soon they were all jumping and cracking open to produce flower petals. Tiny petals of every colour imaginable popped in bunches and fell to the ground. As they continued to multiply, the children scooped the petals up in their own hands and took great delight in scattering them all over the path to their dwelling. Spontaneously, in a gesture of friendship, the children all joined hands around the Stranger and began to sing an old Dwarven chant:

> *"We hallow our shield*
>
> *We hollow our blade*
>
> *For it is penned*
>
> *Hale thy friend*
>
> *And n'er 'gain be afraid*
>
> *Sing again*
>
> *Hale thy friend*
>
> *And n'er 'gain be afraid."*

Extending his right hand, the Stranger bowed low in respect of the honour bestowed upon him. He then motioned them to draw nearer.

"Will I find the Princess within these walls?" he confided in a low whisper.

"The Princess!" cried the children, half shouting and half

covering their mouths as if the words were better left unsaid. A flurry of excited murmurs and quick glances toward the log building followed, before they pulled their new found friend several steps further into their encampment.

"But what can he do all by himself?" argued Byron.

"He came to help!" replied one of the girls, shoving him hard and knocking him to the ground. "Isn't that enough?"

"Milly's right!" defended the others, as Byron slowly picked himself up and brushed off the seat of his trousers. Not the shortest of the bunch but certainly the roundest, Milly had defiant red hair and freckles. She glowered at Byron, then stepped forward with such an air that it was immediately apparent who really held reign over the group.

"And if you find her, do you really think you can help her?" she asked in a hush.

"All I need is a place to start," assured the Stranger. Milly thought hard before replying.

"Most everybody says she was kidnapped and taken to the dungeon," she confided sadly, "but we'll never know 'cause no one ever comes back from there."

"We're not tha'poth to know about nothing," came a tiny voice. The young man looked down to find the littlest of the Dwarven children standing quite bravely beside him. "My name ith Freda," she said with a toothless smile.

"Yeah..." added Byron, with a timid glance toward

Milly, "they always send us out to play whenever they talk about the 'Lord Governor' and those *other* things."

"But couldn't we tell him about our friend with the thmelly breath?" came Freda's voice once again.

"Welll...," began Milly hesitantly, "the old drunk tells us all sorts of stories about the dungeon. Maybe he could tell you stories too, if you ask him real nice."

"And where do you suppose I can find this old drunk?"

"Ha!" cried Milly, pulling on his hand, "in the Tavern, you silly." With laughter and jubilation, the band of Dwarven street urchins grabbed hold of the Stranger's robes and ushered him towards the gates of 'The Keep'.

"Uh oh," moaned Byron, looking up to find two uniformed guards who had just now positioned themselves outside the heavy doors.

"That's okay," exclaimed Milly, "I've got a plan!" And quickly she huddled the group together. Not a moment later, they ran ahead of the Stranger, leaving little Freda to lead him by the hand.

"I'm too thyort," she pouted, as a carefully disguised game of frogs unfolded and leapt ever nearer the unsuspecting guards. Subtly, the child's play became a tug-o-war with the sentrys' capes and sword hilts. Like so many flies, Freda and the other Dwarven pests were shooed away from the Stranger and back to their rickety camp, as, unrestrained, the young man crossed the threshold and entered 'The Keep'.

Chapter Eleven

Inside The Walls Of The Keep

...was a small community enclosed by a great wall. Standing just inside the giant gates, the Stranger pondered on the reason for a guarded courtyard on the top of a meaningless precipice. For an outpost so far from other villages or ports of importance, it was surprisingly ~ unique. The easiest way to protect 'The Keep' would have been to garrison the walls overlooking the bridge. Even stones and clubs would have protected the village at that point, so narrow was the bridge and fatal the drop into the canyon far, far below. The village itself was a continual, although gradual, climb to reach the high parapeted walls of 'The Keep'. Once the gates were closed, archers ~ even half blind ~ would easily have been able to hold off any attack. But why a fortress on the edge of nowhere; to keep something in or to keep something out?

The palace or stronghold inside the gate was built into the stone walls and resembled a villa overlooking the large courtyard. Three towers rose above the walls in each corner ~ triangular, like in the shape of an arrowhead.

The masonry was that of the bridge, ancient, square and smooth, yet not overly artistic. The bleak and unoccupied upper levels were dotted here and there with patios and balconies, suggesting that a once affluent and large population had dwelt within. The only hint of spirit hung from the ironwork railings. These were crimson banners supporting the crest of the Vischan Empire, a black cross pointing to all directions, north, east, south and west. Higher still, only a single guard in full armour walked the battlements as daylight met dusk.

A smooth cobbled road ran a wide path both left and right, in a circular motion from the gates. The courtyard held four buildings that stood apart from the rest of the stone city. To the left stood an Inn, the largest of the buildings. Wooden steps to a high porch and two stories tall, the Inn was built of massive, round timbers and a slate roof. Tucked behind the Inn, a long single-story building with all fashions of goods hanging in the windows, was the Trade Store. The porch was bare, and the lack of light within proclaimed it closed. Directly in front of the young man, and with doors open, stood a spackle-white temple. Three small blocks of stone reached to its entryway and the single-story structure's right wall rose high above the building's slate roof in support of a narrow bell tower. Just below the tower feathered an apple tree, leafy and surprisingly still full of fruit. An empty basket leaned against the base of the tree, surrounded by a scattering of ripe apples. Farther to the right, a thickly thatched roof covered a moderately-sized cottage. Laughter and song could be heard coming from the open door and it was evident from the ruckus within, that the young man was now looking upon the village tavern.

After a careful survey of the inner city, the young man took an eager step toward the Inn, then on second thought, continued in the direction of the Temple. What beliefs this region held, he knew not, but the young man could hear Elan's sage advice beckoning him forward. Two large cressets hung from either side of the entryway, softly lighting the Temple's humble interior. Save for the raised platform directly ahead and a single, lit, pillar candle thereon, the room was empty. His footsteps echoing across the hard tile floor, the young man came to a stop before the altar platform. Drawing his sword, he laid it flat before the altar and lit one of the smaller candles from the lone flame. Before the candles' soft glow, he dropped to one knee and lowered his head in deep thought.

"A pleasant evening," uttered the young man without moving from his reflective pose.

"Outsider…what is your purpose here?" befell a heavy whisper, as a tall, robed figure emerged from the shadows.

"I have come to…help," he replied, his head and body still motionless.

"We are not in need of assistance!" insisted the robed figure, cautiously stepping into the candlelight. He pulled his hood back, revealing his face ~ worn and wrinkled with age. His hair was tousled and white and his eyes deep set and dark. Standing, the young man sheathed his sword and faced the old man.

"The Princess has been found?"

There was not an immediate answer from the old man, but daring one step closer, he eyed the Stranger carefully. "I am Prior here, and all who enter the dungeon are damned!"

"It is not my intention to be damned. I have only come to pledge assistance," replied the young man.

"Will you help us seal the demon-hole forever?"

"Demon-hole?"

"The evil path that leads into the dungeon!" exclaimed the Prior.

"Is this Princess in the dungeon?"

"Some say she is," continued the Prior, "but…" He was about to say more, but stopped abruptly and scowled toward the entryway.

There in the Temple doorway stood a female Dwarf, with a full, dark beard which reached halfway down her gray-tweed tunic. Stoic and demanding in appearance, every inch of her looked to be as solid as stone. A broad, hand-forged branding sword was strapped to her side.

To the young man, she seemed every bit a match for any Knight from his own Realm.

The Prior gaped for a moment in uncertainty, but only for a moment. He turned on his heel and swiftly scurried back into the shadows of the Temple's inner-chamber.

With a nod and a smile, the young man acknowledged the Dwarf's presence. But he might as well have been greeting a statue. Taking a deep breath, he tried again. "Hello," he offered, but still she did not reply. Nodding as if she had, he slowly walked toward her. His height was a good three hands to his advantage, yet she still did not yield the entryway. Flushed with embarrassment, he stopped just short of her and dipping his hand into his robe pocket, he produced a gold coin. Holding it up for her to see it plainly, he stepped lightly around her and deposited the coin into an iron box on the wall and awkwardly continued his way. Thinking that the evening air never felt so refreshing, just outside the door the Stranger encountered three more oddities, standing together in the courtyard.

The first to catch his eye was a Gnome not taller than four feet. His appearance reminded the young man of a festival banner; bright blue leather boots, grass green shirt and trousers; his thinning hair and full beard a colour that could only be described as brilliant orange. He was inclined to laugh aloud at the grinning Gnome, but his eyes were quickly met with those of a full-blooded Elf. She was thin and wispy, and her fine, white hair flowed near the length of her yellow robe. Suddenly remembering his manners, the young man greeted them both and a third member of their party, a beady-eyed Halfling not yet the size of the Gnome and who seemed more at ease hiding behind the other two.

"Greetings," he offered.

"Hello," replied the Elf graciously, "our little friends outside boasted of a Stranger with great magical ability."

"Well…" he chuckled, "I *am* a Stranger to these parts."

"I am Oblio, and these are my friends, Nommie…" she nodded toward the orange bearded Gnome, "…and…" she turned to introduce the Halfling, but he scooted from behind her and darted around the young man into the Temple.

"…and that is Quimby," she added, almost as an excuse. The Stranger turned to follow the Halfling's flight. Not surprisingly, it took him directly to the iron box on the wall. But standing between them and watching his every move was the Dwarf.

"I believe you have already met Moralee?" Oblio asked.

"Not in so many words," remarked the young man, turning back to the Elf with a smile.

"We're late for supper!" announced the Gnome, walking off at a lively gait.

"Will you join us?" offered Oblio, pointing toward

the Inn. It was all the young man needed to hear, and he quickly fell into pace beside the Elf. The Gnome led the trio through the main entrance to the sitting room. It was a large, comfortable space with a rising staircase at one end and a blazing hearth at the other. The polished wood floor was covered with numerous hand-crafted rugs and, throughout the room, there were heavily upholstered chairs, seemingly placed at random.

The three proceeded through the first of two arched doorways and a short hall that led to a dining room and the delightful aroma of food. The Gnome pointed to the hooks on the wall and unbuckled his sword strapping. The Stranger followed suit, peering into the dining hall. The walls were covered in tapestries, mostly hunting scenes, and hung from ceiling to floor. Suspended from the ceiling was an ironwork candelabra filled with scores of candles that hung over the centre of a banquet table. Most of them were lit and the many-flickering lights played against the fabrics on the wall. A dozen chairs surrounded the table, five of which were already occupied at the far end nearest the kitchen by men bent over in deep conversation. So intense was the conversation, the dinner guests stood in the archway for the longest moment, completely unnoticed. Bits and pieces of the discussion were too loud to go unheard.

"…those Dwarves in the hills are a damned nuisance!"

"Even the Vischan armies are powerless to…"

"The Lord Governor's got his own problems!"

"But something must be done about the trade agreements!"

Some of the words were spoken in heavy whispers and others were emphasized with a good hardy fist to the table.

A lanky, big-boned woman rushed into the room from the kitchen. In her arms were three large, clay bowls, whose contents filled the air with delicious, gossamer-like vapors. She opened her mouth in the discovery of the trio standing at the far end of the room and her eyes opened even wider as the Halfling and the Dwarf stumbled in behind them. Quickly she dumped the bowls into the middle of the heated conversation and, wiping her hands on the towel around her waist, she ambled forward.

"Wondered if you were dining in this evening. Come! Come!" she beckoned them all and, upon noticing the Stranger, she added, "Lots of food, lots of room," and she dashed off momentarily, only to reappear with an extra plate, bowl and knife.

The Innkeeper, a tall, muscular man, rose awkwardly from the head of the table and, with some embarrassment, gestured for the rest of them to be seated. He, too, noticed the Newcomer and nodded an extra welcome.

"Well…uh…evenin'," he began.

"And a pleasant evening to you too," came a loud

voice, as a short, fat man rushed into the room just behind the others and quickly took up the end chair opposite the Innkeeper. Beads of perspiration dotted his brow, which he wiped with a purple silk and folded neatly into his vest pocket. He was lavishly dressed, several vests thick and rather well to do, judging by the size of the purse tied around his neck and visible for all to see.

"Ahh…Reushalt," said the Innkeeper, "a meal wouldn't be complete without your presence." With this, the tension around the table was instantly calmed as a good hardy laugh echoed around the room.

No more introductions or speeches were forthcoming as the bowls were quietly passed and helpings quickly drawn. The Innkeeper's wife dashed in and out of the kitchen several times with additional bowls and saucers of gravy, butter and salt. Upon her last trip, she deposited four large pitchers of wine on the table. Pleased that everyone seemed content, she gathered up a pile of yarn, sat down in the vacant chair next to Oblio and began to knit away.

Between bites, the young man noticed her worn hands loop the yarn and weave the thick wooden needles in and out. A constant click-clack was the only sound to carry throughout the hall, in what was becoming an uncomfortable hush.

"The wool was a bit coarse this last time, Mr. Reushalt," remarked the Innkeeper's wife.

"The Gathire wools will be in soon and I'll gladly replace the old with the new," he replied.

"Have you a shop in the village?" asked the young man politely.

"A business here? In 'The Keep'?" laughed the fat man. "No, no, my dear boy...not here!" he denied brazenly. "The *villagers*...all occupy seats at the other end of the table."

"Without me hanging around this forsaken outpost, *Mr. Reushalt*, you wouldn't eat or sleep nearly as well as you do," loudly remarked the man directly to the left of the Innkeeper, his fork jabbing the air. The young man noticed at once his unkempt military manner.

"You do an 'Admirable' job," perked up the Gnome. Then leaning in to the young man, he continued in a softer voice, "for a Lieutenant!" Bold laughter erupted from the young man's end of the table, none so loud as Reushalt, who added...

"Yes...the Corporal and the good Lieutenant indeed do us an honour by lowering themselves so much as to partake of food with us," prodded the fat man, which caused the Innkeeper to rise up quickly from his chair in nervous laughter.

"Now, now...gentlemen..." he pleaded, holding his wine glass high over his head, "let's dish ourselves another helping and pour ourselves a little more wine."

"Here, here!" Reushalt agreed and scooped another

generous portion of steamed turnips onto his plate, although it was far from empty. The Gnome nudged the young man and whispered.

"The man to the right of the Innkeeper is the Levi, or Commander of the guards of 'The Keep'. And the two to our side of the table are the guardian of the mercenaries, the Lieutenant and the Corporal…"

"…of the barracks outside the gate," continued the young man, to which the Gnome affirmed with a nod.

"Secrets?" observed the fat man none too quietly.

"Nommie here was just helping me keep things straight," corrected the young man.

"And who might thou be?" Reushalt's booming voice asked directly of the young man.

"I am…" paused the young man as if caught by surprise, "my name is…Muk."

"Muk! That's a fine name," laughed Quimby from the other side of the table, which resulted in a none-too-soft nudge from the Dwarf sitting beside him.

"Ah, yes," mused Reushalt, leaning toward Quimby and dangling his purse before the Halfling's eyes, "I'll wager there's more to Sir Muk than you'll ever be." Turning back to the young man, he continued. "I have traveled near and far as my trade would take me and I know these regions well, but tell me, surely you do not abide in this Realm?"

"I belong to the City of Brothers…do you know of it?"

queried Muk. Quimby furrowed his brow in thought and Nommie blinked in surprise.

"Valrhun! Of course I know of it," remarked the fat man. "Not only is it a model city of trade and commerce, it is a beautiful city as well. But it is very far from here."

"Uh…yes, I have been on a journey of sorts…"

"Yes, I would say so. Now there's a city for you," claimed Reushalt, downing the last of his wine and pouring another glass. "A spectacular port and a friendly city with arms open to all who enter…regardless of race or circumstance. A wonderful idea, is it not, Lt. Danski?"

"I wouldn't know, ne'er been," answered the good Lieutenant with his mouth full.

"Tis a pity," scorned the fat man, "I would think that we might all do with a slap of social humility during these trying times. Don't you think, Sir Gnome?" Nommie wasted no time in reaching for his drink and, standing tall on his chair, he raised his goblet in a toast.

"It is a Gnome…and I do believe it is also a Dwarven tradition…that one embraces another's shield and lowers their sword in tribute to friendship. To friendship then!" he added boldly.

Abruptly, Moralee the Dwarf stood in salute, jarring the table and nearly upsetting more than one goblet of wine. "To friendship!" she exclaimed, her arm and goblet raised high. One by one, the dinner guests stood and politely sipped their wine, except for Lt. Danski and the Corporal, who was nervously watching his superior out of the corner of his eye.

"Friendship is all good and well," admitted the smiling Lieutenant, rising to his feet, "but I prefer to drink to 'trust'. If you can trust a man…then he is truly your friend. When there is distrust, you find a rebel. When you face this rebel, you usually find a Dwarf! And as everybody knows, you can't trust a Dwarf!" There was a long, cold stare between Moralee and Lt. Danski before he went on. "Therefore, I would like to propose a toast. To 'The Empire', the true symbol of strength and trust!"

The Lieutenant and the Corporal both downed their drinks quickly and left the dining hall with an air of triumph. In the silence that followed, the Levi rose to leave as well, but not before Quimby jumped to the seat of his chair with a toast of his own.

"To the guards of 'The Keep'!" he saluted, to which everyone nodded in agreement. Pleased by the gesture and equally embarrassed, the man sat back down and acknowledged the toast by raising his empty goblet. But before the Innkeeper could reach over and refill his goblet, the fat man exclaimed…

"To the roof over our heads," he saluted, gulping down a full goblet in one swallow. Nommie and Quimby nodded and downed their drinks in similar fashion.

"To the lovely meal," responded Oblio, who turned with an expectant look toward Muk.

"I raise my cup…" Muk began, trying to think first of something profound, and then desperately of anything at all, "I raise my cup…in hopes that the Princess will be found and brought to safety."

"Here, here," voiced the fat man, but the silence that suddenly descended upon the room was deafening.

The Innkeeper's wife stood with her knitting clutched in her hand and left the room in a rush. Her husband rose to follow, but sat back down, his fingers rimming the top of his goblet.

"Please excuse me," he said at last and he followed after his wife through the kitchen door.

"It's her daughter," murmured the villager to Muk's right, but a blank expression was all that Muk could offer in return.

"The Princess is the daughter of our host and hostess," offered Oblio as a means of explanation. Reushalt filled his own cup yet again and waved Muk's cup closer, so that he could fill his as well. Then he continued.

"You see," he began, "Princess is her name, not her title. And not her *real* name, mind you. Somehow, she became mixed up with that Lord Governor fellow and, well, he called her his 'Princess' and now she's just known as 'Princess'. It's as easy as that," he summarized and emptied the last of the wine into his cup.

"My name is Mr. Boggs," suddenly announced the man sitting to Muk's right, "*villager* and shopkeeper extraordinaire. Are you a part of these adventure seekers?" he asked, motioning to the others.

"Adventure seekers?" Muk replied.

"We haven't asked him yet," answered Oblio with a smile.

"And we aren't about to!" Quimby cut in sharply.

"Of course, you must understand…if I were a bit younger…I would gladly lead you into the dungeon myself!" Reushalt stated firmly. "But you," he added, waving a hand at Muk, "with your size and strength, I'm surprised to find they haven't as yet enlisted your aid."

"I think we should consider it," added Nommie and the Dwarf nodded in agreement.

"And I say he can't be trusted!" argued Quimby.

"Excuse me," asserted Muk, "I've only just arrived this evening and I'm afraid I don't quite understand."

"Moralee, Oblio, Quimby and I are attempting to find the Princess. We have been on hold for four days now… waiting for the Lord Governor of 'The Keep' to address us…" Nommie began.

"But he won't see me…us!" Moralee quickly corrected herself.

"All we were asking…was permission to enter the dungeon," explained Oblio.

"*And* bring her back safely," added Nommie.

"*And* let's not forget to mention the word 'treasure'," laughed Reushalt, his eyes wild with expression. "The Ancients, after all, claimed that the dungeon was full of unbelievable riches."

"Far be it from me to be the one to remind you," warned the shopkeeper, rising from his chair and putting a chill to the conversation. "But a bare few have ever entered the dungeon and returned to see the light of day. And those unlucky few are mindless and much better off dead!"

There was a long silent pause, before the shopkeeper and the Levi took their leave from the table. Stopping in the doorway, the shopkeeper added, "Of course, if you should decide to go into the dungeon, and by some miracle you do happen to make it out with anything interesting, you know where you can find a *fair* price." Mr. Boggs turned to leave, but not before directing a false smile toward the fat man.

"He doesn't frighten me!" muttered Quimby.

"He only frightens himself," Moralee added.

"Ah ha, well put, Sir Gnome," yawned Reushalt, "But where you are planning to tread, it is a fearless man who is already dead!" he reminded them, and, with another yawn, he rose, steadied himself and, with apologies, headed for the sitting room.

"If I were entering the Demon Hole or dungeon as you

call it, it would comfort me to know the safety of numbers," Muk offered, once they were alone.

"Nobody cares what you think!" Quimby was quick to point out.

"But a good thing to keep in mind," Nommie contended, looking to Oblio and not the Halfling's glaring stare.

"Let's not discuss it here," Oblio said with a glance toward the kitchen.

"Agreed," Moralee announced, pushing herself from the table.

"Let's retire to our room," suggested Oblio. "Will you join us, Muk?" Quimby's mouth was agape at the offer and, not waiting to hear the young man's reply, he stormed out of the dining hall.

"Thank you," Muk replied with raised eyebrows, "if it's not too much trouble," he added with a nod toward the Halfling's exit. But Oblio quickly assured him by allowing him to take up her arm and together they left the dining hall, Moralee and Nommie bringing up the rear.

The sitting room was warm and peaceful. A cozy blaze crackled in the hearth at the far end of the room, where the fat man had settled himself in the largest chair before the fire. His elbows leaned to the outside of the chair and his feet were already stretched comfortably toward the flames.

Regrettably, Muk was not led toward the warmth of the hearth. Instead, he was directed to the foot of the stairway where Oblio handed him a sconce from a small table covered with an assortment of well-used candles. Standing impatiently at the top of the stairs was Quimby, holding a tin candle holder similar to those on the table.

"Where's Nommie?" he demanded in a huff of frustration, seeing the others standing at the foot of the stairs. They all turned and looked at once, thinking that he had been right behind them.

"...'ight 'ere," he answered, entering from the opposite side of the sitting room. It was also the quickest route to the kitchen.

"Nommie?!" laughed Oblio, pointing to the armful of sausages, fruit and bread.

"I was still hungry," he offered with a swallow and a grin.

"You're always hungry," retorted Moralee, holding her candle high and foraging ahead. Turning at a small landing, Muk climbed the stairs to find a dark hallway. Straight ahead, at the farthest end of the hall, a still muttering Quimby struggled to both hold his candle and push against a door that would not budge.

The first two doors they passed were across from one another and shut. Oblio pointed to the door to the left and whispered, "Necessary Room." The next two doors to the right were open and Muk noticed by the faint light of his candle that the rooms were sparsely furnished. Both rooms were nearly identical, a bed with straw mattress, a nightstand with bowl and pitcher and one chair, piled high with folded blankets. By the time Oblio addressed the troublesome door, Quimby was red-faced and fit-to-be-tied.

"It bent my knife!" he gruffed.

"It just sometimes sticks," she laughed and slowly ran her hand along the face of the door and just above the handle. The door 'popped' and opened inward. Quimby was first to rush in, ducking underneath Oblio's outstretched arm.

On tiptoe, he lit each of the four lamps that hung in the corner of the four bare walls and adjusted their light.

"Home sweet home," Nommie announced upon entering and crossing the room to several blankets and a pack, which he immediately opened and began to stuff with edible treasure.

There were no windows and just the one door and, other than a pile of leather strappings, a shield, some blankets and a few packs, the room was completely ~ humble.

"This used to be a storeroom," explained Oblio, misreading Muk's pained expression. "It was simpler than all of us fighting over one bed and cheaper too." She motioned for him to sit beside her on the floor in the middle of the room. "This room is costing us only half as much as the others and it's twice the size."

"It's not much," added Nommie, "but you'll find it comfort enough."

"But I haven't spoken to the Innkeeper yet!" Muk explained, thinking of the straw mattress down the hall.

"I did it for you," admitted the Gnome, "the Innkeeper's wife, that is. She gave us her blessing as well as the midnight snack."

"He's not staying with us?" complained Quimby, adjusting the light on the last lamp.

"Of course he is," voiced Oblio.

Quimby turned to the others in protest. "I don't think we should add another member to the group now!"

"I think we ought to," chimed in Moralee.

"But it will only take us longer to finance the expedition," Quimby pouted, throwing himself onto a pile of blankets in the corner. "And every day we stay here eats up more of our money."

"How much do you need?" inquired Muk.

"Our goal of ninety pieces gold provides a party of four ample food, arms, armour and rope," Nommie determined, "but to add on another…" he calculated, running a hand through his thick orange beard.

"How many gold pieces have you?"

"Don't tell him!" squealed Quimby, springing up from the corner to join the others.

Oblio gave him a slighting glance and replied, "Almost sixty. Of course, we were counting on some assistance from the Lord Governor…"

"Then…" Muk said, "would you make me a member of the expedition if I can match that amount?" The query was met with silence. But his acceptance into the group was obvious by their expressions….all save one.

"What else would you be good for?" retorted Quimby, finally realizing that he was being outvoted.

"Well," Muk began with a smile, "having lived around a water port all my life…and with all that rope you plan to buy with my money…I suspect I could keep myself busy tying knots."

"Yes, now that's definitely something in your favor," laughed Nommie along with the others. But Quimby was not impressed.

"But can you defend yourself?!" shouted the Halfling, suddenly producing a knife with a slightly bent tip and taking a threatening step toward the unwelcomed guest.

But Muk was just as swift and, from a concealed pocket beneath his cloak, he countered the threat by wielding a blade thrice the size of Quimby's.

"I didn't come this far on my journey without a few tricks up my sleeve," he smiled. But the Halfling didn't back down.

"Boys and the size of their knives!" chuckled Moralee.

"Then it's settled," Nommie decreed, trying to diffuse the situation.

"Should we begin our expedition tomorrow?" It was a

demand Oblio had thrown directly at Quimby, although the question was meant for the Gnome.

Nommie, pulling heavily on his beard, began to think aloud. "If Muk indeed has sixty pieces gold…and if the tavern gossip flows as readily tonight as it did before…and with an early errand or two…" Nommie finally concluded. "There seems to be no reason to keep us from it!"

"Then we go tomorrow!" confirmed Oblio.

"Yes, yes! Tomorrow…tomorrow…" Quimby agreed vigorously, his attitude and facial expression suddenly changed. But only because Muk had pulled the stitching loose from the inside seam of his robe and began producing one shiny gold coin after another, allowing them to drop heavily onto the floor.

Chapter Twelve

The Night Air Was Cool And Fresh

...as the band of five crossed the open courtyard. The moons of Somber were now at arms-length from one another, giving everything in view two soft shadows. The tavern door opened inward with a burst, for it was old and hung a bit oddly and moved only when you gave it a solid push. Moralee stood in the half-light of the entryway to a room smoky and loud, but not yet overcrowded. Instantly, there was a sudden hush. The two tables just inside the door were taken up by a handful of mercenaries who, when they looked up, leaned their heads back together in disgust and carried on with their grumbly conversation. To the far right and closest to the wall and a blazing fire, were tables occupied by a half dozen Dwarves. Beyond the centre of the room against the far wall was the bar. It was as long as the tavern was wide, except for a small space at either end in which to maneuver around. Several local tradesmen were standing at the bar, talking to the barkeep.

Nommie pushed his way around the Dwarf and

proceeded directly to the counter. Oblio, Quimby and Muk followed his lead. A wooden bucket of thick, bubbly ale was ordered and drawn from one of three giant kegs on the wall. As soon as it was placed on the countertop, Quimby was quick to grab it up.

"This ought to do *me* just fine," he announced loudly, bringing laughter from every corner of the room. With both hands struggling to hold up the heavy bucket nearly half his size, he led the group strategically to a table in the centre of the room.

Moralee, however, nodded for yet another bucket to be drawn and joined the tables occupied by the Dwarves. Unbuckling her belt and leaning her sword against the wall, she sat down amongst them. Almost at once, the Dwarven table became an instant buzz of conversation. The gestures, nods and looks were aimed at the newest member of the group ~ Muk!

Muk and the others waited patiently for their cups to be brought to them. The Barkeep's wife, a burly woman with arms as big as posts entered from the storeroom behind the counter, carrying a tray of wooden cups. She lifted the bucket of ale as if it were one large cup and began pouring, each in turn, beginning with Oblio. As she held the bucket much higher than needed, the ale cascaded like a waterfall into each cup with nary a drop lost. And as she poured, she began to sing, in a voice high and shrill:

> "From ancient times…
>
> There is a rhyme
>
> And a story to tell, 'Bout two rivers
>
> A heavy snow
>
> And two crops found in the dell.
>
> On banks of Fain
>
> Came golden grain
>
> Fast upon the melted snow, Ripe hops from Furth
>
> Torn from the earth
>
> And together they did flow.
>
> Water rumbled
>
> Roll and tumbled
>
> Into the pools of Trenkin, Into a vat
>
> Imagine that
>
> 'To us! A night of drinkin.'

Everyone at the table except for Muk, who could not have looked more out of place, sang the last line.

"First time, dearie?" she asked with a suggestive smile that set the whole table to laughing. She returned to the bar, this time for two buckets of ale, and continued to parade around the room, selling more ale and encouraging each table to join another round of song.

Meanwhile, Nommie, Oblio and Quimby were orientating Muk and helping him catch up on the last three days. Nommie pointed to the three men standing at the bar counter. One of them Muk recognized at once as Mr. Boggs, the shopkeeper. The other two, he was told, were the Advisor and the Butler for the Lord Governor.

"While Moralee is busy talking to her kinfolk," Nommie decided, "I think I will see what information I can get out of the soldiers. Oblio, why don't you and Muk find out more about our invisible host, the Lord Governor? If anyone should know what's going on, it must surely be his Advisor."

"What will I do?" Quimby complained, following on the heels of the Gnome.

"My dear Quimby," began Nommie with a reproving look, "who are we about to share our ale with?"

"Dunno! I never met them before," he confessed.

"No, no, no," groaned Nommie, "what are they?"

"Soldiers hired by the Lord of 'The Keep'," Quimby replied. "Mercenaries!"

"Yes! A private army who are well paid for their duties…are they not?"

"Supposedly," answered Quimby in the same matter-of-fact tone used by the Gnome.

"And who do you suppose is the one person who controls most of the wealth in this region?" he pressed with a sly grin.

"Ahh…" answered Quimby with a wink and off the two of them went, Nommie carrying their half bucket of ale as a gift, and the little thief trailing right behind.

Abiding with Nommie's wishes, Muk and Oblio returned to the bar to refill their empty cups. Muk nodded a hello to his former dinner companion and the shopkeeper smiled and nodded in return.

"Entertaining place…" Muk said over the din of the room. "What's it like in the dead of winter?"

"Dead!" Mr. Boggs responded with a chuckle at his own joke. "May I offer you a brimmer?"

"Thank you, Mr. Boggs," accepted Oblio, stepping between the two as if on cue. "Muk has just joined our dungeon expedition and he and I were wondering if your friends here know whether the Lord Governor will be available for an audience tomorrow morning?'"

"It's not for us to decide," apologized the Butler with a forlorn expression. "If it was up to me, I would have invited you all in the very moment that you arrived. Given you a tour for free…just to air out a few of the rooms."

"Things have been a bit strained around here lately," added the Advisor with the same almost mournful look.

"You mean since the Princess disappeared?" asked Muk.

"Well, yes, that and other things," replied the Advisor with a quick glance toward Mr. Boggs that left him silent-tongued.

"Do you plan on venturing down…uhh…that is…"

"Into the dungeon?" Oblio finished the Butler's question for him. "Yes," she affirmed. "In fact, we will be calling on you, Mr. Boggs, very early in the morning to go over a list of things we need."

"Fine! Splendid!" the shopkeeper said excitedly, "catch me in early, while the Lord Governor is still absent and you can be sure of bargain prices," guaranteed Mr. Boggs. The other two men seemed genuinely enthusiastic as well and all five of them raised their cups to celebrate the wonderful news.

"So the Lord Governor is…away?" Muk was quick to ask. But the Advisor had turned to order another brimmer, so the Butler answered for him.

"Not away actually…just…" he began to say, but was cut off.

"Actually, there are three answers to your question," the Advisor said, even before turning to face him. "One, this Dwarven rebellion in the Highlands of Gathire. Two, the greedy Vischan armies gobbling up all the trade routes and agreements. Three, with this Princess thing and their supposed 'wedding intentions'; and on top of all that, the Somber snows are nearly upon us ~ and that in itself, is more than enough to worry about in these regions."

"That's four!" the Butler pointed out.

"Four what?"

"Four reasons…uh…I mean answers to his question."

The Advisor stopped and thought about that for a moment, then responded, "Well…there's your answer then ~ a wagon load of horse dung overturned on a hot day!"

"The Lord Governor should be attending to any one of these problems," inserted the Butler, who seemed to want to add verbal confirmation of his own. "And he soon better be. The population of 'The Keep' has dwindled to much less than half since he was appointed, and things aren't getting any better."

A loud grating of chairs cut into the tavern conversations as the mercenaries all rose and left together. As soon as the door slammed shut, it reopened again quickly, as a handful of villagers entered, headed by the Levi. Apparently, the news of the group's journey into the dungeon had made its rounds; and, overjoyed, the locals began to invade the tavern, all motioning for drinks.

Moralee joined the crowd at the bar and stood beside Muk until he noticed her presence.

"We needn't spend anything on rope," she said with a wry grin, then scrutinizing Muk closely, "what exactly happened down at the dock?"

"Uh…I'm not sure. What do you mean?" Muk replied sheepishly. But Moralee had no time to quiz him further as Nommie and Quimby returned to the bar for another bucket.

"That was a total waste of ale!" muttered the Gnome as he brushed by.

"And I don't think they're all that well paid," added Quimby, holding up the few coins he had pocketed. "And all we found out was that the Lord Governor has been absent for a few days." Muk concurred with a nod and the Halfling motioned toward the last group through the door. "The Smithy is making something for Nommie and we are looking to work some information out of the Levi," he said with importance.

"We must find our drunk!" Nommie whispered heavily, hoisting a full bucket of ale and heading in the direction of the Levi and the fresh gathering of villagers.

When Muk turned to join the conversation around him, the only one looking at him was the barkeep, who was motioning toward his empty cup.

"Do you know of a man known as 'the drunk'?" Muk asked, pushing his cup forward for a refill.

"Oh, him!" answered the barkeep, who was only interested in filling everyone's cup. He proceeded down the bar, nodding and refilling wherever it was needed. But Muk was insistent upon gathering information, so he pulled Mr. Boggs aside, interrupting his conversation with Moralee about supplies.

"I'm sorry, but I must find him this evening," Muk explained. "Do you know where I might find him?"

"Find who?"

"The drunk!" Muk had to shout above the wave of noise coming from behind them.

"Oh...such a poor, poor man...it's unfortunate...it really is!" Mr. Boggs offered with a heavy sigh.

"But where can he be found..." appealed Muk, "tonight?"

"Oh...I don't know," he answered with a wave of one hand and spilling ale on himself with the other. "With this much activity in the tavern, I'm surprised he's not already here," added the shopkeeper, pushing his way through the crowd to join the celebration in the centre of the room.

Nommie and Quimby had gone directly to work pouring ale and asking questions of those townspeople who had just arrived. The room was suddenly a buzz with excitement and talk of the attempted journey into the dungeon.

The Levi was the first to proclaim a toast: "To the noble deed and safe return!"

"To the return of *my* Princess," cried the teary-eyed Innkeeper's wife.

"To her return..." began the Smithy, a burly man who seemed to be mostly beard, "so that I might once again get another decent day's work out of my young apprentice," he added, to which the room erupted in cheers and laughter.

Marcus, the young man seated next to the Smithy, blushed violently. He was about the same age as Muk but thinner, and his blond features were weathered by the rugged outdoors. The young man also, as Muk had noticed upon his entering, was limping and had to be helped to the centre table by his friends. Thinking that he had had enough drink for one evening, Muk looked to Nommie for a sign to leave, but the Gnome had just cornered the Smithy into conversation. Oblio too, had just settled in next to the apprentice, Marcus, and was listening intently to his answers.

"This is all very boring," griped Quimby, who was feeling unimportant and had experienced a very poor night of thievery.

"I am finding myself very tired as well," Muk agreed.

"Nommie says we must find the 'drunk'!" Moralee briskly reminded them both.

"The drunk, the drunk," snapped Quimby. "That could be anyone still in here!" In a huff of frustration, he maneuvered around the group bunched in the middle of the room and headed for the door. He was but a few paces from the door, when it burst open to the cool night air. Only this time, it wasn't a choir of happy villagers, but a return of angry mercenaries. Scanning the festive and noisy room, the soldiers were looking in particular for a short, Halfling thief. But Quimby saw them first and, seeing his escape completely blocked, he reversed his sights and quickly headed for the less populated end of the bar and the side door marked 'Privy'. As he disappeared around the bar, there came a sudden 'yelp' and groan. The conversational roar in the room died to a near silence and heads turned in wonder.

A quick dash was all that could be seen of Quimby, as he darted from behind the bar and between the first pair of legs he could hide behind.

"Whose dog just walked all over me?" yelled a grizzly-bearded man, crawling out from behind the bar and teetering to his feet. He stood, blinking in surprise at a room suddenly filled with people.

"I'm not a dog!" Quimby protested, stepping forward in his defense. Then reconsidering the situation, the Halfling backed up several steps toward Moralee.

"What happened?" Moralee couldn't help but ask with a laugh.

"Some dumb drunk was lying asleep on the floor at the end of the counter and I accidently tripped over him," he admitted.

Chapter Thirteen

"The Drunk!"

...both Moralee and Muk said in unison and the three of them turned to watch the figure disappear behind the bar and a closing door.

"The Halfling Thief!" rang out almost simultaneously, as the solders in the tavern doorway began pushing their way across the crowded room. Only Quimby understood the two causes of the uproar that was now taking place.

"Gotta go!" he cried, dashing around the end of the bar after the drunk.

"Wait, my sword!" exclaimed Moralee, but the Halfling was already out the back door and into the night.

"He didn't look that menacing," Muk shouted over his shoulder and quickly followed on Quimby's heels. Personally, he was thankful for any diversion that took him out of the pandemonium that had suddenly broken out in the tavern.

Seeing their quarry escaping only gave the solders more incentive to push through the crowd, which met with immediate opposition. It was by no means a drunken crowd, but the tensions between the two factions were already near the boiling point. Even though the villagers had no idea why they were being forced aside, they began to push back.

Unknowingly, it was Moralee who escalated the shoving war to drawn knives and swords. Muk and Quimby had been in her charge, and she had hastily grabbed for her belted sword in an attempt to help corral the evasive drunk. With sword in hand, she raced out the back door. But the mercenaries saw her attempt to arm herself as a sign of battle against them, and the metallic sound of steel being drawn sent out an immediate cry of 'War' from the angry crowd.

Oblio and Nommie stood in the middle of the attack. The Gnome, with his bright blue eyes blazing for battle, was being held tight by the grasp of Oblio's hand. He instantly looked to her for some plausible explanation, but her head was bowed as if in prayer.

The first hum of an arcing blade clanged harmlessly over their heads, having been blocked by the Levi's sword and quick action. The second and last blow met with Marcus's wooden crutch, which rendered it worthless; but fortunately, no harm had befallen him. The next sequence of events still has the inhabitants of that region talking about it to this day, as those present swore that the tavern door swung open in the fists of a mighty wind and whisked the three soldiers, blades and all, into the dark shadows of the courtyard from which they never returned.

Meanwhile, out back, the 'drunk' had not gotten far. Not ten paces from the back door stood the surly old man, with Quimby blocking his path with every step he tried to take. It was a strange scene in double shadows, two very different shapes locked in an odd sort of battle.

"Get out of my way…you nasty bag of wind!" hollered the drunk, waving one hand for balance and using the other as a swatting stick. The hand swipes were flailing in the night air and the Halfling dodged them with ease.

"Stop!" shouted Quimby, but the old man continued to do his best to maneuver around him, one blocked step at a time, until suddenly there were two bodies standing in his way.

"Hulic Hilt!" cried the drunk. "What now?" The added presence of a bearded, female Dwarf in his path gave the old man reason to pause.

"Please sir, may we talk with you?" came a voice from behind him.

"Wha…?" he said, spinning to face yet another figure in the dark.

"We don't mean you any harm," Muk assured him. "We just want to ask you some questions."

"Leave me be!" he yelled and, completely forgetting the blockade behind him, he turned and bumped into a solid wall of Dwarf. "I said..." began the old man, but he never finished saying what his fist had intended to do. In one surprisingly agile but wild exaggerated swing, he let his frustration fly. Moralee calmly stepped back. But Quimby, fully surprised at seeing the Dwarf back away from a confrontation, caught a glancing blow across the top of his head. He rolled over once and came to rest against the wheel of an old, broken down cart.

"Ow!" cried the drunk, shaking his hand in pain and looking to find the Dwarf still standing in his way. "You still here?" he demanded, reaching back to swing again. This time, however, he stepped forward awkwardly and slumped to a sitting position facing the direction he had come, his worn features and hapless situation magnified in the moonlight.

While Muk sat down to join him, Moralee walked over to tend to Quimby, dazed and irate. "You moved!" he bellowed in disbelief.

"He wouldn't be any use to us knocked senseless," she assured him, reaching to lend him a hand.

"Right," he grumbled, waving her off. Meanwhile, Muk was trying to gain the old man's trust.

"Please, we need some help," Muk explained.

"Won't talk about it."

"But Milly, Byron and Freda said you might help us."

"Do you know the street muffins?" asked the drunk with sudden interest.

"Yes, I think they made me an honorary member," Muk grinned.

"I tell them stories, you know…about the old days ~ about the dungeon. They like me! Did they tell you where I was?"

"Uh…yes, they did," Muk admitted.

"Poor rag-a-muffins…you know their parents are practically shackled to their jobs. Horrible wages…day after day."

"Here…take this," offered a voice. It was Nommie, holding out a cup of ale. The old man took it gladly. Oblio, too, was there and sat down next to Muk.

"What stories do you tell them?" said Oblio softly, waiting for him to drain his cup.

"They love the story about the unicorn…the flying horse…and the magical dragon. And I show them a gold piece and tell 'em it's from a room filled with piles and piles of gold and silver…you know, faerie tale stuff," he replied with a shrug. "I just made it all up."

"The Levi said that you were once a great swordsman," encouraged Nommie. There was a long moment of silence. The group was beginning to wonder if the old man was going to respond at all. Finally, he opened his mouth to speak, but closed it, as if looking off to the past and deciding where to start.

Suddenly he smiled. "In my younger days, I was the

'Sergeant of the Watch'…yes!" he emphasized as if there was some doubt. "An officer right here in 'The Keep'! Of course those were the days when people came and went from these walls just as they wished. Trade was plentiful and everyone's business was thriving. Not as it is now, the village in shambles and the trade goods stockpiled and hoarded, the best of the harvest sent inside the walls and the rest sold at prices too high for those who can least afford it!"

"Why did you go into the dungeon?" asked Oblio. The drunk looked at her with a blinking stare.

"The party before us was long overdue," he sighed, "and some of them were villagers…friends of mine." He dwelt upon that thought until his eyes filled with tears. "It was my own fault, really," he continued, looking into Muk's eyes for forgiveness. "I…always held tight to the dreams… the legends of riches and fame." He shrugged his shoulders and wiped his eyes with his sleeve. "Anyway…they didn't have to ask me twice…that's for sure. Treasure seekers, they were…done it before…they said. They were strong and brave enough…but young with ideas…no experience at all, ya see. Me neither, now that I think about it!"

"Did you rescue the first party?" asked Quimby, who had crawled over and was now absorbed by the story.

"We never found them…not a trace. Except for the Old Elf, who later, somehow found another way out ~ none of the original group survived."

"What happened to your group?" Moralee prodded.

"Oh…" he painfully recalled, "we all began bickering…set on going in our own selfish directions, we were. 'Tis a pity…a terrible shame, but we didn't know what to expect…what we would run into…" he stopped suddenly.

"What did you run into?" Quimby said wide-eyed, but the old man just buried his face in his hands and began to sob.

"Do you remember anything that might help us?" asked Muk, "a floor plan, a right or wrong way to turn, anything at all?"

"The Great Hall was fascinating!" he said between sobs but only then did he realize the implications and the meaning behind the questions. There was a look of absolute shock frozen on his face. "You're not going down there?" he gasped.

"We're going to find the Princess…" Oblio began.

"You can't! You mustn't!" he implored, looking to each one of them in turn. "We need to seal that gate shut! Close it forever! You don't understand!"

"Understand what?" said more than one voice in unison.

"The traps!" he cried out, "…men screaming…goblins chasing me…*and*…"

"And…?"

"The Big Bugs!" he wept, and as the last memory crossed his mind, he looked about him wildly. He attempted to crawl to his feet but landed in Muk's lap instead. "They're coming…can't you hear them? They're coming!" he screamed, trying to claw his way past Muk. "I'm lost in the maze ~ in the nightmare! I can't find my way out!" he yelled. "Help me! Please, help me!" he pleaded, pinning Muk's arms to his side with a panicked embrace.

"Here, old man," offered a gentle voice, as two strong arms reached for him, pulling him to his feet. It was the Levi, hugging the old man to a stand and trying to help him walk. "It's alright, Papa…I've got you now," he assured him and together they walked slowly back to the tavern. "You're home…you're safe…it's alright…" he said over and over.

The two men staggered off into the shadows, leaving the huddled adventure seekers bathed in the silence of the bright moonlight above.

Chapter Fourteen

In The Safety Of Their Own Room

...the lamps were relit and the group gathered to discuss what they had learned. Secure in the determination that their plan to venture into the dungeon was both noble and necessary, they began to organize their thoughts.

"So nobody actually knows what this Lord Governor looks like?" queried Muk.

"There is a bronze bust of him in the Governor's entry hall, but after waiting two days to be granted an audience, that's *all* we've seen of him," huffed Moralee.

"And we won't go back again!" Quimby declared.

"It really was quite rude of him," chimed in Oblio. "Nommie left him a very formal letter extending our eagerness to help ~ and that we were staying here at the Inn awaiting his reply...but he still hasn't sent word."

"I'm sorry, but there is something that just doesn't make any sense to me," Muk frowned. "If everybody likes the Princess so much...and it seems that they genuinely do... why hasn't someone gone after her? And why the dungeon?"

"Sense has nothing to do with anything about 'The Keep', answered Nommie. "Everything here seems to thrive on power and superstition. The entire region is in the iron grip of the Vischan Empire; the bridges, the ports, the hills ~ everything. The Lord Governor's informants are everywhere."

"Even if you had help in escaping, the mercenaries on horseback would easily run you down and gladly for a price," Moralee added.

"Sounds like the ancient tale of Darmund," Muk muttered. There was a long silence. Oblio continued.

"The Princess must have either run away, or been taken by someone who wanted to get back at the Lord Governor. And from what we have gathered, it could be just about anyone. It just doesn't seem likely that *anyone* got *far* away."

"But why the dungeon?"

"Ahh ~ the superstition ~ ancient Legend!" stated Nommie.

"Supposedly, the dungeon not only holds fabulous riches, but secrets to unlock the Universe as well," laughed Moralee.

"Some people have sworn they saw treasure," insisted Quimby.

"Yes, but claiming an existence outside Father Forest?" scoffed Moralee, "and proving it?"

"Let's not get back into that conversation again," moaned the Halfling.

"We were talking about the dungeon," Oblio reminded them, "which is a mere forty paces from the Governor's front door ~ the perfect place in which to hide *or* be locked up. Either way, thanks to some superstitious old legend, nobody is coming after you."

"Not even an army of mercenaries will go into the dungeon!" exclaimed Quimby.

"Did you know that the Gnomes of Ancient believed that 'The Keep' was originally built to keep something in?" Nommie said with raised eyebrows. "Not a fortress to keep something out."

"That's seems unlikely...why go to that trouble?" Moralee asked.

"The secret of the Universe probably," sighed Quimby.

"Please, not that again...," Nommie grimaced.

"Okay...I get the power struggle and the superstition ~ whatever 'that' is", asserted Muk, " but if the Old Elf and the drunk's stories are even partially true, why are you risking your lives if an army will not?"

"We have Oblio," declared Quimby. Muk gave a puzzled look toward Oblio, while Moralee and Nommie laughed encouragingly. Her face flushed with embarrassment, but as if a command, Oblio threw her shoulders back, her long, yellow robe dangling from her outstretched hand, and she pointed a finger at Muk. Instantly, a whirlwind encompassed him and lifted him off the floor and moved him toward the door, which opened wide and then closed softly, leaving him sitting in the dark hall.

Muk opened the door hesitantly and peered in. "Where did you learn to do that?" he asked in surprise.

"I know of a great wizard," she explained, "he has sought to teach me much."

"Indeed, he has," offered Muk in tribute. "Do you work with a stone or charm?"

"No," she said with a smile, "I just transported you."

"Transported me?" pondered Muk.

"You're a wizard, you should understand that!" belittled Quimby.

"What manner of magic *did* you place on the Dwarven children," Moralee was eager to know.

It was Muk's turn to look embarrassed. With his robe and tricks folded away in his pack, he decided on a verbal explanation. "The bud I used looks much like a bean," he said, holding out an empty hand. "It comes from the fields east of Darmund. The oil…" he said, extending his other hand, "comes by way of Valjhune ~ from the shores of a distant island. Together they create an energy that…'pops'!"

"Pops?" questioned Moralee.

"That's your magic?" said Quimby, his mouth agape in disbelief. "That's all? That's it??"

"Well, I can sometimes pull a coin out of an ear without

fumbling it," Muk offered in response and began to laugh. Oblio and Nommie joined in, but the Dwarf and the Halfling were thinking in darker terms ~ the dungeon.

"We thought you were some kind of wizard!" cried Quimby, jumping up and opening the door for Muk's exit. The Halfling was glaring at Muk, but it was Nommie who broke the tension.

"Catch it!" the Gnome hollered, half crawling and half lunging toward the open door but not before a rat with a long twisted tail scampered under Quimby's feet and disappeared out into the hall.

"It's just a rat," observed Moralee.

"It wasn't thinking like one," was all Nommie offered, picking himself up off the floor and carefully scanning the shadows of the hall before closing the door.

"Well, I certainly feel safe!" Quimby stated, rolling his eyes. "Oblio moves things. We've a wizard who really isn't a wizard, but knows a few tricks and then there's a Gnome ~ who thinks rodent!"

"It was entirely out of character," Nommie defended. "If I had had a chance to talk to it, I would have known for sure if it was just a rat."

"Now he's talking to them," murmured Quimby to himself and receded to the corner of the room where he began to lay out a blanket.

"What did you sense?" Oblio asked, suppressing a

smile, but both Muk and Moralee listened attentively for an answer.

"Not real sure," he replied aloud, then looking over to find Quimby preoccupied with his bedroll, he whispered, "beats gabbing about magic." He laughed to himself while rummaging through his pack. Finding a heavy blanket, he wrapped it about himself and curled up in the corner until he was comfortable.

Muk was left feeling uneasy. He was uncertain as to whether he was wanted and uncomfortable with the prospect of the hard floor when a bed and pillow were just down the hall. And, he was more than a little apprehensive about a 'journey' to a place no one ever returns from. He looked up to find Oblio's Elfan stare and knew that she had been trying to read his thoughts.

"It'll be fine," she assured him. "We'll regroup in the morning."

When nothing more was said, the rest of them spread out and made themselves as comfortable as they could on the floor. Oblio, with one graceful wave of her hand, extinguished the four lamps and the room fell into darkness.

Tired and exhausted, Muk stretched out on his back, his hands coming to rest between his head and his journey bag. He began to reflect upon the long day up river and the events leading him into this sudden and rather strange partnership ~ a Gnome, an Elf, a Dwarf, a Halfling thief and himself ~ how unlikely. Just the possibility of a chance meeting was barely believable. But banding together, members of different races and separate Realms ~ this concept, forbidden in ancient times ~ this odd alliance was incredible. He smiled at the thought of his great-grandfather, who would have been extremely pleased with the situation. And then he fell into a deep sleep.

The day began bright and exceedingly warm. There was no breeze. All around the young Prince, the Forest floor was covered in green, except for the two long dirt stretches thick with dust running side by side in the centre of the arena. On the outskirts of the glen, there was a hubbub of people and activity. Up the hillside and into the surrounding woods, there were countless camps of men and horses from near and far, each flying bright, colourful banners, symbolic of their position and Realm.

Today was to be an accumulation of years of practice and study, the blend of both boy and man ~ the day of truth. Outside, the ancient, metal shell gleamed with manly courage and strength. Inside, the boy shook involuntarily and wanted to run and hide, but the weight of the armour stifled even his breathing. With great effort, he slowly ascended the plank steps of the loading hoist. Without guiding hands, he would most certainly have lost his balance and toppled to the ground. From behind him there was a sound of metal on metal as he was jerked into the air, unseen hands adjusted him ~ pushing and pulling ~ securing him onto his mount. A jousting rod was thrust into his left hand. He grabbed it firmly by its leather strapping and tucked the ribbing under his arm. The merciless sun and lack of trees left no shade in the arena to protect the horse or rider from the scorching heat. Although his visor was still up, there was no air to cool the sweat upon his brow. The horse, too, was restless, as it twitched and swayed and had to be guided to the starting pole by the edge of the field. He tried to gentle his mount with soothing words and took one last, long deep breath before lowering his visor. He wondered briefly if it would be his last. With his right hand, he grabbed a firm hold on the reins and peered through the iron gridding for some glimpse of the red flag or his opponent, but the tightening of the reins only triggered the horse into a sudden twist and bolt.

∞

Crunch! Crash! Muk awoke with a start, flat on his back on the hardwood floor, a blanket wrapped tightly around him where the suit of armour had been only moments before.

"Listen!" whispered Nommie from somewhere in the darkness. Muk shook the dream from his head and sat up blinking, as the oil lamps magically relit. Quimby darted silently across the room, his ear tight to the door. There was a muffled cry and the sounds of a struggle coming from down the hall. It took Nommie and Moralee a few moments to secure their weapons, but they reached the door at the same time, their swords drawn and ready.

"Oblio, open the door," whispered Muk, scrambling to his feet. "Moralee and Nommie can lead us down the hall, Quimby and I will follow."

"What's this?" blurted Quimby, "Now you're telling us what to do?"

"Quickly," hissed Oblio, "now is not the time to argue, someone is in need of help." Quimby was the first to peer into the hall, but finding no wall lamps lit and tall mysterious shadows dancing at the top of the stairwell, he flattened himself against the door and urged to the others to proceed.

"Hurry up, you two, Muk and I are right behind you!"

Nommie and Moralee then rushed into the unknown, their footsteps closely followed by the remaining three. But the end of the hall was silent and they found nobody to rescue. The first door at the top of the landing, however, was now ajar. Prodding it open a little further, showed the room in a mess. The pale flickering of a single candle revealed clothes and belongings thrown about the floor.

"Reushalt's room," Quimby whispered, rummaging through one of the opened trunks, holding up a mauve coloured dress shirt and a pair of plum coloured trousers. Quietly, the group followed one another down the stairwell to the front door of the Inn, which they found wide open.

∽

"Where's the fat man?" Freddy insisted.

"Gone…you idiot!" explained Chief, none too politely.

"Weren't you listening?" Tommy said, shaking his head.

"I know…but who took him? Why?"

"Who took who?" demanded Mr. Wittlesey. He was standing in the doorway of the dormitory, scouring the room with a heavy-eyebrowed expression, hoping to catch a glimpse of someone out of bed or something amiss.

"Nothing!" came a unified chorus, as the boys all dove under their covers and Eff quickly tucked the Pageleaf beneath his pillow.

Chapter Fifteen

The Aroma Of Fresh Bread

...was all the group needed to hurry their packing and get down to breakfast. The five of them were the only ones at the table as the Innkeeper's wife went about providing them with more than enough food with an air of calm and pleasantness. Breakfast was a quiet affair. Half of the food from Nommie's plate went into his mouth and the other half into his backpack. Quimby reached for the plate of fresh bread and poured the remains into his pack. As an afterthought, he added the cheese and, without a further word, both he and Nommie rushed out of the room.

"What are the boys up to this morning?" Oblio asked of Moralee, who had her pack in hand and was about to follow in their footsteps.

"Nommie's plan was to buy a crossbow and some armour from the Smithy," Moralee reported. "Quimby and I are straightaway to see Mr. Boggs. Our task is to fill the list of supplies we will need. Nommie is expecting us to gather in the courtyard by the time the morning sun reaches the dungeon wall." Then, she too, made her way from the room.

Muk took a deep breath and decided to make use of the opportunity to address a few of his concerns.

"You don't seem the least bit anxious about entering the dungeon."

"I should be, I suppose, but somehow I'm not," Oblio smiled in return. "But you are the surprising one. How do you feel about joining us? I mean going down there with four different...well...*really* different people?" It was Muk's turn to smile and, carefully, he chose his words.

"To be honest, I've never experienced an odder group. Before this trip, the closest I've ever been to a full-blooded Dwarf was a conversation with a river dividing us. Halflings usually do the trading for the Gnomes, but if I had really wanted to meet with one, I would have had to go visit their camp."

"Village."

"Hmm?"

"Gnomes live in villages, Dwarves in dwellings, Goblins...uh...camp, I think."

"Well, that's what I mean...I'm still learning to..."

"Eh...sorry, dears...was there anything else I could get you?" interrupted the Innkeeper's wife. Apparently, she had been standing in the entryway for a short while struggling with her inner feelings. Oblio seemed not to notice her uneasiness and simply shook her head.

"No…thank you! It was wonderful…and filling," added Muk, who had been wondering when they might have another meal like it.

"Well…" began their hostess; then she just threw up her hands and walked over and sat down between them. "I just wanted to apologize for last night. Politics always keep the men at odds, but when it just comes down to the people in the village…well…really…I am so relieved that someone wants to help!" She paused and then reached out, putting both her warm, work-worn hands on theirs. "I didn't have any hope left…but now," she smiled and pursed her lips to hold back the tears, "you just be careful. Watch over one another and you'll do fine." She stood and threw her head back and said matter-of-factly, "And if you find my little girl…you bring her back home to me!" She waited a moment for the words to sink in, "You just do that!" she added, barely able to hold back the emotion in her voice. Turning, she quickly rushed back to her business in the kitchen.

Meanwhile, the early morning sun was beginning to fill the courtyard of 'The Keep'. The porch of the Trade Store was bathed in bright sunlight and the door was open to the fresh morning air. The sign in the window read 'Open for Business' but inside, there were only two customers…one Dwarven shopper and one Halfling shoplifter.

When Muk and Oblio arrived, they found Moralee at

the counter, standing toe to toe with Mr. Boggs. They were bartering in grand fashion.

"That rope is from the port of Valvay, the finest grade!" insisted the shopkeeper. "Four golds!"

"We have enough rope already," Moralee said calmly. "One gold."

"Well…three then."

"One!"

"Okay…TWO then," agreed Mr. Boggs. Moralee shook his hand and tossed the coil over her shoulder to the alert Halfling, who shoved it into his pack. Mr. Boggs insisted that each item she inquired about was of top quality or had some long colourful history. The Dwarf seemed totally uninterested but leaned into every transaction, cutting each price in half, if not better. Each time they came to an agreement over an item, there was an affirmative nod or handshake. Moralee quickly pointed to the next item on the list, while Quimby was doing a bit of shopping on his own, but not bothering to pay for any of it. The shopkeeper was so embroiled in the pricing battle with the Dwarf that he was completely unaware of the Halfling, moving here and there from one display of goods to the next, casually sticking things under his belt or shirt.

Wadding up the list that Nommie had given her, Moralee strolled out the door, with Quimby following so closely behind that they could have been attached. Muk was more than a little uneasy by the Halfling's shameless stealing and dug into his trouser pockets for another coin or two, until he saw the prices posted on the baskets and bins. He grimaced, thinking of better ways to waste his money, and followed Oblio into the courtyard, where they organized the goods, both purchased and stolen, equally among four packs.

When all of the sorting and packing was done, Moralee lifted the heaviest of the bags and Quimby the lightest two, leaving the last for Muk to throw over his shoulder. Oblio was left with nothing to carry, Muk noticed, but said nothing. They walked around the rear of the temple now brilliant white in the light of day, and stood between the tavern and the archway over the entrance to the dungeon. They were all waiting on the Gnome. The sun was now high enough to cast direct sunlight over the great wall and into the courtyard between the Temple and the Tavern. Fingers of light were now directly above the sunken arch over the doorway to the dungeon, just steps from where they had confronted the 'drunk' the night before.

"All right then!" came a familiar voice and all turned to find Nommie, in all his readiness, standing before them. He wore armour plated boots, a half-jacket made of chain mail ~ his belt strapped around his waist, securing a sword. One armour clad hand held a cross bow. In the other hand, he carried a red shield. His smiling green eyes were flashing under his new metal helmet, which had a spike sticking out of the top of it. Quimby was the first to speak; and it was a good thing, too, for the other three were desperately holding back fits of laughter.

"Why didn't I get something to wear?" Quimby frowned, carefully inspecting the Gnome. He circled him several times admiring the hardware. "Why didn't I get something to wear?" he asked again, with an imploring look over at the others.

"Sorry," broke in the Levi, realizing that he had just interrupted a tense moment between the adventurers. "Are we all here?" he said, rattling a large metal ring with several keys on it and motioning toward the far corner of 'The Keep'.

"What about the Lord Governor's approval?" inquired Oblio, choosing to ignore Quimby's tirade.

"He is not to be found, nor is Lt. Danski," began the Levi. "I am next in line to decide things, and since there wasn't a single nay vote to be found anywhere in the village…," he nodded to the handful of curious people now beginning to gather in behind him. The Innkeeper's wife too, could be seen waving from the Trade Store porch, where she stood holding hands with several other ladies from the village. On a number of the balconies above them, there were clusters of families staring down at them, some of the children pointing or waving. A few people eyed them from the front of the tavern, but the largest of these groups were those walking toward them from the temple. This included the young man Marcus, badly hobbling without his crutch, and the Prior, who was rushing ahead of the crowd as if trying to stop the proceedings.

"Uh…that is…" the Levi began to say, but the Prior began waving his hands even before he spoke.

"Wait…I must bless the tools of war," he demanded, his hands clutching a leather pouch from around his neck. "Lay out your weapons!"

"But that would leave us unguarded," protested Nommie sarcastically.

No one laughed. The others stood solidly behind the Gnome unmoving, but unsure of how to proceed.

"Well…we'll just have to bless the entire courtyard then," the Prior muttered and began to dust each of them with a fine powder that smelled of lavender and musk. "Blisset thy means…blisset thy self," he repeated over and over as the fragrant dust, with the help of the morning breeze, began to spread over the entire courtyard.

"Well…we are all in agreement then!" exclaimed the Levi nervously, and not waiting for an answer, he turned to lead them under the archway and down several wide, stone steps to a very heavily, secured door. An ancient rune was carved into the solid oak door, and the hinges and braces were made of overly thick iron. There were three oak-beamed horizontal braces which had to be lifted off in order to even spy the lock. Suddenly remembering the Gnome legend, Muk felt that the blocked entryway certainly looked as if 'something' was definitely meant to stay on the other side of the door. Fumbling with the keys to the lock, the Levi, with Mr. Boggs' help, finally pushed the door inward. Taking a lighted torch from the wall, together they led the procession down a spiral stairway into a dark cavern.

Presently, they were all standing on level ground facing a gate with heavy iron bars. It too was locked. Twenty paces ahead was another gate. But on the left, between the two gates, was a pleasant looking log-wood shack, complete with thatched roof. There was a warm light and an odd sort of humming-singing coming from within the open doorway, perhaps coming from someone or something who didn't really know how to do either very well.

"Open up!" yelled the Levi, clanging his keys against the bars and giving them a good shake. The humming-singing stopped immediately and out peeked the face of a large Troll. Moralee let out an audible growl, but the Troll's reaction was one of being pleased with company. He was bare-chested and wore chain mail trousers down to his bare feet. There was an odd odor about the place, either from him, or perhaps to be kind, from the simmering pot near the fire. Tied to the side of his trousers was a long leather thong that held two jangling keys. Slowly and with very deliberate finger movements, he untied the thong and produced a key that opened the gate for them to enter. Hum-singing again, he shuffled to the far gate and opened that door as well, before slowly and deliberately re-tying the thong to his trousers.

"Fair luck!" nervously offered the Levi. Apparently, he had walked as far into the dungeon as he was willing to go. Moralee nearly had to wrench the torch from his grip and, when an insistent Quimby reached for the one Mr. Boggs was holding, the Shopkeeper quickly spun on his heel, clutched tightly to the torch, and hurriedly led the Levi back the way they had come. Meanwhile, the adventurers cautiously filed by the simple Troll.

"Apple...APPLE!" Nommie whispered to Muk, jerking his head toward the back of his own pack. For the first time, Muk noticed the bulging pack the Gnome wore. It must have weighed twice his own. Lifting the top flap, he found at least a bushel of green apples nearly spilling out the top. Nommie reached back for an apple and presented it to the Troll as a thank you gift. With a delighted smile, the Troll reached for the apple, but it somehow dropped from the Gnome's grasp and fell innocently between the Troll's legs and rolled behind him. Nommie booted Quimby to get his attention.

Muk marveled at the simplicity of both the Troll and the plan.

First, the Troll leaned forward to reach behind him, but seeing that wasn't going to work, he turned his back on them and, bending slowly, retrieved the apple. Once the group stepped beyond the gate, they all peered back through the bars to watch. The Troll, sniffing his gift, put the whole thing in his mouth and started to munch. Not noticing the loss of his key, he walked back to his shack, to his simmering supper and to his hum-singing.

"That was brilliant!" Muk laughed.

"That was sad," Moralee countered, but they all began to laugh.

"Didn't like the idea of having to ask for our coming and going!" offered the Gnome.

"You needn't have kicked me!" Quimby protested. "I knew what we were doing!" he added, holding the key up to the torchlight.

"Well then…you keep it. After all…you lifted it."

"Really? I get to keep it?"

"Just don't lose it!" chimed in Moralee, as she thrust their only torch straight ahead. And slowly, carefully, the troop followed the Dwarf over a downward slope into a mouth of inky darkness.

Chapter Sixteen

A Torch

...high on the wall suddenly burst into flames, reminding the group that they were on a mission into the *unknown*. Another ten paces into the darkness and another torch surprised them in similar fashion. Someone or something seemed to be expecting them. Wondering whether it was a friendly light or a warning, they continued their slow descent. No one commented, but they were all thinking the same thing. By the illumination of the fifth light, it was obvious that the group was staring into the mouth of a continuously sinking, dark corridor. The passageway was just wide enough to walk side by side comfortably and, on either side of them, stark, stone walls rose to a curved ceiling, shadows dancing in the torchlight.

"The Great Hall?" Nommie wondered aloud.

At twenty paces, they came to a door. Ahead in partial shadow was another door at about the same distance, only on the opposite wall. As the next torchlight sputtered to life, one could see that the progression of doors repeated for as far as they could see. Moralee hit the first door with the palm of her fist. The result was a resounding echo.

"Empty!" she said, leading the group stealthily down the hall. As Oblio passed the door, she too touched it, but with a soft stroke. If she sensed anything at all, she kept it to herself. Moralee reached the second doorway just ahead of the others. It was like the last, a large wooden door with no handle. This time, however, as her fist slapped against it, it slowly creaked open. Quimby quickly drew his knife and Nommie put an arrow to his cross bow. The door was slow to open and hit the rock wall behind it. Moralee pushed in her torch, revealing a square cold room ~ bare and dusty.

"Let's storm the hall and open all the doors at once!" declared Quimby, his adrenaline pumping. He even ventured a few brave steps down the hall all by himself.

"Let's not forget about the Princess," reminded Muk.

"I think, for safety's sake, we should walk together and with some plan," Oblio said in a cautious tone, which stopped the Halfling in his tracks.

"My thoughts exactly," added Moralee and she took up the lead once again. The third door was different. It had a window in it about face high with three vertical metal bars. On tiptoe, Moralee could see that it wasn't empty. "Whew…Goblins," she said distastefully and quickly continued on.

"Goblins?" Quimby uttered in disbelief and sprang to

the door. With a quick jump up, he peeked through the bars. "Yup!"

"Locked for a good reason," mumbled Nommie. "Trouble."

Muk was shocked to watch everyone move on with so little regard for the Goblins. When he leaned against the door and peered in, he saw three rather unkempt Goblins sitting on grain bags against the far wall. They were bickering loudly amongst themselves and playing some sort of card game.

"Hey!" he shouted into the room. The Goblins stared back at the door completely unfazed by the Stranger looking in on them. "Does anyone want out?" Muk immediately felt Nommie's presence beside him.

"Bad idea," he said, "these three are trouble." But Muk pressed on.

"Hey…for some information, I'll let you out!"

"Come on, Muk," Moralee scowled.

"No, wait. This could be useful," answered Muk. He grabbed an apple out of Nommie's pack before anyone could argue and pushed it through the metal bars. The middle Goblin crawled forward and eyed the apple carefully.

"For some information, I'll let you out," offered Muk.

"What do you wish to know?" the Goblin asked in a high squeaky voice.

"Tell me something important enough and you'll be free."

The Goblin took a bite out of the apple and sat there a moment before answering. "I've seen a flying horse."

"Yes, well…I've heard that one."

A second Goblin joined the first, stealing the apple and a quick bite.

"Which path are you taking?"

"We've just entered the Great Hall."

"Well…" began the second Goblin, "this isn't the Great Hall. So let me out!" he demanded.

"No…" answered Muk, "something really important."

"Well, I'll tell you something that won't be a secret for long…" the third Goblin said in a sinister voice. "He will never let you out alive!"

"You shouldn't have said that!" reprimanded the second Goblin, hitting the third over the head with the remainder of the apple.

"Not right!" added the first, joining in, as the three Goblins grappled their way back to the bags of grain and eventually back to the game of cards.

"Not in a big hurry to get out, are they?" Nommie observed, ushering Muk back in line with the others.

"That wasn't very smart!" Quimby was quick to note.

"Well…one thing for sure," Muk said on his behalf, "this isn't the Great Hall."

"I could have told you that," asserted Moralee, but Muk didn't let the criticism stick and he began to chuckle to himself.

"What?" said Oblio.

"Another thing…" added Muk, looking back over his shoulder and laughing aloud, "those are the stupidest creatures I have ever met!"

"Why?" came the question in unison.

"Well…when I first leaned against the door, it was open. There isn't a handle or a lock on that door!" The others all shot quick glances up the hall, before joining in laughter.

"Still…" offered Nommie, "dumb as axe-handles or not, Goblins are like a hive of bees. It's best you avoid them whenever you can."

The next doorway was open. In fact, there was no door to go along with the hinges that hung loosely from the door frame. Other than the charred remains of the door near the centre of the room, it was dark and empty.

"Hey, here's a find," announced Moralee, pointing to the next indentation in the wall. The stone archway over the door was the same as the others, but this doorway had been bricked up. And not a good job of it either, as the mortar was old and crumbling and looked as if a little prying might easily loosen several of the bricks.

"To keep something in…or keep us out?" queried Muk aloud. But Quimby wasn't going to be dissuaded from his treasure hunt and knocked in several bricks with just one kick. Nommie gave it a shove with his shield and a hole easily opened up, large enough to crawl through.

"It's dark," echoed Nommie's voice, as he stuck his head in.

"Here!" Moralee tapped him on the shoulder with the bottom of her torch.

Nommie took it and thrust into the room.

"Let me try!" insisted Quimby, but the Gnome was pushing aside more bricks and either didn't hear him or chose not to. Nommie leaned in precariously, which was just too much for Quimby, who added a healthy shove from behind. The Gnome tumbled headlong into the pitch black with a loud 'yelp'! Moralee shoved the giggling Halfling aside and quickly followed ~ sword drawn.

Muk dislodged a few more bricks and now the four of them were standing over the Gnome. He was sitting palms down on a gritty floor, staring at a seemingly empty room. The torch lay a few paces ahead revealing a stone-walled room and a sand covered floor. Quimby eyed a small box half-buried in the sand and darted over to it. He eyed it carefully, pronounced it empty, and threw it into the corner. Muk knelt down to a pile of disintegrating cloth and, from the sand, produced a jewel-laden dagger. Instantly, Quimby was by his side, ogling his find.

"I'll trade," he offered, unsheathing his own knife with the bent tip. "Mine's got ancient carving on the handle." But before Muk could turn him down, Nommie had gotten to his knees and crawled over to where the empty box had been. He smiled as he sifted his fingers through the sand. He was sure that he had seen something...something shining in the torchlight.

"Yes!" He cried, holding it up for all to see. "A diamond!"

"Whoa...!" hollered Quimby, giving up on the dagger. And suddenly the two of them were the best of friends, laughing like children at the beach, sifting through the sand together, occasionally showing each other another shiny gem.

Meanwhile, Moralee was more interested in the only other noticeable difference from the other rooms. It was an all metal door, lost in the shadows.

Partially ajar, it opened *into* the room, but was wedged solidly in the sand.

"If we can't close it, we should inspect it," observed Oblio, peering into its depths.

"Should I?" Muk volunteered. Moralee agreed with a nod and gripped the door with both hands.

"It's open...no matter what!" she promised.

'No matter what' Muk thought to himself, as he suddenly regretted his offer. Squeezing through the small space between the wall and the cold door, he inched his way along a very narrow passageway that sloped ever downward. Barely wider than himself, he ran his hand along the wall until it turned diagonally to his right. Without the torch, he was in total darkness; and, still walking downward, he came to another metal door. Cold steel…it was like kissing death. The tiny window in it was barred, but everything beyond it was black. He closed his eyes and breathed deeply. A large room lay beyond. Lots of air. Musty. But the door would not give. Locked or bolted from the other side, he could not tell, but the instant he turned to retraced his footsteps upward away from the door, he immediately felt better. Still, he was covered in a cold sweat, as cold as the metal door, by the time he turned the bend in the passageway and faced his uphill journey. With every step he fought the need to run from his cramped surroundings. Finally, he spied Oblio's outline in the torchlight, with Moralee still holding fast to the metal door.

"Solid metal door," Muk reported and left it at that. He was just so thankful to be back in the room with his friends.

"Time to move on," Moralee announced to the room, but Nommie was in disagreement.

"Not me!" he insisted, struggling to take off his breastplate and readjusting his pack to make room for a few other molded metal strappings from his body. Nommie wasn't publicizing the fact that he had overdressed for the occasion, but it was abundantly clear he was uncomfortable and weighted down by his purchases. Muk too, needed the time to breathe and acclimate to the confinement of the dungeon.

"Yes…just a moment to adjust," he agreed, stripping off his cumbersome robe.

After carefully repacking, Nommie could not find room for everything, which left a handful of green apples.

"I feel like we've been here for days, and I'm hungry," he said passing out the leftovers.

"Me, me..." Quimby pleaded, adding several apples to the treasure of diamonds already in his lap. Surprisingly, Moralee accepted the invitation to join in on the picnic. And there the unlikely group sat cross-legged in the sand in the flickering torchlight, munching on apples.

Chapter Seventeen

From Somewhere In The Hall

...a faint glow of light began to grow, brighter and brighter; and with that intense light, a shrill sound that grew ever louder as the hall beyond the pile of crumbled brick began to resemble the rising sun. Nommie and Quimby, both with their backs to the doorway, scampered behind the other three, all with hands up to their eyes to block the blinding light.

The torch at their feet sputtered. They looked at one another, blinking. Everything looked as it had moments before, but the light and sound from the hall had been replaced by an eerie silence. Again, the torch sputtered. Muk got to his feet and, picking up the torch, he stepped cautiously toward the doorway. Poking his head back into the long hall, he first looked right, finding only the dusty trail of footprints from the direction they had come. He lowered his head and stepped over the bricks and brought the torch up over his head. To his left in the middle of the hall, not ten paces away, stood the figure of a very striking young lady. Her green, Elvan eyes reflected in the torchlight and her hair was a deep burgundy. She stood as tall as her archer's bow, not a hand shorter than himself. She wore a pair of green boots and men's trousers of grass green to just below the knees. A leather strap across her yellow top held a quiver of arrows. A journey bag similar to Muk's hung from her other shoulder. She did not appear frightened or alarmed, nor was she intimidated when Quimby crawled over the rubble and took a stand beside Muk with his dagger clenched between his teeth.

"How came you to this place?" he found himself saying.

"Powers but by magic," she said with a smile. Right away, Muk knew he had been correct in thinking she was not only eastern, but of royalty.

"I am Muk from Valrhun."

"I be Delphinea from Valjhune," she responded, observing Quimby with interest, who was literally pulling on Muk's pants leg.

"Uh…this is my friend Quimby," Muk announced, motioning to his side. "And this is…" But Muk didn't get a chance to finish the introductions, as Nommie had been trying to carry his pack, cover his bald head with his helmet and climb through the brick opening all at the same time.

"Hulic Hilt!" hollered the Gnome, stumbling over the loose rubble and landing with a 'clunk' in the hall. His pack spilt forth apples and his helmet rolled to the opposite wall. He opened his mouth and began to utter something else but stopped short of saying anything embarrassing when he noticed their young guest. Quickly he shot to his feet and dusted himself off. "Pardon my speech," he began. "My name is Albion Gaeyl Penrun ~ my friends call me Nommie," he added with a courtly bow. Muk found himself speechless when he heard the name 'Penrun', and stared at the Gnome in surprise. Oblio made her way around Nommie and introduced herself and Moralee who stood motionless by the collapsed doorway, her hand on the hilt of her sword.

"I am Oblio of the Midplains and this is Morah of Leith, leader of the Highland Leiths. We call her Moralee."

"This be your home?" Delphinea inquired, pointing to the hole in the wall.

"No, no," Oblio assured her, ushering their guest through the crumbled doorway with a short description of their adventure thus far.

"Where did you find a name like that?" Muk laughed, handing the Gnome his helmet.

"My grandfather!" Nommie explained, dumping apples into the helmet and forcing it down into his pack.

"Now you know why we just call him Nommie," Quimby said, rescuing one of the apples from the cold dungeon floor and slipping it into his mouth. "An' 'ere does s'e come fr'm?" he added before swallowing.

"South"…"East," they both concurred simultaneously. Both Nommie and Muk looked at each other and laughed.

"Valjhune is *east* of where I live," Nommie pointed out, "on the ocean."

"Valjhune is an eastern culture but it is *south* of here," explained Muk. The two of them exchanged glances.

"South!"

"East!"

"Are we ready?" Moralee announced, poking her head into the hall.

"Well, if we're not interrupting your gossip party," Quimby shot back, wiping his mouth on his sleeve. Moralee laughed at his quip and leaned out a little farther as if in secret.

"We just wanted to know how she got here," she whispered.

"How did she get here?" Quimby asked. But the Dwarf had ducked back into the room. "Wait! How did she get here?" he demanded a second time, jumping up and scampering over the bricks to follow her. Nommie and Muk laughed at the Halfling's exit.

"East!" Nommie muttered while closing his pack.

"South!" Muk uttered to his journey bag, adjusting the shoulder strap and readying himself to continue.

Chapter Eighteen

A Troupe Of Six

...now wandered the dungeon of 'The Keep'. Where apprehension had once filled the hall, conversation among the three women echoed in its place.

"A Wizard asked you to come *here*?" Oblio questioned.

"I be sent to join the 'journey'," smiled Delphinea. "Presently I be here."

"No one can travel by light!" argued Moralee, but did not seem to doubt the reason for her joining the expedition.

"I not be expecting underground."

"Or three male egos, I doubt," muttered Moralee.

"How could Valjhune know of our plans?" Muk whispered to Nommie, still unconvinced by the possibility. "We only met yesterday."

Completely ignoring the chatter, Quimby took up the lead and attacked the next two doors. One seemed rusted shut, the other bolted from the inside.

"We be treasure finding?"

"Princess finding....supposedly," corrected Moralee.

"We're here for the good of the village," insisted Oblio.

Quimby finally muttered something about a women's social club, and in an effort to get things rolling again, stretched his lead over the others. When the next illuminating torch refused to light on its own, Quimby dropped his pack and, leaping up, grabbed hold of the torch handle and was about to pull the torch out of the metal holder.

"Stop!" Oblio cried out in a voice that echoed up and down the hall. The air went still and everyone looked about instinctively for something wrong.

But the only thing out of the ordinary was Quimby.

Like a monkey hanging from a tree, he hung by one arm, still grasping the metal bracket high up on the wall. His feet were pressed against the wall, and his body leaned out into the hall, his face frozen in the moment. He would have made a delightful stone caricature, if it weren't for the look of terror on his face accentuated by the flickering torchlight. In less than a heartbeat, the dungeon floor directly under Quimby had opened up to swallow him whole. And, from somewhere just up the hall, a solid stone wall slammed down from the ceiling with a 'Thunk!'. Then, to the group's surprise, the wall came grating toward them. Quimby's pack, which had been sitting in the middle of the hall, was swept forward by the wall; and, when it came to a sudden stop flush with the gaping black hole in the floor, the pack fell into the void. Quimby's mouth dropped as he watched all of his possessions sail off into the darkness. It had happened so fast that none of them could have prevented it. And there was Quimby, left hanging out over the void, afraid to or unable to move.

"Put..the..torch..back..in..the..holder," Muk said, enunciating each word very clearly.

"Quimby, please put the torch back into the holder!" Oblio cried louder, just to be sure he understood his predicament. Very slowly, the Halfling replaced the torch, but his facial expression never changed nor did he take his eyes off the black hole in the floor beneath him. There was an audible 'click' the moment the torch handle was reunited with its holder and the wall and floor slid back into its former position, as if the whole thing had never happened. Quimby, however, did not recover that quickly. Nommie had to stomp around the trap door to show him that it was securely in place and Muk had to help unclench his fingers before his grip on the wall bracket loosened. Once he was down and on solid ground, however, it was quite a different story.

"Did you see that?" he exclaimed. "I could have been on the other side and been pushed in to…there!" he pointed to the floor. "I could still be falling, but I'm not. Am I? Didn't let it. Did I? It tried to swallow me up! But I was too quick. It was a trick to get me, but I was too smart," he said excitedly.

"Got your pack though, didn't it?" Nommie chuckled and the Halfling suddenly became mute.

"Quimby…I'm sorry," Oblio said, "I should have been paying more attention."

"I know not how to see this coming," said Delphinea. Moralee took her turn stepping over the trick stones and added, "I don't sense any depth beneath these stones…that could just as easily been any one of us."

"Well…we weren't actually invited in here now, were we?" Nommie said as a joke, but nobody laughed.

"Perhaps that was just a warning…to prepare us," cautioned Muk, who stopped just before the next unlit metal holder and motioned for Moralee's torch. "The torches don't seem to be cooperating anymore either," he pointed out and carefully held the flame against the charred sconce. The torch sputtered to life. Everyone waited an anxious moment for some sound or cause and effect, but thankfully they were only met with silence.

"Here's a door we can enter," Quimby noticed, "but why is it bolted from the outside?"

"Let's see what's up ahead," Nommie suggested, "we can always come back."

"Fine by me…let someone else lead for a while," offered Quimby. It was Muk who lit the next torch as they moved further down the hall. After lighting the second, the entire group almost simultaneously took a step backward.

A heavy curtain of cobwebs blocked their path. Muk pushed the flame into the thick webbing and, immediately, a handful of 'dark somethings' scurried from the light.

⸙

"What's a dark something?" Alex wanted to know.

"Sssh!" cried several voices at once. Sam tiptoed to the hallway and peered down the hall. He nodded that the coast was clear and jumped back into his lower bunk. It was way past their bedtime, and the last thing any of the boys wanted was to lose Eff's Pageleaf to Mr. Wittlesey and his habit of prowling the hallways after lights out. Charlie, who was draped over the top bunk, pointed eagerly to the Pageleaf and Eff continued.

⸙

Chapter Nineteen

"I'm Not Going That Way,"

…Quimby said, finding comfort at the rear of the group.

"What be such creatures?" uttered Delphinea.

"The scurrying kind," Nommie grimaced.

"It doesn't appear as though too many people have gone this way," was Muk's comment as they retreated to the bolted door.

"Torch!" summoned Moralee, who had already lifted the timber off the door brackets and stood facing the others. There was a hushed pause. The hinges squeaked as she pulled the door toward her. Inside, a row of torches lit, revealing a small, furnished sitting room. There were several comfortable looking armchairs against the walls of the room, while two straight-back chairs sat at either end of the wooden table in the centre of the room. A thickly woven rug covered most of the stone floor and, except for the two skeletons occupying the chairs at the table and another sitting against the far wall smiling at them, the room had an air of livability and comfort.

"Skeletons!" announced Nommie.

"Better than creepy-crawlies," replied Quimby. His eyes quickly scanned the room, looking primarily for wooden chests or furniture that might contain treasure or trinkets.

Uninterested in bones, Moralee continued with her torch through another small passageway into an adjoining room. Upon entering the threshold of the second chamber, she found the ceiling illuminated in a strange, magic light ~ no torches or sconces, no candles or fire. It was a smooth, stone room with just the one narrow passageway in and one door straight ahead leading out. In between, sitting on wooden risers, were four ancient stone crypts. The first stone tomb was open and empty and the heavy lid lay to one side. Carved into the top of the lid was the likeness of a sword plus images that seemed to be telling a story. The other three crypts were sealed and they too, had engravings on their lids.

"This is odd," Moralee was heard to say. Having not found any shiny baubles, Quimby scooted quickly through the passageway to join her, while the others slowly combed through the sitting room.

"Ah hah!" Nommie declared, stopping to confer with one of the skeleton guests that rather looked like it was waiting for tea. On one of the boney fingers was a ring. He carefully slid it off from its former owner and eyed it with glee. Muk too, found a surprise waiting him as he surveyed its luncheon companion. He reached down and unfastened a belt from around its waist. He brought it up to the light and remarked, "I think it is woven in gold!" Muk held the belt out to Oblio, who studied it carefully.

"Yes…the gold braiding appears to be very old. Did you notice the script on the reverse side?" she asked, handing it back. Muk carefully turned the belt over and repeated the inscription:

"bi ritt: Magnis ferend de ark 'Batas',

Wisan e beorn, wield oer wald,

Gyrdel be trum wen."

Muk looked over to the others as if asking for a translation, but all he got were blank stares. Making certain that Quimby's attention was focused in the other room, Muk took the extra time to take out his robe and push the belt deep into his pack before placing the neatly folded robe back on top. But Quimby didn't seem to be at all interested in Muk or Nommie's find. He had found another item all by himself; in fact, it was so obvious that he almost missed it altogether. It was a shiny sword handle that was simply sticking out of a stone block. He pulled it out of its stone cradle and, holding on to the hilt with both hands, he dragged the sword, which was as long as he was tall, across the rug and back into the sitting room.

"Do you think it's magical?" he asked, looking to no one in particular. Delphinea saw the gemmed handle and ancient craftsmanship and turned it over in her hands.

"It be very handsome."

"Not at all a common piece of weaponry ~ and much too heavy for either of us to use," added Oblio.

Quimby attempted to lift the sword, to show them all that he was man enough to handle it, but failed to get it off the ground. Having caught sight of his find, Moralee approached and roughly grabbed it out of his grasp.

"Where did you find this?" she demanded. Everyone stepped back as she drew her sword out of its sheath and handed it to the speechless Halfling. A strange look came over her as she touched the new sword. When both hands found the handle, she stepped into the middle of the room and swung it twice over her head. It hummed loudly with both swings.

Without word of explanation, she sheathed it and demanded that Quimby show her where he had found it. Quimby dropped the used sword and led the Dwarf back into the stone coffin room.

"What do you think it is worth?"

"Exactly where did you find it?"

"I'll trade with you if you like. Or I could let you use it for a while. You could…Yipes!…"

'Yipes' was the last word that the rest of the group heard, and they instinctively hurried through the passageway toward the second room.

A grinding sound of stone upon stone held Moralee and Quimby in their tracks. Slowly, the heavy crypt lids fell to the floor with a loud 'thud', and up popped three gruesome, smiling skeletal heads to greet them. But, by the time Moralee and Quimby backed up into the passageway, the other four were pushing their way forward, trying to determine the actual meaning of the word 'Yipes' and the frighteningly heavy, loud sounds.

When Quimby saw that all three skeletons were drawing swords and stepping out of the coffins towards them armed, he let out a scream and began clawing his way back through the bottleneck.

"Everybody…get back!" was all that Moralee could yell, because the words to describe the scene and the time to do it were not available to her.

Still unable to comprehend the situation, the others stumbled over one another back into the sitting room. By then, it was almost too late. To their total surprise, the other three skeletons were standing erect. One was eyeing its ringless finger ~ another was feeling for its belt and all three were advancing upon them menacingly. Fortunately, the first two were flailing nothing but boney arms, but the third skeleton had spied the heavy Dwarven sword that had been carelessly left on the floor and began waving it around like it was a feather.

"Looks like they want their stuff back!" hollered Muk, holding off the first skeletal warrior with nothing but his pack. Nommie had dropped his crossbow in the confusion in the passageway and was using his shield as best he could, hoping to force the skeletal army back into the first room. But, because he had been taken by surprise, he was having a devil of a time getting to his sword while fending off the surprisingly vicious assault.

Quimby had slipped through everyone's legs and had grasped the situation behind them. In an instant, he produced a leather sling from his belt and a rock from a pouch he tossed on the floor in front of him. From a kneeling position, he slung a perfectly aimed rock at the sword-wielding skeleton, but it somehow found its way through the boney ribcage and smacked hard against the opposite wall, bouncing harmlessly away.

Moralee had no Idea why her friends weren't backing out of her way. Left to fend for herself, the best she could manage to do was ward off the deadly blows with her shield and back up one step at a time, letting her three adversaries slowly advance down the narrow passageway in single file. Oblio was stuck in the middle, not being able to see clearly what was happening on either side of her.

With Quimby now crouched and slinging rocks from

the floor, Delphinea was able to take aim at Muk's attacker. Her first arrow hit a flailing arm, sending the bone clattering across the room. As the skeleton looked down at the missing limb, Muk found the precious time to lower his pack and secure his blade. Seeing the opportunity, Delphinea quickly drew another arrow.

"Hey!" she yelled to get the skeleton's attention, and her second arrow hit its breast bone and it crumpled to the ground. Meanwhile, Nommie had successfully retrieved his sword and was whittling away pieces of the second skeleton left and right until it literally bit the dust.

Now the sword-wielding skeleton had nothing blocking its way and it lunged at Muk with a straightforward jab. Falling backwards, he instinctively brought his journey bag up for protection as the sword sliced through the canvas and into the wall next to his ear. He released his pack as the skeleton stepped back to attempt yet another deadly blow, but it had to stop in midswing to shake loose the heavy obstruction hanging on the end of its sword.

In that moment, Quimby jumped up with a war cry and slung a rock that hit the third skeleton in its fighting shoulder with a loud 'clack' that might have been heard clear up to the parapets of 'The Keep'. Even though its arm and sword fell to the floor, it quickly retrieved the sword with its left hand, and, with an evil grin, it came directly for Quimby. But Nommie stepped in front of the Halfling and blocked the first several swings with his shield. Delphinea had found room to move in behind Quimby, but her attempt to loose another arrow was blocked by the Gnome's heroics.

Nommie was quick and agile as he parried with his shield and, with a swing of his own, snapped off several ribs. But even broken-ribbed and one-armed, the skeleton did not back down. With one unexpected and swift blow, the hilt of its sword came down directly on top of the Gnome's bald head.

Nommie blinked, closed his eyes and dropped to the rug.

Delphinea wasted no time in taking aim, but neither did Moralee who stormed into the room with a war cry of her own and, with one flat-bladed swing through the rib cage, sent bones flying everywhere.

Yet the battle was not over. The five adventure-seekers rallied to Nommie's side, who was now ~ with Oblio's help ~ sitting up and conscious. Everyone but Moralee and Quimby were astonished to look up and see three more skeletal warriors stepping menacingly into the room. Their swords were drawn and faces were intent on battle to the death. This time, the group knew exactly what to do. Moralee stepped forward to greet them. Delphinea, already a quiver to her bow, took the left flank. Muk eyed Moralee's old sword near his feet and, when he reached to pick it up, Quimby quickly filled in the space between them, his sling already in motion.

Although they were outnumbered, the three skeleton warriors wasted no time in lunging forward in attack. Delphinea's first arrow struck the jaw of her attacker and the bones fell lifelessly to the ground. Meanwhile, Moralee waited for her attacker's first blow, blocking it easily and countering with a sword hum louder than the sound of the second skeleton's bones as they rattled against the wall. Muk took his cue from Moralee and blocked the first blow, but his first swing was blocked as well. Quimby, though, had more than enough time to take careful aim and let fly with a rock that bounced off its bony forehead. Muk stepped back, ready to block the next blow, but the skeleton just stood there, dazed. Moralee took one quick step sideways and, in one quick movement, took the head off the last remaining skeleton. Its bones fell haphazardly at her feet and the skull ricocheted of the wall and rolled to a stop at Nommie's feet. Picking up the head with both hands, Nommie motioned the jaw up and down. "I give up!" he mimed.

Chapter Twenty

The Battle Was Won

...mostly on the strength of Moralee's sword and Nommie's shield, but that did not keep Quimby from recounting his own version of the conflict.

"Did you see that shot...did you see that shot?" Quimby cried, mimicking the skeleton's dazed look caused by his rock, just before it was beheaded.

"It was an excellent shot," Muk agreed, "but I think we were very lucky."

"At least Nommie was," added Oblio, helping him to his feet. "Something tells me that your skeleton wasn't left handed."

"Obviously..." the Gnome agreed, now standing on his own and rubbing the lump on the top of his head, "and something tells me that I should never have taken my helmet off!"

"Can you be traveling?" Delphinea said, handing him his crossbow.

"'Course!" he frowned, sheathing his sword and grabbing the crossbow and shield. "I would really like to know what these critters were put here to protect."

"Maybe the Princess?" offered Oblio.

"Maybe more treasure!" said Quimby.

"Perhaps both," Muk said thoughtfully, walking a circular path around the room and picking out a bone here and there. "But first, I'm going to make sure these 'critters' don't bother *us* again!" Righting the table, he used it as a chopping block. Using Moralee's old broad sword, he chopped the six long femur bones in half and tossed them strategically around the room. "That should do it!" he reckoned. Delphinea looked to the others for an explanation, but none was forthcoming.

With renewed energy, Nommie marched into the crypt room and scrutinized the four empty coffins. Nothing unusual was found – only a bright, clean marble room and four empty crypts. He then pushed his shield against the wooden door on the far side of the room. It swung inward easily. Cautiously, with sword drawn, he entered first, wary of another skeleton, but hoping for an unguarded treasure or perhaps, if the fates would have it, the Princess.

The room that met his eyes was astounding. Bathed in self light as the crypt had been, it was an eight-sided room with a painted dome ceiling, smooth stone walls and a colourful, checkered marble floor. The most striking thing about the room was the large statue standing in the middle of it. It was in the image of a wizard, a staff firmly in one hand and the other pointing at them. It stood at least twenty hands high and was made entirely out of green marble. The group toured the room and Moralee tested each of the seven remaining doors. They were masterfully crafted wooden doors with heavy metal fittings. She pulled on each of the brass looped handles, but not one of them so much as budged.

"Good!" voiced Nommie, as he dropped his pack and sat down to rest. He was a lot wearier than he'd realized. The knot on his head was now quite pronounced and noticeably purple. It wasn't until they sat down, that they all felt extremely exhausted. Muk wasn't at all sure how long they had been in the dungeon. His stomach said days. He dug into the bottom of his pack and brought out the meal provided by the Innkeeper's wife. He offered a muffin to Delphinea.

"I was in Valjhune once…a long time ago." His statement didn't seem to surprise her.

"You found it to your liking?"

"Yes, it was lovely. The castle, the air off the sea ~ and the *boats* ~ all tied up in the rock slips outside the castle walls. I wanted my father to take me fishing."

"What time of year?"

"It was…the first festival of Awgust. I remember playing in the sand, burying my mother's feet…on a beach somewhere."

"That not be the city. That be hallowed place."

"No, I don't think so…it was just a sandy beach…but they said the Emerald Castle was Sacred!"

"You know Emerald Castle?" As Delphinea spoke these words, her green eyes lit up as bright as the room.

"Is that the castle you left from, just before you arrived here?" Oblio asked, moving closer to the conversation.

"Yes, I be waiting all of dawn for Reza. Reza is my Wizard," she answered with pride.

"How long did it take you to get here?" inquired Moralee, stripping off her armour and laying her pack on the floor next to Nommie's. Delphinea acted as if it were a strange statement.

"Immediate!"

"No, I think she means from the time you left until the time you got here," Quimby explained, sitting purposefully next to Muk, since his pack and extra breakfast had sailed off into the unknown.

Delphinea blushed, then repeated softly, "Immediate." Muk looked at her in disbelief. He quickly calculated the distances and shook his head.

"How is that possible? We are a quarter-moon from Valrhun, and Valjhune is at least…" he stopped to re-calculate. Delphinea saw his thinking and replied.

"It be a strong light?" she guessed and smiled at Nommie, who had opened his pack and began handing out his left-over breakfast to the group.

"A strong light," Quimby repeated and, helping himself to a piece of cheese and a hard roll, he sat contemplating the thought. They all must have been in a thoughtful mood, because the room soon fell into a heavy silence. So heavy in fact, that, one by one, the adventurous group fell fast into a restful sleep.

It was not the same at the Rafferty Home For Boys, where more than a few of the orphans had had a fitful sleep. Skeletons jumping over fences instead of sheep, or Mr. Wittlesey as a skeleton walking aimlessly through the halls, were only a few of the fitful dreams that kept even some of the older boys tossing in their sleep. Rumours of stories about skeletons had not escaped the 'all-knowing' Mr. Wittlesey on the very next day. He stormed into the mess hall at breakfast and waggled his finger in the direction of McNaught, Freddie and Tommy, for what he thought was an attempt to frighten the younger boys.

Eff's story was put on hold that night by more than a few votes. But, by the following evening, they were all begging Eff to continue from where he had left off.

Chapter Twenty One

The Eight Sided Room

…was still there when Muk opened his eyes. He had no idea how long he had been asleep, but he quickly took in what he saw and then closed his eyes again. It was true, he thought ~ that darkness holds no time. For the first time in his memory's reach, he had truly rested. Was magic involved? He took in a deep breath, but did not stir. He let his insight feel the room for him. Nommie and Oblio were awake. He could smell the fruit-salve that Oblio was dabbing on the crown of the Gnome's bald head. Moralee was pacing the room as if in deep thought. Delphinea was still sitting next to him, where she had been before, only now her head was resting on his shoulder. Muk smiled at the warmth, until Quimby came to mind. The Halfling's presence hadn't been accounted for; but then, it wasn't unlike him to be off skulking somewhere. Instinctively, without drawing notice, Muk reached a hand to where his pack once lay. Good, he thought, it was still there. But something in the room was amiss. Besides Moralee's behavior, there was one other thing that seemed odd. He raised an eyelid. Either someone had moved him while he slept, or the statue was now pointing in a different direction entirely.

"Nothing else!" hollered Quimby. The voice came from somewhere above Muk, startling him and forcing his eyes wide open. The Halfling's head suddenly appeared high above him, over the shoulder of the green marble statue.

"Shhh!" scolded Oblio, as Delphinea's head jerked to attention.

"Morn?"

"It sure feels like it," Muk answered, his limbs aching from the hard floor and wall.

"That's okay, Muk...don't get up," cautioned Oblio, pointing him back down to a sitting position.

"What?" Muk started to laugh.

"Number one..." Moralee announced, rounding the other side of the statue and scrutinizing every step, "we've had a visitor."

"And number two..." Oblio said, handing a red cloth covered in fruit pulp to Delphinea and pointing to Muk, "You've been hurt."

Muk started to laugh again, as he slid back down to the floor. He thought that they were talking about someone else, until Delphinea pressed the cloth against the back of his head, causing a searing pain.

"Ow...Flaming Fire Ants!" he hollered loudly, trying to scoot away from her.

"You have funny words," she laughed, but continued to press the cloth against his head. Muk wanted to say that she had a gentle touch ~ which would have been a lie ~ but he focused his mind instead on his memory of the skeleton's glinting sword that came slicing through his pack.

"I thought I remembered it missing me," he murmured.

Quimby jumped down from the statue and stood with his hands on his hips. From the glare on his face, you would have thought that he was wishing he had been hurt too.

"Well…here's the situation," he said at last. "Someone or something came through that door, attacked Muk, left behind that red rag and then went out the same door and closed it behind him or her…or it."

"That doesn't explain how the statue moved," was Moralee's response, hands on *her* hips.

"Maybe the floor moved?" speculated Nommie. Quimby let out a dubious laugh, but his expression changed the moment he saw that everyone was seriously considering the thought.

"Uh…I be…lost," admitted Delphinea.

Nommie grunted and got to his feet. He took several steps toward the door that Quimby was leaning against, then said, "The only door that opens and was left ajar is that one," he pointed over the Halfling thief's shoulder. He then took two steps toward Muk, pointing. "Someone attacked Muk!"

"No…" Muk shook his head, "I think it happened during the battle."

"So…" Nommie continued, "you weren't attacked while we slept?" Muk suddenly wasn't sure of anything, but absently shook his head no.

"Well… then there's the red cloth," Nommie stated, reaching for the cloth. He stared at it as if it were about to speak. "The cloth was placed in the statue's hand while we slept, because it certainly wasn't there when we came in." Finally, he turned and faced the statue. "And *'somehow'*, the statue moved with no fewer than three of us resting against it! Is that all of it?" he said, looking to Moralee, who nodded in agreement.

"No, not quite…" smiled Quimby, seeing that it was his turn. With great satisfaction, he motioned to the door he was leaning against and pulled it open. "You see…we have a different room, definitely not the same door we came through," he announced. "Well…okay, not a room really…" he took a second look inside it, "more like a large closet with a hole in it, actually."

"Quimby and I explored the room," cut in Moralee, "stairwell down is barely large enough to follow in single file, but it is sturdy and descends deeper into the dungeon."

"The cloth," pointed Delphinea, taking the rag from the Gnome and examining it closely, "it be of a dress…torn."

"That's what Oblio thought too," Nommie said, "she thinks it's a clue."

"I think we're supposed to follow the clue…in order to find the Princess," stated Moralee.

"Uh…sounds a little too obvious, but I'm all set," Muk agreed, hoisting his journey bag.

"What if it is a *trap*?" cautioned Quimby, now eyeing the open doorway warily.

"Ahh…but what if it's treasure?" Nommie countered.

"First of all, there is no mystery to the room," explained Muk, lifting the bag strap over his shoulder. "And, secondly, it makes sense that somebody is helping us to find the Princess. After all, he or she could easily have slain us in our sleep." While saying this, he buckled his prize belt around his waist and, securing Moralee's discarded sword in the empty sheath, he pointed toward Quimby's large closet door. But nobody moved. They just gaped at him.

"Is mystery solved?" Delphinea had to ask.

"Yes…I do believe that it is…" Muk insisted, observing nothing but perplexed expressions. It was obvious to him that they were at the crossroads where several roads or pathways intersected. His castle had numerous intersections. And the pointing statue wasn't unusual either. "Do we have something to mark with?" he asked, eyeing the apples that filled Nommie's pack. Oblio offered him the two pieces of squashed fruit that had been in her lap. He took the one least mashed and smelled it.

"I mixed them to heal the wounds," Oblio explained.

"Right…" he began. Holding up the piece of fruit and taking the cloth from Delphinea, he went back two doors to his right. "Well…this is what I think happened. *This* door was open when we first came in." Muk pushed the fruit against it, making an 'X'. "We fell asleep. Somebody stole in ~ it was the only door that *could* open. Then they closed the door…and deposited this," Muk held up the red cloth, "and left. But not by the same door." Muk turned to muddled expressions, so he went on. "First, someone needed to get our attention, before sending us in the right direction," then, frowning, he added, "…or sending us into a trap." He laughed at the thought, but nobody else joined in. "Okay, here… hopefully, this will leave no doubt. Moralee, you push here," he pointed to the base of the statue, "and I'll push here." Muk went to the opposite side and yelled…"Push!" Nothing happened. "Ahh…of course," Muk realized a little red-faced, "Quimby, could you close your door?" It was easy to see by Quimby's expression that he didn't like being told what to do, but his curiosity got the better of him and he slowly closed the door shut. "Once again, push!"

She did as she was instructed and, immediately, the huge marble statue began to rotate. It wanted to make stops at each door, but Muk continued three doors and stopped. The hand of the statue was now pointing to the 'X'.

"There! Quimby, check your door." This time, the Halfling eagerly did as he was instructed and pulled on the brass ring. But it wouldn't give.

"Let me!" Nommie insisted and ran over to find that the door marked 'X' opened in without effort. He disappeared into the next room and everyone heard him exclaim, "This is the crypt room alright!" Muk had an accomplished grin on his face until Nommie's frightened voice cried out. "Aaargh!"

Instantly, Delphinea grabbed her bow and Moralee darted to her pile of armour. Together with Muk, who quickly drew the broad sword from his belt, they bolted through the doorway, ready to attack anything that moved.

"Ha ha ha ha!" cried Nommie, tears watering his eyes. He was standing on top of the first crypt and pointing at them. "You should have seen your faces!"

"Shame on you!" Oblio scolded, but broke into a smile.

"Somebody could have gotten hurt," grumbled Quimby.

"That was a pretty good one," Muk admitted, sharing in his laughter.

Moments later, Nommie was the only one still chuckling to himself, as the group rejoined at the base of the statue and double-checked their packs and weapons. Rested and in bright spirits ~ with the possible exception of Quimby who seemed to enjoy walking under a perpetual cloud of surliness ~ together they spun the marble statue back three doors, pointing their adventure in a new direction.

Chapter Twenty Two

A Heavy Drizzle

…blanketed the boys as they stood at the end of 'Old Line Road'. They were waiting on Mr. Wittlesey and the slowpokes who were lagging behind. The kids at St. Mary's called it 'Orphan Street'. Most people missed the sign altogether. The faded green letters were almost invisible, and the post itself leaned into saplings and was half-covered by blackberry brambles.

Eff thought that standing under the large, leafless oak would somehow protect him from the rain, but a large drip found him and ran down the back of his neck. Eff hated the gravel drive that led to the orphanage. He thought it was an eyesore, an afterthought, especially when compared to the black paved road, the sidewalks, the neat, groomed lawn and the white cement steps that led into the vestibule of St. Mary's Catholic Church. It was Sunday morning, and the Church doors were wide open and inviting. The cross and steeple were invisible behind a grey mist, but like a beacon, the tall stained glass windows emitted a warm, welcoming light.

When they were all finally huddled together, the Headmaster led them across the street (looking both ways) and directly into Church. They always stopped before the Holy Water basin to bless themselves before filing quietly into 'their' place ~ always the last three pews to the left. Eff crossed himself, but Tommy Jacobson must have thought Eff needed baptizing as well, because he flipped Holy Water down the front of him. Acting accordingly, Eff evened the score, but was met with a hand to the back of his head. As if that wasn't unfair enough, Mr. Wittlesey steered him roughly to the last pew and proceeded to sit down next to him. Wet and defeated, Eff folded his hands and bowed his head. 'What have I done to deserve this miserable day?' he thought, but he was too far away from the statue of baby Jesus to hear the answer. He sighed heavily. The head-slap was nothing compared to sitting through Sunday Mass with Mr. Wittlesey leaning over you the entire time.

Father Griffin had once told the boys that miracles happened every day. Eff wondered suddenly if maybe he had been right, as he heard Tommy moan and, out of the corner of his eye, saw him slump to the kneeling pad. Mr. Wittlesey was up like a shot. The Headmaster rounded the back pew only to deposit himself beside the ailing boy. He didn't find any sign of unruliness, but that didn't keep him from raking the boys both left and right with a grim stare. Chief was looking rather pleased with himself and winked at Eff, who slowly eased back into the extra wide space. Enjoying the 'miracle', he sat unchaperoned with his feet rocking back and forth.

Monsignor Smith was saying Mass. He was old and slow, but fortunately, Father Griffin stepped up to give the sermon. Eff always liked Father's voice and the way that he explained things to the boys in a way they could understand. Today, he talked about Advent and preparing themselves for the blessed miracle of Christ's birth. Eff was listening intently, but soon began mulling over the miraculous events in *his* own life. Why was it that he could read from the Pageleaf when the others could not? The boys seemed to have forgotten about it long ago, but the question 'why could he' had never wandered far from his mind.

Frank had once remarked that Eff was 'Special'. Perhaps that was all it took to read what others could not. On the other hand, perhaps it was time to entrust the idea of the Pageleaf to a 'Higher Power'. As the sermon ended, Eff finally came to the conclusion that the Pageleaf needed to remain a secret from the adults...at least for now.

After the church service, Mr. Wittlesey ushered the boys back across the street, just as another mini miracle occurred. Father Griffin parted the endless procession of cars and skirted over to invite Mr. Wittlesey to brunch with the Monsignor. The Headmaster was at first delighted but quickly began to weigh the consequences.

"I'm certain the boys will behave!" Father reassured him with a fixed stare toward McNaught. "And look...the Good Lord has put an end to the constant drizzle. That's a good sign."

"Well...I'm sure you're right," Mr. Wittlesey said begrudgingly, although the frown on his face wasn't saying that at all. In the end, Father got his way and the two men chatted their way toward the Church and disappeared into the rectory.

The boys had begun their walk down the uneven road to the Home, when McNaught pointed to a break in the trees on the far side of the field.

"That's where I'm going!" he said proudly.

"But...you'll get us all in trouble," whined Tommy.

"Not today...you idiot!" he replied.

"What's in there?" Sam asked softly, but just loud enough that everyone heard him.

"It's a path into the swamp. McNaught thinks it leads to the train tracks," Eff answered.

"It does?" doubted Charlie.

"Where else would it go?" McNaught retorted, picking up a rock and flinging it halfway across the field. A flurry of rocks followed, but not one matched the distance of the eldest orphan.

"What the hell!" cried Freddy, as several of the boys jumped back from the edge of the road. Sam's very first attempt at rock throwing had gone straight up and right straight back down.

"Hey...we could have a race back to the knoll," Eff quickly pointed out, hoping to change the focus to something other than the errant rock.

"Ya know what I would like?" asked McNaught, draping a muscular arm across Eff's shoulders. "I'd like to know where Muk and the rest of them went."

"Yeah," chimed in several voices at once, while everyone pushed and shoved to circle the 'storyteller'. Eff winked at Sam and smiled.

From that moment on, the young boy with the 'points' on his ears, never again questioned the reason why only *he* could read the story. Because now *he* was one of *them* and that was all he needed to know.

Chapter Twenty Three

The Blocks Of Stone Echoed

...underfoot as, one by one, in single file, the adventurous group stepped down a swirling staircase. With the red cloth as their flag of purpose and battle scars attended to, they once again descended into darkness. Quimby led the group slowly, checking over his shoulder to be sure that Moralee was directly behind him. Her shield was strapped over her back. One hand clutched tight to her sword hilt, the other hand held a torch high out as far as she could reach. The lone light was their only guide. Muk brought up the rear, with the discarded Dwarven sword in hand, wary of anything that might be attacking from behind. A poorly lit passageway met them, iron-barred cell doors on either side. The only occupants seemed to be rats.

"Dungeon cells," muttered Moralee bitterly. "Not an inviting sort of place," Nommie added, "but so far…no Princess." Quimby led them down a damp walkway that not only narrowed with each step, but the ceiling was lowering as well. Both Delphinea and Muk found it increasingly uncomfortable, but held their silence.

"Whoa...what's this?" came a cry from the front of the pack. It was Quimby, as the flame from Moralee's torch suddenly jumped and sputtered. A sucking breeze seemed to be coming from up ahead. Nommie edged his way forward and readied his crossbow. Within ten paces, the torch began scraping the ceiling. The corridor was becoming lower still. They advanced cautiously until the hall emptied into some sort of circular, black ~ nothingness?

"Green Father Forest!" cried Moralee. "Quimby, come back!"

"I am here!" his voice answered not a foot in front of her. But not one of the group could see him. Moralee reached out and pulled him back into the light. Everyone was shocked, but no one more than Quimby. "You disappeared!" she said with alarm, poking the torch into the inky darkness. Quimby jumped back in surprise, when he saw the hand, torch handle and flame immediately dissolve in front of him. More surprisingly still was the fact that when Moralee brought the torch back into view...it was extinguished.

"It ate torchlight!" exclaimed Delphinea, her voice echoing down the dark passageway. The only thing to answer her was a small flicker of candlelight that emanated from within the barred, dungeon cell doors.

"Supposedly, there are curtains of darkness as well as curtains of light," Muk assured them, he being more concerned with the narrowing of the passageway than the consequences of the dark.

"There is magic afoot," agreed Oblio. "But I am not sensing any danger."

"Still, we need to be cautious," Nommie reminded them and began rummaging through his pack in the dark. Producing a long coil of rope, he reached around Moralee and gave one end to Quimby.

"Here…you're in front, let's use this magic rope."

"Oblio, are you sure there isn't any danger?" squeaked Quimby.

"Well, I don't sense anything evil."

"Are you in the lead, or aren't you?" snapped Nommie.

"Yes I am!" Quimby replied defiantly. "But uh…I don't believe in magic."

"Well, good…then you have nothing to be afraid of," retorted Moralee who was losing her patience with the conversations on either side of her.

"Besides…there's no such thing as a magic rope," Nommie chuckled.

"Nommie? Can you trade places with him?" There was a pleading to Muk's voice. His knees were starting to shake from the strain of bending and the lack of space. Apparently, that was all Quimby needed to hear, as he grabbed the rope, sucked in a deep breath and disappeared into the nothingness.

The rope inched slowly out of Nommie's grasp. The breathing and shuffling echoed as if Quimby was crawling upward, when abruptly, the rope slipped from Nommie's hands. By the time he got a secure grip on it again, the rope had gone limp. A long silence met them.

"You've got to see this! You've got to see this!" yelled Quimby, whose face suddenly popped out of the inky darkness and just as quickly disappeared.

"Wait here!" cautioned Nommie, as he entrusted the rope to Moralee and followed in Quimby's footsteps.

"If you three could just back up a bit...I would really like to go next," Muk said nervously.

"Quimby be in trouble?"

"No...didn't he sound...pleased?" Oblio asked.

"Oh...he sounded chipper, but you know those two... they can get themselves into a lot of trouble without meaning to," Moralee reminded them.

Wrapping the end of the rope around her waist, Moralee proceeded to back up until the rope was taut. Seizing the opportunity, Muk quickly squeezed by the lot of them. Slipping the sword under his belt, he used the rope to guide him into the dark void. When his hand came to a flat, rounded edge, he pulled himself out of the curtain of blackness.

A blinding light found him sitting on the edge of a bright, white surface and his legs dangling into a pitch-black circle.

But it wasn't the only black circle in the room. Or was it a room? He leaned back on the palms of his hands and surveyed the strangest space he had ever seen in his life. It was a cave of sorts, completely circular and bathed in a magical white light. It was like sitting inside a spacious, giant white ball, but with holes ~ black holes, and lots of them.

The most shocking spectacle wasn't the room, however, as Muk's eyes followed the path of the length of rope stretched out in front of him. Quimby was halfway up the wall, standing perpendicular to the hole they had entered, the rope tied to his waist. Muk was so dumbfounded that Nommie had to holler to him in order to get his attention. The Gnome was behind him and halfway up the other side of the room, standing on the curved wall with his arms outstretched for balance. He ran back toward Muk, successfully avoiding all the black holes, and sat down next to him. Nommie laughed, took hold of the taut rope and pointed a finger at Quimby. The Halfling's backside was in full view and he was leaning far forward into one of the many black holes.

There was a sudden shrill of high-pitched laughter directly above them. It was the other half of Quimby, waving to them from the blackness from an entirely different hole. His expression was one of childlike joy, so delighted was he with the discovery that he could be in two places at the same time.

"I think we ought to find out more about this room

before the others chance it!" an excited Quimby exclaimed from above them.

"That's an excellent idea!" Nommie shouted back, as he reached into his boot for a small knife.

"What's this?" frowned Muk.

"Sweet revenge!" smiled the Gnome, reaching out and severing the rope with one quick flick.

There was a hand on Muk's ankle and Delphinea's head suddenly appeared. She propped herself up on the ledge next to the boys and was slowly adjusting to her strange new surroundings. Noticeably the most bizarre was Nommie and Muk laughing hysterically at the flying Halfling as he fell from the ceiling. Nommie ducked as Quimby sailed right by the three of them into a black hole, only to reappear from another on the other side of the room. Disappearing immediately, he appeared on the far left, then on the right, the whole time, half-giggling, half-screaming, arms and legs motioning frantically ~ until he finally fell into a hole and did not reappear.

"Moralee said the rope broke," Oblio uttered, as she popped up next to Delphinea.

"Tell Moralee everything is fine," answered Muk, who stood and was now taking several awkward steps forward. "Is this not the strangest thing?"

"Once you find your balance," Nommie said, "there is an energy to this place that just makes you want to laugh."

Moralee appeared and slowly crawled into the room. She flung her end of the rope to the floor. Her 'you forgot about me' expression covered her like a cloak. She opened her mouth to express her displeasure, but not before Nommie burst into a dance. It was a jig of sorts, complete with cartwheel. He picked up the short length of rope and used it to complete his dance over the walls of the cave to where Quimby had disappeared earlier.

"Where's Quimby?" demanded Moralee. Nommie stopped in the middle of his celebration, his eyebrows knitted up and expression sobered.

"Oh..." he answered, letting out a little laugh. He picked up his dance where he had left off. Then he turned, bowed low and jumped high into the air over a black hole ~ and was gone ~ the rope fragment trailing along behind him.

Muk was amused by the impromptu dance and laughed aloud when the green-clad Gnome with the orange beard vanished from the room. But Moralee wasn't overjoyed by either the celebration or the strangeness of the room, so Muk decided to lead them without any fanfare directly to the exit. He cautiously slid into the hole, only to momentarily pop back up and say..."It's more fun if you jump!"

Delphinea thought it a curious statement. She waited a moment, pondering the situation. Seeing her hesitation, Oblio smiled and jumped feet first into the hole. Delphinea and Moralee followed close behind. The reason for the jump, they soon found out, was that beyond the black hole was a short smooth slide onto soft, woven floor pillows.

When the girls arrived, Muk was standing with his arms raised, Quimby and Nommie on either side of him. Their weapons were drawn and they were attacking each other ~ a thrust and parry around Muk's right side and another thrust and parry to his left. Moralee drew her own sword and rushed the three of them.

"I don't like being left behind!" she declared, raising her sword in the air. One loud 'swoop' in their direction and the Gnome and the Halfling quickly gave up on the horseplay.

It wasn't a moment later that the group was suddenly bathed in a warm light. At once, they all realized they were standing together in the foyer of a grand room with a thickly woven rug beneath them and a large, circular candleholder high overhead. Richly coloured frescos of pastoral scenes covered the ceiling and the walls were oak paneled and covered in tapestries of ancient design. There were three arched doorways. The one they had come through was inky black. The other two were identical ~ heavy oak and precise metal fittings with knobs and key-locks. In the centre of the room sat a large desk and an ornately carved chair.

"Feels much like someone's home." Quimby was in awe.

"Maybe we should go back?" whispered Moralee.

"No, the way open to us pointed this direction," Oblio assured her.

"Carpeted hallway!" shouted Nommie from one doorway.

"Locked!" reported Quimby from the other. While the others were securing the exits, Muk focused his attention on the desk. He pulled out the chair and checked underneath the desk carefully. There was nothing but open space, so he sat and pulled himself up to the desk.

"It does feel like home," he said pensively, eyeing the drawers and slated round top.

"What do you suppose is inside?" asked Quimby.

"I wouldn't mess with something you know nothing about," stated Moralee, looking around the room nervously and running her hand over her sword hilt.

"It wouldn't hurt to check," offered Muk, thinking that the desk looked much like the one in his father's map room. Unlike the other desk, this one had three drawers on either side. Muk tried the top drawer on his right, but it wouldn't open.

"It might be a trick drawer!" suggested Quimby.

"Just what I was thinking," Muk acknowledged, remembering the secret compartment in his father's desk. He carefully opened the bottom drawer and it released easily. But it was empty. Leaving the bottom drawer open, he retried the top one and it suddenly slid open by itself.

"Ah ha!" Nommie reported, leaning around the desk and spying a half dozen scrolls. Oblio reached in and carefully lifted them out. She was looking for a place to unroll them. "I'm pretty sure this opens up," Muk said, lifting up on the wood slates. With a funny rattle, the wood lid slipped up to fully open, revealing a flat desk top, inks, quills and many odd shaped, small, wood drawers and cubicles.

Oblio laid out the first scroll, but it was in a language that no one recognized. The second scroll appeared to be a map, but upon unrolling it, the ink suddenly disappeared.

"Uh oh," Oblio uttered. "Perhaps we shouldn't open the others."

"Let me hold them!" offered Quimby, crawling over the back of the desk.

"They belong to someone with a pack," Nommie retorted and Oblio carefully scooped them up and helped the Gnome place them into his pack.

"What's in here?" Quimby asked, opening one of the many sliding drawers to the inside of the desk.

"Quimby!" shouted Oblio, as a green gas shot out into the room.

"Get out!" cried Muk, much too late to cover his eyes. He pushed the chair back from the desk, toppling it and sending him crashing to the floor. Moralee shielded Oblio, carrying her to the only open doorway. Delphinea backed away to the centre of the room, her hand firmly in Nommie's grasp.

Quimby had climbed over the back of the desk only because he had been interested in the enthusiasm of the others. The anticipation of finding a treasure map rolled up in one of the scrolls was just too much for him. When the scrolls not only proved fruitless but were stuffed away in someone else's pack, the Halfling thief felt betrayed. All he wanted to do was to prove himself useful. With so many compartments just waiting to be explored, he knew that great rewards were waiting for them all, but he never envisioned anything like this. The very instant the gas escaped, he had scurried back to his locked door and watched helplessly while it hovered over the desk for a brief moment and then vanished. With each reaction by his friends, as they shouted out to one another, he felt more and more alone.

"Nommie? Muk?" Moralee called out from the doorway. She had picked up Oblio without realizing it and was cradling her like a baby doll. "Where are you?"

"Here!" Nommie answered. "Delphinea and I are here," he added, rushing over to help Oblio out of the Dwarf's tight grasp.

"I can't see. Is Oblio okay?"

"I am fine. You can put me down now," she insisted. "The gas is gone."

"Nommie, is that you?" said Moralee, grabbing his hand.

"Yes, may I have my hand back, please?"

"Oh…of course…good. I can see…sort of. The more I blink, the better I see."

From the middle of the room, Delphinea, too, saw that the gas was no longer a threat and quickly ran over to aid Muk. "You're eyes are all glassy. Can you see anything?"

"No, I got it straight on…I'm pretty much blind. Quimby?" he hollered, as Delphinea helped him to his feet. Even sightless, Muk was intent on hearing how everyone fared and where everyone was, but the Halfling's presence was not yet accounted for. "Quimby, you still here?"

The Halfling sat in the doorway on the far side of the room, watching the results of his actions take place. He sat shamefaced and jealous.

"No…I'm as blind as a bat!" he cried, and covering his eyes with his hands, he began to weep.

Chapter Twenty Four

"This Door Be Bolted

...from the other side," Delphinea announced pushing hard on the door Quimby was sitting against. She knelt down to console the blind, woeful Halfling.

"I already said that!" Quimby scolded, wiping away the tears. "Just leave me alone," he muttered, unwilling to take hold of her outstretched hand.

Delphinea maneuvered Muk around the desk to Moralee's side, while Nommie patrolled on ahead. Moralee stepped forward slowly, while Muk followed with one hand on her shoulder.

"Bolted!" came Nommie's voice.

"Mind if I keep you two company?" asked Muk.

"It's okay, Muk," Oblio encouraged. "It doesn't seem to last very long. You'll be fine."

"I think I can see now!" Moralee said cheerily, only a moment before she rammed her shoulder into a doorframe.

"Well, that's encouraging," laughed Muk, reaching his hand along the wall to help find the obstacle before it found him.

"Down here," called out Delphinea's voice, "Nommie finds special room!"

"Here you two…follow me," said Oblio, as she guided them through an open archway.

"We should go back for Quimby," Muk reminded them. "Quimby…can you hear us?" he called out over his shoulder.

"Of course," the Halfling replied in a peculiar tone as he quickly brushed by them.

"You mean…you're alright? You can see?" Oblio asked.

"Nope, not yet," he lied, but only then did he remember to raise his hands out in front of him as if he couldn't see.

"Here…here!" Nommie said excitedly, pointing to a large, open window high upon the far wall.

"It's a big room," Moralee was explaining to Muk, "stone walls and bare furnishings."

"Wait until you see this!" exclaimed Nommie. "Oh, sorry, Muk."

Muk followed the sounds of energetic voices and listened to the others describe a window that looked out onto a vast landscape.

"Hold still," Quimby was saying, crawling over Nommie's shoulder and hoisting himself up to the window sill. Muk could feel a fresh breeze and the unmistakable sound of distance, before he could perceive the light. "You can practically see forever," remarked Quimby.

"That castle must once have been spectacular," Nommie mused, speaking of a large ruin that Muk could not see.

Layer after layer of collapsed white marble dotted the opposite cliff face, overgrown with a dark green Forest of vegetation. A long, thin waterfall ran through the center of the castle ruin and fell in a myst into the dark canyon far, far below.

"Could it be an illusion?" offered Moralee.

"I think not. Look at the depth and the sunlight off of the wings of the birds," Oblio pointed out.

"That's true…it certainly seems real!"

"Uh…I've been thinking," pondered Muk, seeing only diffused light through a darkened window frame, "perhaps we could find our way back to the desk and search it further. There may be an antidote in one of those drawers."

"No! Muk, you don't want to go back in there!" Quimby almost shouted, "it isn't safe!"

"Safe from what?" Oblio demanded to know.

"Safe from…the…" but he never got the chance to finish his thought, as a door on the far side of the room swung inward and three high pitched voices invaded their space.

"And I'm telling you I don't know!" squeaked one voice. "He just said…do it! So I hurried…" but here the voice cut off sharply to a long pause.

"Arghh…it's them!" mocked a familiar voice.

"Goblins!" shouted Moralee, fumbling for her sword. "Three of them," she whispered for Muk's benefit, but he recognized both their smell and their voices. Both groups just stood their ground, staring at one another.

"Rope!" Nommie insisted.

"Ohh…look at you!" came a high pitched whine.

"Aren't they scary?" said another, while the Gnome quickly made a slipknot and threaded the end of the rope through to create a lasso. Muk heard the swoosh of the rope as Nommie tossed it into the air. There was a scurrying of feet and a 'plunk' as the rope hit the ground.

"Missed!" grimaced Nommie, and Moralee took a threatening step toward the Goblin trio. As they backed away in mock fear, one of the Goblins purposefully backed a foot into the noose. "Got one!" yelled the Gnome and began reeling in his catch.

"Please…please, don't eat me!" the Goblin squealed in a voice that quickly turned into an uncontrollable giggle. Moralee grabbed hold of the rope and reeled in the snared foot. Not three paces apart, the two stood gawking at one another. Easily slipping his foot free, the little Goblin's red eyes began to tear from laughter.

"Dare you mock a Dwarf!" she bellowed.

"Yikes!" screamed the Goblin and ran hurriedly to join the others, where all three continued to laugh and jump up and down. This time, Moralee found the hilt of her sword and, brandishing it into the air, she charged at them with an angry vengeance.

Muk could make out the shapes of the Goblins, but he could not see their genuinely horror-stricken faces as the bearded, female Dwarf gave out a piercing war cry and charged the threesome. Their laughter quickly changed to cries of fear as they scrambled out of the room. The angry Dwarf burst into a spacious hallway but came to a sudden halt. Her sword continued to swoop the air over her head, but when she looked around, there was no one there to chase.

Quimby had his dagger drawn, as did Nommie. Both were right behind her when she put her arms out, bringing them to a halt.

"That'll teach them!" she shouted into the deserted hall.

"What? Let's go!" Quimby frowned.

"Well, I would," she began. "I saw him real good when he was up close, but I'm still a little fuzzy at a distance."

"Anyway…not a good idea to attack the unknown," Nommie muttered. "Besides," he nodded back toward the room.

"Go ahead," Muk said, no longer needing a shoulder to cling to. "I can see your shapes well enough and there isn't any place you can go that I can't follow you with my ears."

"We should be rested and ready, if we need to take on a pack of Goblins," warned Oblio.

"They seemed be waiting for us."

"Definitely they were expecting us," added Moralee.

"Nommie, is that your orange beard?" Muk asked, reaching out and tugging on it twice.

"So it is...so it is," he laughed, stealing it back from Muk's grip. "Here," Nommie said, "let's sit and finish off these apples and figure out our next move. We are almost back in action. Moralee has recovered, Muk can hear everything and see anything that looks orange and Quimby seems…"

"Quimby!" they all turned and yelled at once.

"Quimby what?" quizzed McNaught.

"Not *what*...but where," corrected Eff. "He's gone."

"Gone where?" Sam asked, but the answer to that question did not get immediately answered. Apparently, this particular Sunday was to be full of surprises and several other events were waiting to be unraveled by the time the boys got to the top of the drive.

Chapter Twenty Five

God Bless Sister Margaret

...who stood in the doorway, hands on her hips. The words she wanted to say looked like they were already well etched in her mind.

"Father Griffin called to say you'd be along in a minute!" she snapped. "Just look at the time," she added, pointing them to the cafeteria. "Breakfast must be cold by now." And it was. Cold scrambled eggs and a piece of rubbery ham. Eff was the first to stock up on extra toast. It was hard to ruin toast. He was determined to finish his Sunday chores and hurry back to the Pageleaf. He had a feeling that the Goblins might have had something to do with Quimby's disappearance and he wanted to take advantage of the Headmaster's miraculous but brief absence.

Alex, Sam, Charlie and the McKirdy twins were on laundry duty and, together with Eff, they stripped the bunk beds into even piles and tied the outside sheets into a knot. It took all their strength to push and slide the bundles into the hall and flop them step by step down three floors to the laundry room. The stairs to the poorly lit basement were long and narrow and Sam hesitated about half way down.

"I can't help you if you're just gonna stand around!" Eff shouted over the din of tumbling dryers. The second he said it, though, he wished he hadn't. He just now realized that the Newbie had never been into the basement before. It was nearly as scary as the attic. It was windowless and stuffy. The air was thick with a combination of bleach, soap, damp and an overwhelming, grimey smell of oil from the boiler room. Even for Eff, the poor lighting and cramped working space had taken a lot of getting used to. So he took a deep breath of damp air and began by helping Sam pull his bundle toward the washers, calling out instructions as he loaded each washer.

"Sheets ~ six sets in. Check! Soap ~ half cup in. Check! Shut…push start…go!" Next he pushed Sam to the towel pile. The Newbie was fearful of the lack of light and wary of everything around him, so Eff grabbed his attention by again calling out the proper instructions.

"Towels ~ twelve. Check! Soap ~ half cup in. Check! Shut…push start and go!" he hollered.

The other boys had finished way ahead of them and Eff could hear mischievous laughter coming from the top of the steps. When they finished, he lead Sam out of the spooky basement. At the top of the stairs they found the door locked. Or, more likely, one of the boys was pushing against it from the other side.

"Poop on you!" he yelled, not caring if Sister Margaret was in hearing distance or not. He shook the door, but it didn't budge. "I'll set the Goblins after you," he warned to more muffled laughter from the other side.

"You don't really think Goblins live down here?" Sam whimpered.

"Okay...that's it!" Eff yelled, kicking the door in frustration. He then turned to the younger boy and grumbled, "No, of course I don't," and stomped back down into the basement. "Listen!" he said, stopping at the bottom of the stairs. "Let's just pretend we're on a journey."

"Are there gonna be any Goblins?"

"No..." Eff said, trying to figure a way to prepare Sam for what he had decided to do next. "*You* and *I* are going to be the Goblins...and *we* are going to kick their butts!" The Newbie looked startled. Whether it was because he was unsure about becoming a Goblin or because he very much doubted whether the two of them could physically kick anyone's butt, Eff didn't care. He was about to charge his way through uncharted waters ~ The Boiler Room ~ and he was going to need all the extra courage he could muster. With anger as his muse and revenge his motive, he charged right through the cobwebbed door at the rear of the laundry room. Instantly, he was enveloped by total darkness and a kind of sweet, oily scent that permeated the sand under their feet. Eff was vaguely aware of Sam's presence as he almost tripped over one of the partially buried floorboards that lead them to the exit ~ a wafer-thin shaft of light way off in the distance. Eff pushed open the boiler room doors to the welcoming daylight of the back yard, which was a small patch of grass bordered by endless swamp. Even though it had started drizzling again, Eff felt invigorated. Glancing behind him to be sure that he hadn't lost Sam to the evil darkness, Eff marched up the kitchen porch steps, forged his way through the pantry and caught the boys totally unaware.

"Goblins gotcha!" he screeched, rounding the corner and advancing upon them. The amount of ruckus that followed was embarrassing. Eff thought it sounded like a bunch of girls screaming bloody murder, but he was too caught up in the moment to back down. He, and Sam to some degree, chased the other four into the hall entryway. For some unknown reason, one of the McKirdy brothers turned to fight them off, his eyes shut tight as if blind and an invisible sword in his hand. Undaunted, Eff continued his relentless attack.

"Big Goblins!" he hollered all the louder and charged ahead. Five of the boys ran full tilt through the cafeteria archway, screaming and yelling. One of them, however, bounced off the wall and ended up lying in a pool of blood.

Sister Margaret shrieked. Frank moaned, "Oh, Christ!" Thankfully, quite some time later, Mr. Wittlesey found them all huddled just inside the door to the infirmary. Without knowing exactly what had transpired, he stood there mumbling, "I knew it…I knew it…I knew it!"

Later, after Frank retreated to the kitchen and Sister ran to find the Headmaster, it was Pat McKirdy's story that everybody wanted to hear.

"I was pretending to be Muk," he said proudly, sitting up in the infirmary bed, supported by a mound of pillows. "And I was running blindly through the dungeon with my sword drawn." The boys all laughed. There was no doubt that they all had dreamt themselves in a similar situation.

Of course, now that Mr. Wittlesey was standing in the room, the boy's story suddenly failed him, along with the truth.

"I was running…" Pat had said, shaking uncontrollably, more afraid of Mr. Wittlesey than the stitches, "from…" He hesitated.

"…the spiders," came a soft voice, finishing the sentence for him. Everyone turned to Sam. Witnessing the tearful, Newbie's face made the lie true. It was instantly obvious to them all, that the youngest of orphans had been trapped in the laundry room with more than the smell and the darkness.

'What an odd day' Eff thought to himself, looking from Sam's downcast face to the black-and-blue stitched knot on Pat's forehead. But two things suddenly occurred to him that made him smile. The biggest one was that Mr. Wittlesey had not lost his temper. In fact, he had stepped forward, carefully scrutinized the doctor's stitches, added an extra pillow for the injured boy's comfort and then left the room and the boys to themselves, making them all feel as if they were ~ cared for. And secondly, all because of an innocent little scar, Eff was never again going to be wondering which McKirdy twin was Pat or which one was Mike.

Chapter Twenty Six

"Greasy Little Devils"

...muttered Quimby, the Goblin's laughter and taunting still fresh in his mind. "They didn't seem that frightening," he told himself, following their bare-footed tracks down the sand covered hall. Just as the sand diminished and the tracks stopped altogether on the stone floor, the Halfling sensed he was going the wrong direction. He didn't understand the calling, but something was prodding him to turn around and go back. 'Back to what?' he thought.

Meanwhile, back in the room, the apples were quickly shoved back into Nommie's pack and weapons were readied. The idea of taking a break was short-lived, seeing that one of the troupe was missing. Their meal, treasure and the Princess would have to wait; the group now went searching for one of their own. The Halfling's footprints, fresh in the sand, especially those with boots and metal strappings, were not hard to follow.

"You know he's out to get all the treasure for himself!" Nommie reminded them, as their pursuit of Quimby came to a crossroad. The sand was thicker here and all the tracks turned to the left. Cautiously, Moralee peered around the corner and, finding only a dimly lit hall, she led them forward with sword drawn.

"Curious!" stated Moralee, coming to a stop and pointing to where Quimby tracks had apparently reversed direction and walked directly up to a solid stone wall and disappeared. There were footprints, but no Halfling.

"It be damp," Delphinea said, describing the smell.

"You mean he peed on the wall?" Muk asked, stepping closer to better see what the others were describing.

"No," laughed Nommie, "there's a unique scent coming from behind this wall…and somehow…" It was Oblio who ran her hand over the wall and caused the loud 'Click' that spun the stone slab open. A dark cavernous entrance awaited them and Quimby's footprints continued straight ahead up a large dune of sand that was enveloped by darkness. Fortunately, on the backside of the stone slab, there was a lit torch high on the wall. Beneath it was a wrought iron basket full of torch handles. Each member of the group lit their own torch and proceeded in the direction of the Halfling's tracks.

Soon, both Nommie and Moralee were laboring under the weight of their armour, as the depth and the softness of the sand increased. The smooth stone walls of the entrance gave way to rough, jutted rock and the ceiling rose high into dark shadows that the torchlight could not reach.

"Now we know where all that sand in the hall came from," puffed Moralee, stopping to take several deep breaths. Just as the sand began to level out, they were bathed in a heavy scent, damp and musky. As they struggled over the top of the dune, the deep silence of an enormous cavern greeted them.

Moralee's torch shone in the distance. It had been thrust into the sand and its reddish glow danced in the mouth of an ancient cave. From the top of the dune, it appeared as if they were walking into the gaping jaw of a many-toothed dragon.

"Stalactites!" declared Muk.

"Quimby?" Oblio called out. The name echoed much longer than the time it took to find him. He had stripped himself to the waist and was kneeling beside a pool of dark water that lapped gently against the sand.

"I saw some beady, red eyes peeping at me, but I think they're gone now," he offered as an excuse. No one commented on the lie, but they all knew that the Goblin's footprints had headed off in a different direction.

"We all have to learn to stick together!" Moralee reminded him sharply. As they approached, the torches illuminated the scene, revealing the depth of the cavern and a clear water lake.

"Did you sense it or smell it?" Oblio asked, as she joined him in the sand. Quimby looked at her, his face abnormally calm.

"Those vilings were taunting us. So I set out after them to teach them a lesson. But then I sensed..," Quimby stopped to collect the right words, "...something like a memory. It was an overpowering emotion ~ maybe it was the smell. I come from a long line of sailors. I have an excellent sense of smell, you know!"

"Well, I'm for a rest," stated Nommie, wanting to strip down and sit for a spell.

Moralee too, dropped her shield, belt and armour leggings and added, "But one of us should probably stand watch up on the dune."

"Goblins have a great fear of water," declared Oblio. "I think we're clear of them for a while."

"Good...let's rest," said Moralee, a decision that surprised them all.

"I've still got cheese and leftover breakfast," Muk remembered, emptying the contents of his pack onto his robe.

"Picnic anybody?" announced Nommie, wiping off his boot knife and slicing away at the cheese.

"Picnic be good!" agreed Delphinea, laying out her cloak on the sand and breaking the bread into equal portions. Once they began eating, there was a peace to the place that went beyond the quiet. Eventually, the conversation turned back to food.

"Back to 'The Keep'? I don't want them to see us coming up empty handed," Moralee admitted.

"But we're down to an apple apiece," Nommie reminded them.

"Going back up isn't going to help," Muk said, "because I don't have any more gold."

"All the more reason to continue the search," pressed Moralee.

"On an empty stomach?" Quimby whined.

"That or we go back up with something of worth," suggested Oblio. "The scrolls might be worth something or Nommie's ring."

"Speaking of ring..." Nommie muttered, running his hands through empty pockets.

"No...not the ring! Why not the belt? Or the sword?" sputtered the Halfling.

"Muk, why don't you try to decipher the articles we have," Oblio insisted. "At least that will give us an idea of their value."

"Perhaps...one of them is a spell for all the food we can eat," frowned Nommie, still unable to locate his prized skeleton trophy.

Muk fixed a long stare at Quimby, then motioned to the sand. "There! In the sand!"

"Look at me," smiled Quimby. "I found a ring."

"Wondered where that thing went," Nommie grumbled, plucking the ring from the Halfling thief's grasp and handing it to Muk.

"Oblio, maybe you ought to be the one to read them," encouraged Muk.

"No, you should do it," she insisted, "but I'll hand them to you so that you'll have plenty of time to read them all."

Muk, Delphinea and Oblio wandered to the far end of the beach planting torches on either side of them and laying out the scrolls on Delphinea's cloak. Quimby followed closely, never letting the ring out of his sight. When asked about her new sword, Moralee refused to give it up, saying that she already knew all anyone needed to know about it.

While they were setting up the scrolls, Moralee and Nommie began building a wall of sand by the water. Moralee scooped up the wetter sand by the lake with her shield and Nommie with his shield. They started together at the middle and went at opposite angles, recreating the walls of 'The Keep'.

Meanwhile, Muk sat himself down next to the carefully laid out items. He took a deep breath to calm himself and said nothing about the butterflies in his stomach. "Be quick to open the scrolls, there's no telling how long the spell will last," he reminded them. He smiled. He was ready.

He lifted the heavy parchment entitled:

"Enchantment ~ The Power To See & Read".

It was only four lines long, but before his fingers ran across the first line, Muk's head began to swim and his eyes to burn, spots pulsating before them. He felt a flame from somewhere inside sweep over him and a strangeness crawl through his body, down through his arms to the very end of his toes. An overwhelming sense of being pulled backward enveloped him. He flashed upon a brief moment, seeing himself standing on the bow of a barge and looking up at a steep mountain and seeing 'The Keep' for the very first time. He saw a foggy dock and Elan's friendly face. He smiled as he remembered his Mirthday and his uncles' raging war of arm wrestling. He saw an all too brief glimpse of his father and mother, but could not hold the memory long enough, bringing tears to his eyes.

Quimby had stopped his fretting and decided to join Delphinea, who sat in great anticipation. Oblio knelt beside Muk, scrolls in hand, waiting for him to give her some sort of sign that he was ready. She watched his lips silently move as he read the incantation and then, almost instantly, his cheeks flushed and then turned a sickly pale. His eyes glassed over as if he were once again blind and he sat motionless, as in a trance.

"He be waiting for power of understanding?"

"Maybe it doesn't work. Maybe he's bewitched!" warned Quimby.

"I get water!" offered Delphinea and she rushed to the

lakeside. Seeing Nommie's shield, she scooped up some water and started back up to the others.

"Hey!" hollered Nommie, looking up from their play and recognizing trouble. Muk was trance-like, staring at the sand in front of him, mouth open and face white with sickness.

When Oblio saw the tears running down Muk's cheeks, she only then dared grab hold of him. There was an electrical 'zap' and Muk shook with the sudden awareness that someone else was there. Then, looking down, his eyes focused on the gold-braided belt. He smiled at it for an instant and tossed it aside. He held up Quimby's ring and began to laugh. To the Halfling's disbelief, Muk slipped it on to his own finger. Oblio fumbled with the scrolls, then, carefully handed them over one by one. Muk nodded at the first one, made a face at the second, and, after each was only glanced at, he rolled them up and placed them in his lap.

"Is that all?" he said sleepily, turning to Oblio with a vacant smile. She responded with a nod. "Except for the Gathire Sword, I see."

"I'll not give up!" Moralee nearly shouted with a defiant step back from the others, her hand tight to the hilt of her sword.

"No, it was not meant for any one of us. I just hope you know what will be required of you..."

"Uh…the ring…?" Quimby reminded everyone, reaching to take it back.

A sudden burst of light illuminated the dark cavern and, for a brief second, lit the sandy beach like the light of day. What felt like a bolt of lightning shot through Quimby, leaving him on his backside several yards away. And there he remained for several moments, counting the stars that circled before his eyes.

For Muk, the jolt was like being shaken awake from a troubled dream. The Halfling's touch had released a torrent of troubling images that were foreign to him. He shot forward, unable to rid himself of them and unable to stand. His limbs became jelly and, when at last his mind was free of the unwanted energy, he rolled face first into the cool sand.

"Just a little nap," he replied, plopping his head back on the soft sand.

"Quimby?" asked Moralee, as the Halfling jumped up and pushed his way by her. He stood by the lake, kicking at the castle walls made of sand.

Oblio picked up the scrolls and placed them carefully into Muk's pack. It was Delphinea who took the cloak lying in the sand and placed it under Muk's head. "Be you okay?"

"Yes, I'm fine…just a little rest," Muk said with a deep sigh. "Rosslyn says hello," he mumbled and closed his eyes.

"Is he asleep?" Moralee asked.

"I think he be resting."

"Remind me to never touch that ring!" joked Nommie, shaking the water and sand out of his shield.

"Who's Rosslyn?" wondered Moralee. Delphinea's face blushed slightly, but she said nothing.

"Strange business, magic," observed Nommie.

"I thought you didn't believe in magic," countered Oblio.

"I don't," replied the Gnome, "but I do believe in the power of a short nap."

Chapter Twenty Seven

The Best That Quimby Could Do

...was wander, while everyone else was at rest. In frustration, he kicked down the walls of the sand castle and paced back and forth on the water's edge. He was not in the mood to sleep. Quimby wanted to wear his ring. After all, he had found it ~ well ~ stolen it. Somehow, Muk realized that he had 'lifted' it off the unsuspecting Gnome while climbing up the window to see the valley. But that wasn't what was really bothering him. Muk's 'Vision' had included the Halfling's best kept secrets ~ both of them! In one swift bolt of energy, Muk had read Quimby's mind. He was sure of it. He had seen the shock of sudden understanding in Muk's eyes. The one piece of twisted metal hidden deep in his pocket ~ the magic key that he had never told anyone about, the one item that defined who he truly was, was now discovered. But it was the second secret. It was the frown and troubled expression that had washed over Muk's face that really worried him the most. Muk must have seen a vision of 'The Room'. It was a glimpse of something so strange that even he, Quimby, did not know what to think.

It wasn't his fault they thought he was crying because he was blind. And earlier, in the thick of battle with the skeletons, only because he was quicker and smarter, did Muk and Nommie get hurt and not him. Why did they receive extra support and comfort? And the disaster at the desk, anyone could have accidently opened that drawer. Sure, Moralee and Muk might have been blinded by the gas, but did anyone race immediately over to him? Did anyone rush to him with a comforting word? No! He was an afterthought! So he cried. It was just a moment of weakness. And when they finally left him alone, he snatched up his opportunity. With one quick turn using the magic key that had truly made him a legendary thief, he was in. They would never know.

But what had he found? Not a room full of treasure or meaningful scrolls. *What had he found?* It was so odd that there were no words to describe it, yet his instincts cried out to him to quickly turn and go. He felt as if he had uncovered something so sinister, that he was in mortal danger. So he acted as if he had seen nothing ~ he pretended to play blind. What else could he do? If everybody thought he was blind, then maybe he could get away with it, at least until he could figure out the meaning behind what he saw.

But now Muk knew. Quimby wasn't sure if this was a good thing or a bad thing. He didn't know if Muk could make any more sense out of it than he had, or even if he could trust Muk enough to talk about it. Until he was sure about what to do, 'The Room' needed to remain a secret. Quimby stood at the edge of the lake, grumpy as hell. And, while pondering what to do next, he found himself staring at some glimmering, shiny objects out in the water.

"Ahh…ha…foun…gol…!" came a drowning voice, shaking the others out of their slumber. It was Quimby's voice coming from somewhere out in the lake. Moralee ran to the water's edge, but all that remained of the Halfling was a handful of bubbles. An anxious moment later, Quimby was crawling out of the water on all fours, a shiny round coin in his mouth.

"I'm rich!" he coughed, shaking himself off like a dog. "Gold!"

"Not gold," corrected Nommie, reaching for the coin.

"Oh, no. Not this time!" shrieked the waterlogged Halfling, pulling the coin back. He timidly handed it to Oblio instead. Surely he could trust her.

She held it up to the torch light.

"Platinum!" cried several voices at once.

"Does that mean it's worthless?" Quimby moaned, as a tragically pained expression creased his face.

"No…not worthless," Muk appraised, as the open-mouthed Halfling once again stood on the edge of tears. "In fact, it is very rare ~ only worth about a hundred gold pieces!"

"Then I am rich!" he shouted, jumping into the air and diving back into the water. Twice, his diving attempts could not reach the shiny objects below him. On the third failed attempt, he came up coughing water and sucking air at the same time.

"Quimby not be good swimmer."

"No...he's not much of a swimmer," Nommie agreed, reaching down to take off his boots, "and he's going to drown before he gets any richer."

"He's going to be long gone before you get all your clothes off," Muk pointed out. "Do you really want to get all wet?"

Nommie just looked up with a 'do you have a better plan' sort of look. Muk smiled.

"This ought to be interesting if nothing else," he muttered and walked down to the lapping water.

"You better take off..." Nommie started to say, stopping in mid-sentence. Muk took several wobbly steps out on the water surface, found his balance, and took several more steps before reaching down and grabbing the soaked Quimby by the scruff of his neck. He lifted the Halfling up out of the water until their faces met, eye to eye.

"So...you want to go fishing for coins?"

Quimby offered a nervous laugh, first looking over at the stunned expressions of the others, then down and wondering what Muk could possibly be standing on.

"Equal split, or do I tell the others about your 'special' room?"

"Lotsa coins...down there," Quimby muttered.

"You ready?"

"Sssurre!" replied the Halfling, still puzzled by Muk's presence out on the water.

"Let's get rich!" hollered Muk, trading handholds on Quimby's collar for a secure grasp of his ankles and turning him upside down.

Muk walked slowly and carefully, at times waving a free hand in the air to steady himself out over the deeper waters. When he figured he was standing directly over a pile of shiny objects, he raised Quimby's feet high into the air and plunged him, arms and head first, into the water.

Each time Quimby was pulled up, he came up sputtering and squealing like a child. Joyfully, he pitched the coins to the beach, where the other four playfully pushed and shoved one another to come away the holder of a shiny piece of platinum. Every time Quimby threw the coins to the beach, he immediately began wiggling, as a message to Muk that he was ready to return to the bottom once again. At one point, Muk lost his balance and fell over backwards. He found himself sitting on the water ~ not touching it, but resting on it, slowly rising and falling with its movement. To the fit of laughter coming from the beach,

Muk found that the only way he could get back up was by rolling to his knees and then slowly pushing his hands up to where he could stand once more. Of course, Quimby did not have the luxury of floating on water. He floundered about, splashing and cursing until Muk could pluck him up out of the water. And, again, to Quimby's great delight, they went fishing for more coins.

Quimby dried himself off with Muk's robe when Muk wasn't looking and, with his curly locks drying every which way, he sat down to join the others. Oblio doled out the coins in front of her one at a time, then plunked Quimby's share into his eager outstretched hands.

"Thirty-eight!" she announced. "That's six apiece for us and eight for you, Quimby. After all, you're the one who had to go fishing for them."

The Halfling let them clink in his hand for a moment. Then to everyone's surprise, he offered one to Muk. Nommie raised a bushy orange eyebrow.

"That be a kind offer of Quimby," remarked Delphinea, making the Halfling blush.

"Bribe?" smiled Muk.

"Let's just not mention it here," he whispered.

"Holding out on us?" inquired the Gnome, leaning in to listen to their conversation.

"No!" Quimby insisted, stealing off with his hard-fought treasure. Without his pack of meager belongings, he was going to have to hide his treasure somewhere on his body. Nommie gave Muk a quizzical turn of the head.

"No really...it's nothing..." Muk hesitated a moment. He then turned to Moralee. "Besides the Sword of Gathire, doesn't Dwarven lore also recount tales of a magical suit of armour?"

"Suit of armour?" inquired Nommie, his eyes coming alive.

"Yes, it's an old tale about a Dwarven King who falls into a sea of water during battle," began Muk, "and his Lackey who dives in to save him."

"The 'Magical Suit of Armour' is a story we Dwarves all know very well." Moralee acknowledged.

"A true story?" Nommie demanded.

"Of course!" nodded the Dwarf.

"Well..," Muk continued excitedly, "beyond the shallows, when I fell backwards out in the deeper part of the lake, I saw something reflective and large. It could have been a large pile of coins, but it looked solid. Of course, there wasn't any light to see properly and it was out in the deepest part of the water."

"The magical suit of armour?" Moralee thought out loud.

"I always thought that Dwarves didn't believe in magic," tossed in Quimby as he rejoined the group.

"It's Gnomes who don't believe in magic," Nommie

corrected, then chuckled, "Dwarves don't believe they can swim."

"Huh?" frowned Quimby.

"A Dwarve's biggest fear is *water!*" laughed Nommie.

"Actually, the suit is said to possess great powers," Oblio asserted.

"I'm not being dunked for no suit of armour!" protested Quimby.

"Don't look to me!" Moralee was quick to say.

"I'm up to it, if you are," Nommie agreed, peering into the dark recesses of the cave. Piece by piece, he placed his weapons and armour neatly into the curve of his shield. Rolling up his bright blue trousers, he walked to the water's edge. His beaming smile flickered in the torchlight, his toes wiggling in the sand.

"Ready!" said Nommie, grabbing a torch from the beach and climbing onto Muk's back.

Stepping slowly out on the water, Muk made his way back to the centre of the lake. Standing and facing the dark open water with torchlight, Muk was now able to detect a narrow sandy trail between the murky water and the cave wall, leading around the outside perimeter of the lake. Once above the solid reflection and with one arm clutching tightly around Muk's neck, Nommie thrust the bright torch even farther into the darkness. From that vantage point, the two could now see that the lake was actually kidney-shaped with a much larger beach of sand off to the opposite end.

"Big beach!" shouted the Gnome, encouraging the others to follow the narrow trail. It was Moralee's turn to grumble, something about 'unknown things' jumping out of the water at them. Meanwhile, Quimby struggled with Muk's pack and Delphinea pulled the rest of their belongings by tying a rope to Nommie's shield and dragging it like a sled.

"I'm going to bend down on my knees," warned Muk, allowing the Gnome to ride his back like a horse. They were directly over the object, but even as Nommie extended the torch to just above the water, they were still not able to identify the shininess that lay beneath them. And so Muk crawled back toward the others and the sand trail.

"We need another torch," Muk said breathlessly. Quimby was only too happy to drop the heavy pack and wade out with the extra torch. Moralee followed on Oblio's heals, protesting every time she had to wade any higher than ankle deep. Now with three torches illuminating the cavernous opening, the shiny white in the centre of the lake was even more pronounced, as was the large beach at the other end.

"Great place for a picnic," groaned Nommie.

"We're all out of food!" asserted Quimby, who had just realized that he was the only one getting wet.

"That's what I meant," sighed the Gnome. "Well, my friend…one more try?"

"Just needed to catch my breath," Muk replied, getting back down on hands and knees and allowing the Gnome to climb back on board. "You know…you're a lot heavier than you look."

Nommie balanced himself on Muk's back, a torch in either hand. "This armour thing of any value?"

"You mean a magical suit of armour whose wearer has never lost a battle?" asked Muk.

"I see your point. But how is it that it's in forty paces of water?"

"Well…in the original story, the King and his lackey die."

"Ahh…I'm thinking that that information might have been better said sooner!" grumbled the Gnome.

"Yes, but over time, the story and the suit of armour pops up again and again," continued Muk. "Wouldn't it be likely that a suit of magic and a place like the dungeon would suit each other?"

"Suit each other…that's clever," grinned Nommie.

"Well…how about this? What if that sliding trap door in the long hallway is right above us?"

"Hmm…nothing about being strapped to anything magical at the bottom of a lake…sounds very lucky to me!" grunted Nommie.

"Well, it fits the story…" Muk thought aloud, coming to a stop.

The rock shapes suspended from the cave ceiling seemed to come alive with the added flicker of two red flames. The image below was also more pronounced; the extra light greatly aided peering into the water's depths.

"It looks like…" Muk shouted for all to hear, forcing one hand down into the water to get a better look. "I think it's…" he started again, this time thrusting both hands flat into the water, making a glass portal with which to see more clearly to the bottom.

But this simple motion forward, coupled with Nommie's being caught leaning forward to make his own discovery, unseated the Gnome and caused him to topple over forward. Muk heard a 'squawk' and was surprised when he saw two torches spinning topsy-turvy into the air. Nommie splashed headlong into the cold, deep water. The first torch landed nearby, noisily fizzing into the water, while the second torch spun round and round and landed on the edge of the far shore, illuminating the large, sandy beach and deep cavern beyond.

"Holy shivers!" were the first words out of Nommie's mouth when his head popped out of the water.

"I'm sorry!" Muk apologized at once, quickly trying to get to his feet. He had to join the others in laughter though, when he pulled the balding orange mop out of the cold water. Muk was prepared for a long barrage of Gnomish slang, but it stopped in mid-sentence, replaced by a look of horror on Nommie's face.

That is when Muk heard the rustling noise. It was coming from behind him, echoing from the caverns above the beach. From the cave's dark recesses, a long stick was thrust out into the sand, followed by another which landed nearer the water. Like magic, the first stick lifted itself out of the sand and sent itself forward, spearing the shallow water. With the last movement, high above them, a gruesome face appeared from the cavern's shadows.

Muk turned to see who was throwing spears at him and got a quick glimpse of the danger that Nommie was reacting to. Looking something like a gigantic praying mantis, a huge insect beast revealed itself. Its intentions of feasting on the both of them was evident by its continuously clacking pinchers. Without time enough to shout, Muk turned and flung Nommie as far as he could toward the others, then followed at a run.

"Stay down! Stay down!" Moralee shouted. Instinctively, Muk tried to dive under water, but ended up knocking the wind out of himself and bouncing to a stop. Bobbing up and down, he turned to face the oncoming monster just as two arrows flashed by, singing dangerously close to his head. Both struck the beast, one hitting its stick-like leg and crumpling it into the sand, the other lodging itself into its pincher-like mouth.

Delphinea ran through the shallow water and onto the beach before planting one more perfectly aimed arrow into the beast's forehead, leaving it lying motionless in the sand. Muk was shaking too much to stand, so he crawled onto the beach, where he could see by the lone torch spitting in the sand, the mammoth size of the creature that had intended to devour him.

"Wow!" Quimby exclaimed, running up and the first to reach the beast. He surveyed its perimeter, poking at it with the torch shaft. When it did not move, he pronounced it dead. A water-drenched Gnome came up behind Muk and reclaimed the torch from the beach.

"The problem with you young-uns, is that you are always trying to wear out us older folks," Nommie said in a father-like fashion, patting Muk on the back and walking on up the beach to inspect the giant bug.

"Sorry about the bath," Muk called out after him. Delphinea approached with a smile of relief. "Did you get all three shots off?" asked Muk.

"I slowed it in leg and Moralee keep mouth busy," she replied. "She be good with Nommie's crossbow!" Moralee and Oblio were the last to plod up the beach, the sled in tow.

Muk turned to thank Moralee. "I didn't know you were an expert shot!"

"I'm not," Moralee laughed, "I was aiming at you!"

∞

"I've never heard of a bug *that* big before," Alex doubted.

"You better hope you never do!" laughed Tommy in his annoying high-pitched giggle.

"My uncle told me once that the mosquitos in Montana were pretty big," claimed Charlie. The boys were all sitting in the classroom, waiting on Mr. Brister. Besides Sister Celeste, more often than not, he was their regular teacher. He and a third teacher, Miss Markley, handled most of the teaching chores. She was ancient and couldn't teach every day and Mr. Brister was young and still taking night classes. He had been called into the Headmaster's office instead of one of the boys, for a change. Sam stood just inside the hallway with an ear tuned to any disturbance in the stairwell. He gave the thumbs up and Eff continued with the story.

Chapter Twenty Eight

"No Suit Of Armour?"

...echoed Quimby's voice throughout the cavern.

"All that 'shiny' at the bottom were bones!" Nommie answered for the second time.

"Just bones," added Muk, "and I nearly saw mine lying down there with them." For a moment, the cavern entrance was silent, except for the soft lapping of water from the beach. Quimby was trying to think of some other cutting remark, but his stomach was making all the noise.

"No armour...but be door," Delphinea called to the group, pointing to the direction of the insect's lair. They followed Delphinea up the sand dune and into the back of a cave full of bones.

"Great...more skeletons!" commented Nommie, as Moralee drew her sword.

"Bones...not be human."

"Just the same...holler if you see one of them move," Muk laughed uneasily.

As the torches drew nearer the rear of the cavern, beyond the hill of sand and skeletal fragments, they came upon the remains of a fishing village. Against a wall of stone was a heavy door and beneath that a wooden planked dock. Pilings jutted up at odd angles and a broken-bottomed boat lay to the side, half exposed in the sand. On the far end of the dock, a broken timber lay across empty crates and old nets.

"Looks like the water was once a lot higher," Muk observed. They were all standing around the dock, wondering if the planks would hold the weight of investigating the door. Moralee pointed her torch to the remains of a different skeleton farther off into the shadows.

"What's left of a barge. There must have been a lot more trading and hauling once."

"You mean like…food?" Nommie muttered.

"Shhh…" Quimby alerted, dropping to the sand beneath the dock. From his view, he had been eye-level with the bottom of the door and a faint light from the other side had been disturbed by moving shadows ~ approaching feet. "Torches…" he added and instantly smothered his into the sand. The other torches were quickly extinguished as well, as there wasn't time enough to run and hide into the shadows. A key from inside turned and the door opened.

Two pairs of skinny, little Goblin arms pushed the door out a little less than half way. One of the Goblins walked to the edge of the deck, untied his trousers and began to pee.

"Here...grasshopper!" he laughed in a high-pitched giggle.

"You'll be sorry the day it's waiting for ya," squeaked the other, not willing to come out all the way into the open.

"I wouldn't even be here now if it weren't for Peevis!"

"Why *are* we on double duty?"

"Dopey outsiders...but Peevis figured they musta run off."

"So what's Peevis' gripe?"

"He was losing at cards and got up and left."

"Well, wherever he hides out during one of his fits, I doubt if it's in the cave or anywhere near that monster."

"Not unless he's temperamental *and* crazy."

"He's temperamental alright, but not crazy like you. Get in here before it takes a bite out of your water hose!"

The thick door shut with a thud and a key slapped against metal. Quimby rested his chin on the dock and watched through the space at the bottom of the door until the moving of shadows and feet were gone.

"Free!" Quimby whispered.

"Torches are dead," Moralee reported, brushing the sand off her knees and elbows. Instinctively, they had buried their torches and now, except for a tiny ribbon of light emitting from under the bottom of the door, they were all standing in total darkness.

"It's a long walk back for another torch," Muk reminded them.

"Two of us could go back up top for food and more torches," offered Nommie.

"Colony of Goblins be watching," warned Delphinea.

"Not a good time to split up," said Moralee. "I say we stay together. In force, we can protect ourselves or even take them by surprise."

"If we get close enough, I could work a sleeping spell," offered Oblio.

"Sounds good to me," said Nommie, "but how do we get past the locked door?"

"Me...of course!" said Quimby proudly, crawling silently over the dock and eyeing the keyhole. There came a muffled click and the door slowly opened outward without a sound. Deciding on a quick peek, they stuffed their packs beneath the dock. Moralee followed behind Quimby, her shield raised and sword drawn. One by one, they slipped into the hall unnoticed. Muk was the last one to enter, closing the door softly behind him. Ten paces ahead, Quimby poked his head into an open doorway.

"Warehouse!" he whispered heavily, waving the others forward. The room was full of supplies: shovels, spades, picks and other tools, clothing and crates full of small bows and arrows. Quimby snitched the first coil of rope he came to and Nommie an armful of arrows for his crossbow.

"Let's go load these into our packs and come back," Quimby suggested.

"Two be better!" warned Delphinea.

"Yes, you two sneak out and we'll wait here," Moralee decided, but Nommie had a different idea. Surprising everyone, he turned in the doorway and began walking up the hall instead.

"Come on," he motioned with a mischievous smile. Moralee's protests, mostly 'psst's' and 'ssst's' just bounced off his backside. Wondering if the Gnome had gone 'tiddly', the rest of them followed him hesitantly into the quiet hall and through another open doorway.

A very disgruntled Dwarf was the last to enter the second room, but she wasn't troubled for long. To all of their amazement, Nommie was sitting on a crate of apples, beaming with satisfaction. With muffled exclamations, the group rummaged through a room completely filled with boxes, sacks and crates of food. They quickly cleared a chopping table and covered it with their delicious newfound treasures: fresh carrots, hardloaf bread, cheese, apples, figs, nuts, jerky and the 'unanimous favorite', Muk's discovery of several kegs of wine. He found the kegs behind a burrowing of grain sacks piled up like a wall. And when he went to lift the first keg and hand it to Moralee, he unearthed another type of find altogether.

Chapter Twenty Nine

"Peevis? Right?"

...asked Muk, gazing down at a very inebriated Goblin.

"Yep-up," came the half-answer, half-hiccup.

"You wouldn't want to come out from under there and meet everyone, would you, Mr. Peevis?"

"Me-heep?"

Muk lifted him under one arm and Moralee under the other and sat him down on a bag of grain by the table. He just sat there, back straight, mouth open with a pair of disbelieving red eyes that went from one strange creature to the next.

"Help yourself," Quimby laughed. "It's probably your last meal."

"Heep!" he answered, cautiously reaching for the portions being placed in front of him. Except for the occasional hiccup, they ate and drank in silence. Muk had been looking around the room and tallying in his head before he thought aloud.

"There must be a whole garrison of Goblins somewhere in these halls. Forty or fifty."

"Thirtee-heep!" popped the answer from their dinner guest, without looking up from his food.

"Which means a lot of trouble!" muttered Moralee.

"Yeah-huc!"

"Do you have the Princess locked up?" grilled Nommie. The Goblin answered him with a vacant stare.

"Do you know of the Great Hall?"

"Nooo…" he said, "but more great wine?"

"Is there a room full of treasure?" Quimby asked, but the Goblin didn't seem to recognize the word 'treasure'.

"Do you work for the Lord Governor?"

"I don't tha-hic-so."

"What do you do down here?"

"We steal from…hiccup…dock. They think it's…" here the little Goblin looked at each one of them before pointing to Moralee, "you!" he admitted.

"Well, that's probably why they don't use the insect route anymore," said Muk. "Why work, when you can steal it?"

"That must mean there is another way in!" replied Nommie.

"And out!" added Moralee.

"Yep! But…shhh…don't go out that way…hiccup! Bug eats everything up!"

"Can you show us the other way…or is there a map of the dungeon?" queried Muk.

"King has lotsa maps," admitted the little Goblin, taking the last piece of bread and stuffing it onto his mouth.

"King? You have a King?" laughed Quimby.

"King takes orders from Wiz-heep!"

"Wizard! Here in the dungeon?" Muk was shocked.

"Wizard lives in…hic…dungeon. Watches everyone! Hiccup…Zap! Goodbye!"

"I think we really need to go…Now!" Quimby was adamant.

"Where can we find this map?" Nommie asked.

"Kingroom," Peevis said, jumping down from the table and wobbling to the door as if he had been ordered.

"Wait! Are we ready for this?" cautioned Moralee.

"We really shouldn't!" insisted Quimby, grabbing Muk's arm. "We're being watched," he nearly shouted. "Didn't you see it?"

"But a map would help us," Oblio voted in favor.

"An army of Goblins won't," warned Moralee.

"Maybe we could make a deal with the King?" suggested Nommie.

"Muk…we really need to go…"

"Kingroom…heep…just next door."

It was Muk who finally made the decision. "That does it then, if we're this close to a map."

"A sleeping charm will help," offered Oblio, as they stood and made ready to proceed.

"I'd rather go back the other way," muttered Quimby, just loud enough to be sure that everyone knew exactly how he felt about the decision. They all considered the Halfling's statement in silence and then all eyes fell on the Goblin, teetering in the doorway.

"I'll keep him busy, by the scruff of his neck," said Nommie, making absolutely certain that Peevis's motivation wasn't treachery.

Moralee listened intently in the doorway before the group entered the hall. Although Peevis was held tightly about his collar, he either didn't notice or didn't seem to care, as he led them casually to the next doorway. It didn't look to be a King's entrance or a door to a throne room, but it was closed and secured from the inside. It had a keyhole, but no handle.

"Now what do we do?" uttered Moralee.

"Peevis! Get us in!" Muk whispered. Quimby grumbled from the back of the procession and pressed forward with his services. But before he could take his 'secret' from his pocket and into the lock, the Goblin stepped up to the door and simply knocked.

"Who is it? Who's there?" cried a high-pitched voice from the other side. Everyone froze still, as still as the silence in the hall. "Well, speak up!" Nommie shook the Goblin for lack of knowing what else to do.

"It's me, Pee-hup!"

"Who! What did you say?"

"It's Peevis!" Muk said in a squeaky voice and as close to the door as possible, hoping to keep the sound to a minimum. Peevis looked up at Muk, shocked that a poor imitation of his voice was necessary.

"What do *you* want?" demanded an angry voice.

"Arghh!" Nommie cried in pain, as the little Goblin turned in defiance and chomped down on his hand with his razor sharp teeth. Nommie quickly dropped his grip from the creature's collar, but Quimby replaced the collar-grip by slipping his slightly bent dagger directly into the little Goblin's view.

"Arghh?" came the inside voice.

"Arrr…" Muk looked to the others in desperation. "Are…you wanting us to feed the outsiders to the bug?" he squeaked.

"You captured them!" a delighted voice came from within. A heavy latch was lifted and a bolt was thrown from inside the door. Then a second latch was heard rattling above the keyhole. Unfortunately, the next sound they heard was not a key unlocking the door, but an alarm bell that rang loudly in the hall.

Muk heard muffled cries from within and then the bolt as it started to slide back across the door. Grasping for Quimby's dagger and shoving with all his might against the door, Muk slammed the dagger into the doorjamb. Luckily, the upper half caved in enough to stop the bolt from completing its task. What Muk could not see, however, was the first wave of Goblins as they rounded the corner into the hallway toward them. Six of them in total, with bows in hand, knelt and fired, even before a cry of warning or surrender could be given.

Although Moralee would not have deemed it a blessing, she and Oblio were the farthest into the hall, or at least closest to the Goblin attack. Her shield followed the flight of the first barrage of arrows and she knocked them away from Muk's frantic attempts to force open the door. A second wave of Goblins, easily a score, skirted the corner, took aim and, immediately fired. Oblio threw up her hands and, to the Goblin army's great surprise, the force of her actions ricocheted the arrows in all directions ~ hitting walls, ceiling or sailing clear down the hall behind their intended target.

For Peevis, the chipping and slapping of arrows was very unnerving and he quickly sobered enough to realize the gravity of his situation. He was standing in the middle of the hallway with the enemy. Without warning, he kicked Quimby hard in the shin and began biting at him insanely with his little, razor-sharp teeth.

Reacting to the creature's sudden rebellion, the Halfling moved his hands out of bite's reach and the little Goblin turned, squirmed and ran. Pushing by Oblio and Moralee just enough to get by, he frantically waved his skinny arms in an attempt to hold fire long enough for him to reach safety. But it was not to be. Now a third volley was already on its way. Thirty arrows sang out; six of them found their mark. Peevis the Goblin dropped to the floor, never to move again, and a seventh arrow somehow skirted through Oblio's defensive shield and struck Quimby full in the chest.

Muk sensed disaster looming. The harder he pushed on the door, the more they couldn't set the second bolt, but still he couldn't get in. He was at a stalemate with the door, yet he knew that it was a battle they dearly needed to win. So he was dumbfounded when he saw Nommie turn and run back down the hall.

"Muk, please hurry," Delphinea pleaded, as she cradled Quimby and helped him to the floor.

Muk had been faced away from the attack and now switched shoulders in an attempt to find some added or buried energy, anything to get them out of harm's way. He knew the longer they remained in the hall, the less the chances were of survival. As his eyes focused on the scene around him, it was as if time was standing still. He saw Moralee protecting him with her shield and heard the hum of Oblio's outstretched hands. Delphinea was countering with an occasional arrow, but the stream of Goblin arrows was unrelenting and gave her no hope of retaliation.

And then he noticed Quimby, lying on the floor, staring up at him. His eyes were nearly lifeless, a faint smile on his lips. He had gotten Muk's attention at last. The dying Halfling's arm flopped out and his fist landed against Muk's foot. When Quimby closed his eyes for the last time, his hand opened and went lifeless. There in his outstretched fingers was the 'Key' ~ the strength and secret to the legend and the mastery that had been Quimby. Muk realized at once the importance of his last action and, the very instant he reached down to snatch it, there came an ear-splitting 'crack'. It was Nommie's doing. The moment Muk bent to reach for the key, it had given the Gnome the opening he needed to launch a pick axe to the center of the door. A large chunk fell to the floor. His second swing shook the door with a mighty crack that reverberated down the hall. Through the splintered hole in the door, Muk could see into the room. The Goblins had given up on the bolt and were now shoving with all their might against the door.

"Delphinea…push!" Muk shouted in desperation, shoving Quimby's key into the lock and turning it.

"One…two…three!" yelled Nommie and all three of them pushed the door in with such a force it knocked the barricade of Goblins to the floor. Swiftly, they were up again and on the attack ~ two with sharp pointed daggers and the King with a gleaming sword. Delphinea used her bow end as a club and whacked the first Goblin she came to across the nose. Nommie had rushed into the room with nothing but the handle of the pick axe, the heavy, iron head still embedded in the door. He easily knocked the small dagger from his adversary's hand and brought the axe handle down full on his attacker's head. Filled with the temper of battle, Muk charged ahead.

The last to fall was the Goblin King. Although he had a confident smile on his face as he raised his sword high over his head and prepared to vanquish the would-be intruders, the enemy's swift entry and a slightly bent dagger was first to find its mark. The Goblin leader could not believe his eyes. Out of nowhere, it was as if a drawbridge had somehow dropped, allowing a handful of strange creatures access to his sanctuary. With a high-pitched war cry, he had challenged the invaders only to fall silent, a puzzled expression of death upon his face. His sword dropped to the stone floor and he slumped back into his regal-padded chair. His eyes closed for the last time and his crown slipped to the side of his head in defeat.

Chapter Thirty

"I Don't Understand,"

...piped up a quiet voice. This came after a long minute of total silence. It was late and the boys should have been asleep by now, but something had gone amiss with the story.

"What don't you understand about someone dying?" answered an abrupt voice. It was Pat McKirdy. One didn't need the lights on to notice the still purple bump on his forehead or the pained expression in his words.

"You mean Quimby's hurt, right?" Charlie asked.

"No," Eff swallowed hard, "it was a Goblin arrow. He died."

"He really died?" uttered Sam.

"It's okay," reassured Alex, who was always looking to the brighter side of things. "When you die you get to go to heaven."

"Or hell!" McNaught reminded them, quickly bringing the conversation to a hush.

"Maybe Oblio has a magic potion," someone from the back of the room suggested.

"God could bring him back, Eff," Sam said, trying to sound cheerful. "He brought Jesus back!"

"I don't think it works that way," Eff tried to explain.

"I didn't like him anyway," Tommy finally admitted.

"That's stupid," Chief said, "he was their friend!"

"He was a thief!" Mike pointed out.

"Like you never stole any apples out of the kitchen," laughed his brother.

"Look who's talking," Mike retorted. "What about a certain piece of jigsaw puzzle?"

"That wasn't me!"

"Was too!"

It was survival instinct that brought everything to an instant halt. For a half second, nothing moved. A creak on the steps sent everybody diving under their covers.

"I'm not sure what all the noise is about up here, but it better stop immediately!" warned Mr. Wittlesey, snapping on the stairwell light. He stopped at the top of the stairs with his hands on his hips. He didn't need to take another step. With the light shining behind him, his dark shadow completely covered the far wall. It was not unlike a giant Troll threatening to club anything that moved.

It must have been a full ten minutes before anyone breathed. Not until they saw the light go out and had waited for the last receding footsteps followed by the click of Mr. Wittlesey's office door shutting tight, did anyone stir.

No one wanted to tempt the return of the Headmaster Troll. There was a momentary rustle of blankets and bodies turning and a pounding of pillows being adjusted, before a brief calm floated over the dormitory.

"Was to!" whispered Mike. "Was not!" muttered Pat.

Chapter Thirty One

Goblin Bodies

...had fallen where they stood. Once the group had fled the hall for the safety of the Throne room, Oblio was able to cast the sleeping charm that she had intended, before being rained upon by arrows. The Goblin horde was asleep for the moment, but nobody knew for how long. Delphinea sat just inside the room, visibly weak and shaken. Oblio, showing little emotion, was there by her side.

"The energy shield should have held," explained Oblio, "but the creature pushed through it and left it open for…"

"There was no fault," mourned Delphinea, wiping away a tear. But her biggest concern was for Muk. She had seen the look on his face when he dropped Quimby's bent and bloodied knife to the floor. Muk said nothing.

Moralee had taken it upon herself to guard the two injured Goblins, her sword waving before their frightened faces. Both sat in the corner. One was tending the lump on his head and wondering where he was.

"Bokin doz," cried out the other, eyeing the sword as if it were a snake about to strike.

Meanwhile, Nommie and Muk were quick with their business. The girls looked up to see them carrying Quimby's body back down the hallway to the beach. Delphinea once again began to cry.

Moralee tied the two captives back to back with a length of rope taken from the warehouse. Leaving Oblio and Delphinea to their thoughts, she lifted the King's body from his throne and joined the boys in the hall. There was a brief discussion and the three of them went separate ways, Moralee to the beach with the King's remains and the boys in opposite directions at the crossroads up the hall. Stepping over sleeping Goblins, each was assigned the same task. Soon there was a sound of activity in the hall, as furniture moved and scraped over the stone floor.

"Once I conjured the shield, it was all I could do."

"I know...I know," consoled Delphinea. "Bow even had no effect. I feel sorrow." As she said this, a procession of wooden tables, chairs and benches paraded by. It took three trips to build a pyre large enough to satisfy Nommie. It had to be respectable enough to honor their fallen companion, he said.

Muk appeared in the doorway with two buckets of lamp fuel, one in each hand. "We're ready!"

Delphinea and Oblio held hands out the door and all the way onto the beach. Moralee had already lit the pile of wood and the flames were inching closer and closer to the rock outcroppings suspended from the ceiling. They stood in the sand, circling the blaze, staring not so much at the flames as into the memory of the last few days they all had shared with their friend Quimby.

"He is gone," Nommie said, turning and walking the sandy trail back up to the hallway.

"We must go," pressed Muk, waiting for everyone to pass, so that he could bring up the rear.

"They sleep how long?" inquired Delphinea.

"It was a strong spell, but I'm not sure," Oblio replied.

"What do we do now?" asked Moralee, carrying a crate of apples from the storeroom into the Throne room.

"I'm looking over the wall maps," Muk said dejectedly, "but there doesn't seem to be a point of reference. After all that trouble to get in here, I'm afraid they're of no use."

"Well…plan B then!" huffed Nommie, approaching the two captives, knife in hand. The bruised Goblin still had that tiddly-look about him, so Nommie confronted the Goblin with the broken nose.

"Doan kill be," he moaned.

Nommie allowed the knife to trail down the frightened creature's arm, before he cut the rope binding his hands. "Follow me!" commanded the Gnome and walked out of the room. The little Goblin could but blink. The one called 'Muk' towered over him and the bearded Dwarf looked like she was thinking of cooking him alive. He chose to quickly leave the Throne room for the comfort of the hall; but then, he had absolutely no idea of what had transpired in the hall.

"Eiyee…" cried the Goblin, when he saw that all his comrades had fallen in battle. Believing them dead, he shook in terror. Nommie leaned him against the wall, knife pressed against his throat.

"I'm in a generous mood, I am," the Gnome said with a smile. "Take us to the eight-sided room and you won't end up like the others." It was impossible to tell if the poor creature had just given a nod…yes or no, he was trembling so badly.

"And?" queried Muk, as he and the others approached.

"It is my belief that he wants to help us," Nommie smiled.

"We should be moving soon," Oblio insisted.

The terrified Goblin was left to take the lead, but he was so nervous, he could hardly walk. Moralee grabbed him by the scruff of the neck, lifted him over the sleeping Goblin bodies and dropped him in the middle of the four way crossroads and grunted.

"Dat way," he affirmed, pointing a nervous finger to the left. The procession continued with a sense of urgency, knowing that the fierce little creatures left behind would awaken very soon.

The group, moving silently and with an occasional prod

from a knife blade, was led through a kitchen; wooden chairs overturned and tables missing. A gaming room followed, with an unattended fire dying in the corner and decks of cards strewn about the room as if the inhabitants had been called away to an urgent situation. At last, they came to a long, narrow hall that led to a familiar looking, arched, wooden door. Muk pushed against it, but it would not give.

"By turn," said the Goblin, shaking his head. He stepped forward and pressed his bony fingers against the wall. Immediately, a heavy rolling sound was heard from the other side of the door. He pointed back to the door. Muk opened it inward with ease. The green marble statue greeted them in the bright light of the eight-sided room.

"What do we do with eyeballs over there?" Nommie asked, referring to the wide-eyed Goblin, pressed against a wall as far away from them as he could get.

"Well…I'd feel safer if he didn't see which way we were going," said Muk, running his fingers over the dried pulp of door 'X'. With Delphinea's help, Moralee rolled the marble statue clockwise one door. Muk opened the door and the square, open stone room with the yawning spiral stairway lay before them. Bowing low and bidding the Goblin to enter, Muk and the others were surprised when the creature backed up to the door that he had been hugging earlier. The little Goblin stared at them for a moment.

"One-doo-dree," he said. They all looked to one another curiously and then back to the Goblin. "One…doo…dree…," he said much slower, this time nodding to the three doors. One, being the door exiting the Goblin lair; two was the descending spiral staircase and three, the door he was visibly eager to pass through. Muk closed the door and motioned to Moralee for one more turn. It was the little Goblin who opened the door all by himself. Cool air entered the room from what looked like a long, dark tunnel. The creature stood in the entryway, looking to his captors as if waiting for someone to change their mind. But when nothing was said and no one threatened him with a weapon, he turned and ran as fast as he could go.

Chapter Thirty Two

A Cloud Of Sadness

…hung over the group as they sat resting against their packs. A decision needed to be made and it was not to be an easy one. Pushing the thought of bloodshed from his mind, Muk struggled with their predicament ~ to continue on or to return to 'The Keep'. To the positive, they now had full packs of food. But of course, now they were without Quimby.

At Nommie's insistence, they rolled the statue one turn to the left of the Goblins' hasty exit. It was an empty closet. At that point, Muk determined to try the room directly across from it. He smiled to himself, even though it turned out to be nothing but a large, empty space. The decision boiled down to taking either of the two unknown doorways, any one of the 'known' passages, or returning to the Inn to rest and regroup. The stillness in the room was thick as Muk contemplated the yin and yang of each of his thoughts.

"I have a theory," Muk said, interrupting the silence.

"Uh, oh!" chided Nommie, rolling his eyes.

"I want to continue!" Moralee proclaimed loudly. She shot to her feet when she said this, as if a vote of confidence were being polled.

"Delphinea has a plan," offered Oblio. All eyes focused on Delphinea, whose cheeks blushed nearly as dark as her hair.

"We *must* find Princess. There yet be two paths not taken," she said with purpose.

"Great! Let's go!" affirmed Muk, looking to the others for any objections.

"Seems like we are down to two choices," Nommie said, deferring back to Muk.

"As to my theory," explained Muk. "In this room, it seems that opposite doors are similar. The door across from the exit up to 'The Keep' led down. Therefore, the door across from the Goblin lair seems more promising. At the very least it should lead on."

The marble statue moved once more and the door opened slowly, revealing a room that took their breath away. There was a soft glow that emitted from the white marble floor. Two contrasting black columns rose from the center of the room to a domed ceiling. It was an oval room with many sturdy doors, each with wood inlays ~ perhaps art patterns or ancient runes. The spacing between doors was exact and there was an aura of precision to the room.

They walked to the center of the room and stood in

awe, although Moralee huffed her disapproval when she noticed that all of the doors opened in.

"Eleven!" Nommie reported.

"Eleven?" queried Delphinea.

"Eleven aggressive doors," Moralee explained. "Not good!"

"Any ideas?" Nommie asked.

"Well…we could open them all at once and let whatever comes in attack themselves for a change," laughed Muk. No one else so much as grinned.

"Let's try one door at a time," Oblio cautioned the group, pressing her hand against the first door she came to. A bowl shaped swatch of indigo paint full of bright red lines decorated the door. She nodded to Delphinea, who opened the door and quickly jumped back from a deep pit of flames and molten rock. Oblio stepped in front of her, with her hands raised. She smiled.

"Just an illusion!" she assured her before closing the door to the cold, empty room. Muk ran his hand over a door with what looked like a stained glass window design on it.

"Long dark hallway!" he shouted, as he both opened and shut his door in one quick motion. It set the others to laughing. A triangle of spots headed Nommie's door of choice.

"Could be snow…" he chuckled. "Whaa…?" was all

Nommie had time to say as the door burst open at his touch and hit him squarely in the jaw. A wall of sand poured into the room at an alarming rate, and flailing arms and orange hair was all one could see by the time Moralee could grab his outstretched hand. The door had burst off its hinges and there was no visible means to stop the flow of sand into the room.

"Check the doors!" Oblio shouted from her knees, as the first burst of sand had cut her feet out from under her. Muk saw at once that the doors adjacent to the sand torrent were already blocked completely by the wall of sand. It took both Muk and Delphinea to unbury Oblio. Like water, the force of the sand current was pushing her across the room like a rag doll.

"We must be quick with the doors!" she managed to say through the grit in her mouth. The surge of sand attacking the middle of the room was now as tall as Muk. Four more doors were now hopelessly forced shut. Hugging one of the pillars, Muk jumped over the sand current washing by him and ripped open the first door he came to. But it opened inward only enough to peer into, as the fine granules became wedged beneath the door. Muk bent down and dug away some of the sand when he thought he heard a faint cry for help. Straightaway, he gave the door a rigorous pull. It gave a little, but not wide enough to get in or out.

"Please, don't leave me in here!" cried a girl's frightened

voice. A hand appeared around the door...a soft hand, with long, thin fingers and nails.

"Delphinea!" Muk hollered, as he grabbed the door with both hands and pulled. But it wasn't going to do.

"Be not wide enough!"

"I know," grunted Muk, falling to his knees and scooping sand away from behind the door. The door moved again and Muk quickly wedged his shoulder against the door, his feet pushing from the wall. He looked up to see Delphinea's hand reach into the room and someone dressed in red step over him.

"Is there anyone else...?" he started to ask, but the door slammed shut to the pressure behind it, nearly taking his fingers with it.

It was Nommie who first heard the odd sound and movement from the ceiling. A trap door had opened to reveal a long hose, which swung into the room over their heads, the end of it landing at Moralee's feet. In an instant, the Dwarf had her sword out and had it poised to strike, but the hose just laid there, like a dead snake. She tapped it with the end of her blade, but it did not respond. Not until Nommie dared crawl out to inspect it and grab hold of it did it suddenly come to life. To his great surprise, the hose began sucking with such a force it pulled from his grip. With a loud whine, it reared up its ugly head and knocked the Gnome backwards. Flipping into the air, it wheeled about and hit Moralee full in the chest, attaching itself to her beard.

"Get it off!" she cried, unable to pull it off by herself. Nommie climbed over the dune and climbed on the back of the shiny, round hose. At once it released her, but it then began to noisily fly about the room. Its gyrations and quirky movements soon had the Gnome hanging on to it for dear life. In some other circumstance, it might have been a humorous sight, but as Muk surveyed the rest of the room, only two of the eleven doors were even visible: the one they came through and the one to its left, behind where Oblio, Delphinea and the girl in red stood in a frozen stance.

"Del!" he shouted over the sound of the sucking machine, "the only way out," he pointed. Delphinea reacted with a nod of understanding and, pulling the girl in red behind her with one arm, she directed Moralee and Oblio with the other.

Nommie was still on the ride of his life, more afraid of letting go and being swallowed up by the sand than the beating he was taking by holding on. As Muk worked his way slowly over the dune of sand, the bizarre scene continued, as the hose, with Nommie attached, acted like a giant, beheaded worm, contorting with its last moments of life. At the top of the dune, Muk finally reached the end of the hose suspended from the ceiling. It was vibrating, but stationary. Once atop the dune, he was able to straddle the hose and slide down its back, forcing the angry beast into the sand. At last Nommie could release his death grip on the hose and roll down the dune. Although he came to a rather abrupt stop against the wall, he immediately joined the others in trying to unbury the last doorway. Muk kept his weight on the hose and its head buried in the sand so that the sucking force wouldn't find air again and become uncontrollable. But once the hose was submerged and doing its job, Muk was amazed at how easy it was to control the machine. Slowly he was able to maneuver the hose to the back of the escape door. Progress was instantaneous and the door was free to swing in almost at once. The once hopeless task had been so easy, in fact, Muk felt that once he had found control of the sucking devise, he could have conquered the whole room. But the moment the door opened and everyone was safely tucked into the adjoining hallway, he tossed the hose end into the centre of the dune. Like a vengeful snake though, it coiled right back at him. He had to duck to escape its wrath and he stumbled into the cool hallway, landing unceremoniously on his hands and knees.

Over breakfast the next morning, there waged a major

debate. Every time they looked to Eff for an answer, he quickly shoved another large spoonful of rolled oats or toast into his mouth.

"Well, I think she's pretty," insisted Alex.

"All Princesses are pretty," Walter added.

"You think everything is pretty," Tommy said, batting his eyes.

"Not you!" answered Alex. The cafeteria burst into laughter.

"What does Muk think?" was again the question addressed to Eff, who shrugged and filled his mouth full for the third time.

"We could put it to a vote," offered Freckles.

"What would we be voting on," said McNaught frowning, "whether or not Muk and the Princess get married? That's stupid."

"Besides, Muk likes Delphinea," Chief pointed out.

"I like Delphinea," Sam admitted shyly. The room once again filled with laughter. Eff looked up to see Frank standing in the kitchen doorway, shaking his head in disbelief. He turned and disappeared back into the kitchen. Just minutes later, they were all out on the knoll, awaiting what they all were hoping would be the final verdict.

Chapter Thirty Three

"And This Be Muk!"

...said Delphinea, pointing to the floor. Muk realized, as he rose to his feet and brushed the sand from his clothes, that he had been waiting a long while for just this moment. Since he had first overheard 'The Plight of the Princess' in that Ale House in Beauly; the encouragement from the Dwarven Bargemen at the lake; the reaction of the local street urchins in the village of 'The Keep', and then the unlikely bonding of fellowship with his new friends in a dungeon of all places, there had been a hope from the very beginning that this was a special moment, something destined.

"It is an honor," bowed Muk, offering his hand. The Princess looked his hand over carefully and when she spied his ring she offered but a faint smile. She was truly thankful to have been released from captivity, but she somehow felt safer hugging close to Delphinea's side. Muk could sense the shyness and couldn't help but stare at her beautiful blond hair. The colour of honey, it bunched on her shoulders where it curled every which way, as if twirled nervously, again and again. She was as tall as Delphinea, but wider, and when she pushed her hair away from her face, Muk could discern her mother's eyes and her father's broad face. If anything about her was short of perfect, it might have the sadness that kept her from offering a smile.

"Muk, this be Mairi," Delphinea added to the already growing silence between them. It was Nommie who finally acted.

"My name is Gael Albion Penrun, but everybody here calls me Nommie," he interjected, taking her other hand and leading her away from the disastrous room of sand.

Muk was left standing in the hall, feeling useless and abandoned. He quickly composed himself, grabbed up his pack and hurried to bring up the rear. Moralee, with sword ready, led the group over a flagged stone walkway. As in the main hall, a burst of flame illuminated the hall as they proceeded, but here the lighting was more stylish, coming from half-moon, oil cressets hugging high on the walls. Nommie was still chatting away.

"My friends and I...master warriors all, banded together in hopes of finding you and returning you to the safety of 'The Keep'."

"Did Edmund send you?" Mairi asked, pulling them to a sudden halt.

"The Lord Governor? No...no one even knows where

he is!" assured Oblio. It was an answer that immediately put her to ease.

Muk lagged behind the others, trying to tell himself that first impressions weren't always that important. After all, the main thing and their primary objective had been reached. Find the Princess. Only now, they had to safely find their way out. So far, Muk had been absolutely correct. Everything since the eight-sided room had been on a much grander scale. The beautiful marbled hall had been a disaster, but expertly crafted nonetheless. And now, the echoing of their footsteps over the smooth, stone walkway suggested that they were entering a vast space on a much larger scale. It reminded Muk of wandering the side streets of Valrhun, with its brightly coloured storefronts and sitting areas, the difference of course, being the dark, high cave ceiling overhead instead of the bright, airy sky of home.

The troupe of six came to a stop before a storefront, whose shingled front window protruded into the walkway. There were small, dark shapes on the shelves in the glass window and the recessed doorway was partially ajar.

"Maybe we should continue on?" Moralee commented, but Nommie was in a much more gallant mood.

"We really shouldn't leave anything unturned," he said fearlessly.

"Have we torch?" Delphinea asked, unsure of the shadowy figures in the window and the beckoning doorway.

"No," Muk answered, peering into the shop's dark recesses. Nommie stepped boldly up to the threshold of the open door, sword in hand. Upon breaking the plane of the doorway, the ceiling's vertical beams magically lit in rows, one after the other, revealing a large shop full of children's toys. The figures in the front window came alive and began to move. On the bottom shelf of the window display, a funny contraption ~ long, connected cylinders on metal wheels, rattled along a grid of metal, round and round, belching great puffs of smoke.

"What in the green world..." Moralee uttered in amazement.

"Well...see there. Not so scary!" Nommie said, as he sauntered through the entryway. The others stood at the door, looking in at the exhibition of strange and wondrous items displayed before them. There were animals from many realms. Some of the reproductions were life-like ~ a unicorn and a Dikkelrops. Some of the animals were ridiculous ~ rainbow coloured horses; a pink, fuzzy cow and an all-white wolf. There were a myriad of dolls with dresses and dolls with faerie wings. There was a table devoted to unusually strange animals playing instruments and furniture pieces the size of small children, toys of someone's very unique imagination filled the shop as well as hung from the ceiling. Standing tall, prominently in the center of the store, was a wooden likeness of a castle. From behind the protection of its walls popped up a toy wooden soldier ~ complete with a tall, red hat and dark blue coat, its face painted like a lady. It moved as if to attention, raising a black, shiny metal stick that began projecting tiny, silver balls directly at the Gnome.

"Ouch! Hulic hilt that hurts!" cried Nommie, taking refuge behind a stand of red, yarn-haired dolls. The 'ping' and 'pang' of projectiles slapped all around him. When the doll display suddenly collapsed, he was once again bombarded by a constant rain of pellets. Quickly, the Gnome raced back to the door and picked up his discarded shield. Now properly defended, he turned to face the wooden assassin. With sword raised, he charged full ahead, muttering insults as he went. To the pure amusement of the others, Nommie did not choose either the right or left aisle provided him. He chose instead to charge right through the displays of other toys, hacking and swearing and fending off the stinging pellets with his shield. The toy soldier yielded not a step to the crazed, oncoming orange-bearded giant. Even confronted with a slashing sword, the brave soldier fired undaunted, until the blade had had its say, leaving metal and wooden chips strewn across the floor.

"Nommie...are you alright?" Muk asked, trying to put some sense of honest concern into his voice.

"That ought to keep the little wood-nymph quiet for a while!" Nommie huffed. "Now...let's see..." he thought aloud, searching the rear of the store. Muk followed the Gnome's path, carefully stepping over the chaotic mess.

"Do you really think it was protecting something?" Muk asked in earnest.

"Wait...hold yourself!" warned Nommie, raising his shield. "What have we here?"

"Name!" called out a lone toy soldier, standing straight at attention beside a shelf of stuffed bears. It held no black metal object, but Nommie proceeded with extreme caution just the same. "Name!" it said.

"What'ya mean name...?" mumbled the Gnome, bravely advancing to within a few paces of the wooden sentry.

"Name!" it repeated boldly. Nommie stared at it a moment, then threw his name out like an object.

"Nommie!"

The toy soldier raised a knee and turned sharply toward the row of bears that lined the shelf. It repeated his name. "Nommie!"

Immediately, a small, curly brown bear jumped from the shelf and came to stand next to the giant warrior. "Nommie!" it said. "Theodore!"

"Careful...it's holding a spear!" cautioned Muk with a chuckle.

Nommie turned to Muk with a confident smile. "His name is Theodore," he said cheerfully. "And he wants to join our group."

"Oh, great!" was Muk's reply. "A mascot we don't need...we already have a Nommie," he called out after him. But the Gnome took no notice of his affront, and the little bear followed right behind him, quickly padding his tiny feet to catch up.

"I've found a new friend," Nommie announced, as he and the teddy bear crossed paths with the group in the doorway and continued up the cobbled stone walkway.

Chapter Thirty Four

Nommie And Theodore

...wandered down the cobbled walkway together, seemingly uncaring if the others followed their lead or not. When Muk exited the Toy Shoppe, the door closed by itself and the interior lights went out.

"Mairi feels we be finding our way out," offered Delphinea.

"The sand room is not an option," Moralee reminded them.

"Do you know another way out?" asked Oblio, reaching out to hold Mairi's hand. But the Princess sadly shook her head.

"I was blindfolded and taken against my will."

"It seems the only thing to do is move forward," Muk determined. "Somewhere ahead of us must be a way back into the long entry hall, or to the marble statue."

"Muk, bear wants you," smiled Delphinea, pointing to the stuffed animal tugging on his robe.

They all looked up at once, but could see no sign of the orange-bearded Gnome. Theodore moved off quickly past the storefronts, beckoning the rest to follow. As they rounded a corner, the cobbled walkway opened into a large courtyard surrounded by a high brick wall. Tables and chairs hugged the perimeter and at the far end of the courtyard stood a tall, round, many-pillared coliseum. The pillars were made of huge blocks of carved, white stone; and although the building seemed sturdy and secure, much of the masonry looked to be molded after something that had once been in ruins.

Nommie's spiked helmet, shield and metal leggings were piled before the coliseum entryway marked 'Gate Alpha'. But Gnome was nowhere to be seen. Theodore stood by the pile, looking at them with a bewildered expression. It was obvious that he, too, had no clue as to the Gnome's whereabouts. Muk lifted the bright red shield. Beneath it were Nommie's pack and crossbow.

"Well, at least he's armed with a sword," Muk muttered, searching both left and right for any other clues.

"I know of this place!" exclaimed Delphinea, backing into the courtyard area and surveying the building once again. The sudden realization of what she was looking at opened her eyes wide with a look of incredibility. "But I thought it be myth!"

"It's the Great Hall!" proclaimed a voice from behind them. It was Nommie. He dropped his sword, vest and belt on top of his other belongings and stood before them, clad all in green and soaking wet. His face was beaming as he reported, 'Gate Alpha' is a theatre and 'Gate Beta' is an aquatic pool."

"Nommie, what happened to *you*?" laughed Moralee.

"Wellll…" he began, looking rather pleased with himself. "I just peeked into 'Alpha' and saw an empty theatre in the round. And as I passed the second entry, I looked in again…although I'm not really sure why…and the large, empty seating area of the theatre had somehow become a large pool of water. And I thought, oh well…an illusion…right?! But it wasn't ~ was it?" he remarked with a laugh, gesturing down at his soaked self.

Chapter Thirty Five

"Bravo...Well Done!"

...shouted an unexpected voice. The group turned to find a short man in a black robe and a bright red tunic down his chest. His head was bald and weather-burnt and a black patch covered his right eye. He was casually sitting on one of the courtyard tables, his feet resting on one of the chairs.

"Edmund!" Mairi cursed and cowered behind Oblio.

"Princess dear!" he called out, stepping from the chair to the table top in an attempt to tower over them. "You left your room, I see. Naughty girl!" There was a certain look, an evil glint in his eye as he said 'naughty girl' that had Moralee and Muk reaching for their sword hilts. Nommie backed up to his pile of belongings and ever so slowly lifted his crossbow, but Edmund pretended not to notice.

"What...no introductions, my Princess? I must apologize for the lack of manners these villagers have. I am Edmund," he stated officially, bowing to the others, *"former* Lord Governor of this District. You see, while I was away, they made me Governor of the Realm. They just couldn't help themselves really," he added with a wicked smile.

"As I was saying, congratulations upon finding the Great Hall," Edmund continued. "From what I have learned, and I've studied the legends thoroughly, none of the past expeditions ever made it beyond this courtyard. It doesn't appear that you are carrying any of the so-called, lost treasures? The golden staff? The solid silver unicorn or the magical suit of armour? No? Not a single mound of gold? And I suppose the Princess here has yet to mention that it was her grandfather who wrote about the many treasures lost to the depths of the Dungeon. Or that her uncle was the leader of the last expedition ~ a failed expedition, I might add. You wouldn't have confided all your family secrets to a pack of complete strangers without telling me first? Would you, my dear?"

"Please Edmund, I just want to go home!"

"And soon you shall…" sneered Edmund, pointing at them with a threatening finger, a finger laden with a noticeably large, dark ring. "Just as soon as I take care of your friends."

At that, Muk stepped forward with his sword drawn. In that one moment, several things happened at once; Mairi cried out, Oblio threw her arms out wide as if to fly, and an unseen force sent Muk reeling backwards into a stone column. Even before the impact with the stone column, Muk was positive that the courtyard had suddenly been enveloped in total darkness. At least, that was what he thought had been the sequence of events, when he awoke sometime later, only to find himself lying alone on the courtyard's hard cobbled surface.

Muk's head was still spinning and his back ached as he slowly got to his feet. When he reached for his sword, which lay near him on the ground, his body only complained a little. He thought this was a good sign, because he was fairly certain that he had been knocked unconscious for a considerable amount of time.

The worst feeling was coming from the pit of his stomach however, as he looked around him to find that he was all alone in the courtyard, with no sign of his companions. Only a few of Nommie's possessions were left in a pile, but the Gnome's weapons and pack were missing. Muk hoped that meant they must have had the time to grab things and make good their escape. The logical assumption would be that the four of them would defend the Princess at all costs and then come back for him.

Muk was still shaking his head, trying to clear his mind, when the darkness finally made some sense. At least it seemed to be more likely that it was Oblio's sudden actions that had summoned the darkness spell. That diversion would have given them the time to defend, grab and run. It was only a theory, but it helped Muk feel a little better about the safety of his friends and his situation.

The courtyard and the surrounding buildings were unearthly still, waiting for some sign of life or movement. Muk knew in his heart that the others would return for him, but felt powerless to rush to their aid, especially since he did not know which direction to run off to. Perhaps, a little 'wandering about' was in order, he told himself. Not that he was planning to wander far, but Nommie had made the Great Hall sound so very intriguing.

Muk began walking in the opposite direction from the one that Nommie had taken. He was standing before 'Gate Omega', when Muk heard something calling to him. He turned back toward the courtyard, but all seemed as quiet as before. After a long moment of unbreathing silence, he turned back to the entryway.

'Yes' was the answer that whispered inside his head.

"Hello?" Muk tilted his head to catch any direction of the sound. Oddly, it was the entryway that seemed to be drawing him forward. "Hello!" Muk said again, but this time with earnest. The reply was immediate.

'Yes!' a voice sounded in his head, both definite and audible.

When Muk passed through the shadows of the entryway, he could see at once why Nommie had been so struck by the Great Hall. Even dimly lit, the craftsmanship and the attention to detail was breathtaking. The height of the open space was dizzying. From the floor clear to the top of the arena were numerous, huge marble columns that supported the massive ceiling. The columns were carved in a myriad of images and the ceiling depicted scenes of the Celestial Heavens on the one side and the Forest Fathers on the other. Tapestries and marble statues aligned the walls and hand-carved wooden benches began where he stood and dropped row by row by row to the main floor, which was completely surrounded by amphitheatre.

Nommie had been amazed to have found an empty banquet hall in one door and an aquatic pool in another. But Muk was looking…no, gawking, at a sight even the Gnome would have found most unbelievable. For in the middle of the theatre stage sprawled a large living and breathing Dragon. Its orange-red scales rose and fell with each breath, and all around the Dragon was a brilliance of warm golden light. What little light shone in the Great Hall came from the floor. Piles upon piles of gold coins surrounded the Dragon, leaving a wavy light reflecting over the marble columns and spots of light all over the frescoed ceiling, like bright stars in the heavens. The scene was mesmerizing and it drew Muk ever forward.

"Yes…come closer," Muk heard quite clearly, but there was nobody there responsible for the voice. He proceeded slowly and cautiously down over the amphitheatre seats. The Great Hall looked much more impressive the closer he drew to the stage, as did the Dragon. The ceiling looked as big as the night sky and the Dragon as large as a building. The mound of gold beneath the Dragon seemed to spread out endlessly in all directions. Certainly, it wasn't the gold that beckoned him forward? When Muk reached a position just above the Dragon's height, he stopped purposely, just to prove to himself that he could resist the pleasant and alluring voice calling him forward.

"Come closer," said the voice, but Muk had no problem in denying it.

"No!" he stated flatly. And then, "No, thank you," he added in the same calm and polite manner as the mysterious voice.

"You do not want the gold?" asked the voice. Muk was indeed impressed by the sheer volume of sparkly, bright coins, but felt the draw to the room went far beyond any riches. It had to have something to do with the Dragon, he thought. And the most important thing at the moment was his careful attention to the slow, up and down breathing of what appeared to be a sleeping Dragon.

"Uh…no," Muk answered truthfully. "I just…I've never been this close to a live Dragon before. Are you real?" Upon those words, the Dragon's eyelids slowly opened.

"Of course, I'm real," stated the voice. Muk inhaled deeply and exhaled slowly in order to calm himself. The voice was the Dragon, although its massive jaws remained shut. He stared intently into the Dragon's blue-green eyes, judging its intent. It was like gazing into a deep mountain pool with a sprinkling of dried fall leaves. *They* were beckoning him closer.

"I'm armed," he countered, running his hand down the side of his sword.

"Sadly...I am no match for you," came the voice. With an anguished, "uughh," the Dragon stretched its right foot forward to reveal the handle of a dagger, stuck deep behind its right shoulder. Muk felt an overwhelming compassion for the animal, but the thought of advancing upon an injured beast stopped him short of taking another step. The Dragon seemed to sense this.

"Sit!" insisted the Dragon. For the first time, Muk noticed that beneath both the Dragon and the gold was a layer of sand that seemed to make up the floor of the whole arena. "Sit," repeated the Dragon, "and the gold can be yours." This time, the offer sounded more like gesture of kindness.

The animal's forefoot slowly pushed a hunkerstool across the patch of sand between them. Its long fingers were bony and narrow, tipped with sharp and deadly talons. The Dragon's invitation ended with a moan ~ a heavy, pained exhale that forced a dry, hot air in all directions. Muk held his ground and fought off his inner feelings: the first, an overwhelming compassion to advance, and the other, the immediate necessity to turn and run like the wind. 'What is it playing at?' he thought, frowning at the mountain of gold too big to move and too plentiful to count in a lifetime. The Dragon grimaced and then completely took Muk by surprise.

"Game of tic-tac-toe?"

Muk watched as the beast painfully etched two perpendicular lines across the sand and two more down through them. The sand made a perfect game board.

"I'm pretty good!" stated the Dragon proudly, giving the stool an added little push. The animal's eyes suddenly seemed to sparkle with a childlike enthusiasm. Muk smiled and shook his head in resignation.

"Alright!" Muk agreed. Shaking off any remaining feelings of apprehension, he quickly descended the remaining steps. He unbelted his sword scabbard and placed it on the sandy floor before taking his position on the hunkerstool. "Who's first?"

"Guests go first," smiled the Dragon, "as long as I am the X's." With that said, Muk immediately reached out and, with a finger, etched his first 'O' in the middle square. The Dragon frowned and thought long and hard before scratching an 'X' through an adjacent square. The movement was very slow and forceful, cutting deep into the sand. Perhaps it was Muk's imagination, but the force of the Dragon's sharp talon over the sand sounded as if it were meant to be a warning, meant to frighten or, at the very least, unnerve its opponent. Muk forced a smile and retaliated by unsheathing the sword on the floor. On his next move, he slowly carved a deep and perfect 'O'. His adversary was amused and smiled.

The first game ended in a stalemate and the Dragon swiped the board clean and once again drew up the game lines. He patiently waited for Muk to go first.

"So how does this work?" queried Muk. The Dragon blinked in surprise.

"You do not know this game?"

"No…I mean, if I win…I get the gold? If you win, you cook me for supper?" The Dragon closed his eyes and chuckled; when he opened them again, his expression was sincere.

"Oh…the game has nothing to do with our circumstances. I just like to play tic-tac-toe. It passes the time."

"Then it comes down to the dagger," Muk assumed.

"Ahhh…I was wondering when you would get around to that," hissed the Dragon. "Yes…everything turns with the dagger."

"Well…now what do we do?"

"Simple," stated the Dragon. "You take out the dagger and I go back to the exact spot that it was inflicted upon me."

"And the gold…" Muk was quick to add.

"Sadly, only a small portion remains behind."

"And if I refuse to take out the dagger?"

"Well…I probably have strength for just one small puff, perhaps enough to engulf you in flames," replied the Dragon voice.

"Good point!" Muk conceded. "But how do I know I won't return to that spot with you?"

"The holder of the dagger, my friend, never goes. Only those who are the object, shall we say, of its other point ~ the sharp one, that is. It makes for an incredible weapon, does it not?"

"I don't suppose I could have three wishes instead?" To this, the Dragon actually laughed up a hot cloud of steam that burned at Muk's face as it whipped by.

"Uh-hah…unfortunately, no. But perhaps on our next chance meeting, I could do you and your friends here a favour."

Muk looked up to see Nommie and Delphinea moving cautiously down the steps on the opposite side of the arena. Delphinea had an arrow strung taut in her bow, but the Gnome's sword point wasn't aimed at the beast. It was busily scratching the side of his head.

"Are you ready?" Muk asked, placing a hand on the dagger's shiny handle.

"Phalrig."

"I'm sorry?"

"My name is Phalrig."

"Phalrig...are you ready?"

"I have been ready for a long, long time,' was his reply.

Stepping over the loose mound of gold coins, Muk raised a foot upon the Dragon's scales and pulled hard, releasing the dagger from its former owner. The result was instantaneous. True to his word, the Dragon was gone and a modest pile of gold remained.

"Nicely done!" Nommie exclaimed. His eyes were wide in surprise with the sudden vanishing of the beast and the small shiny pile of gold that remained. Not the mountain of treasure they had witnessed moments before, but probably more than the three of them could carry. Even Theodore, the walking teddy bear, seemed to be impressed.

"You be jolted by ring," said Delphinea.

"We weren't sure if you were a stiffer," Nommie added, "but the next thing we saw was total darkness. Then Oblio grabbed us and told us to run for it." Delphinea frowned and turned to Nommie.

"Why open Gate and throw us in?"

"Well...I suspect she thought splitting up would confuse the Lord...er, Edmund. It sure did me!"

"Any idea where they went?" queried Muk.

"Only one possibility left," Nommie stated with a certainty.

"Well...let's pack up some of this gold. If nothing else, maybe we can buy the Princess back." Muk was eager to scoop all the gold pieces up, but just as his pack became noticeably heavy, he remembered the dagger and stepped back from the remaining gold pieces. "I think maybe we shouldn't make it obvious that we found the Dragon's gold. In fact, I think we shouldn't even tell the others."

"It's not fair to hide it from the others!" huffed the Gnome.

"Muk not meaning to be Quisling," clarified Delphinea.

"Thank you!" acknowledged Muk with a humble bow. "I just meant that Edmund ought to be left in the dark."

"Ahh…" Nommie comprised. "That leaves us with the only building that Del and I haven't yet ferreted. Shall we?" he added, lifting Theodore to a sitting position atop his pack. Re-climbing the amphitheatre seats to the exit, Nommie led the small group from the beautiful surroundings of the Great Hall.

Chapter Thirty Six

The Sign Read

...'Art Museum', but neither Muk, Nommie nor Delphinea were familiar with the meaning of the word 'museum'. Once beyond the heavy, ornately carved double doors, understanding came instantly, as they were immersed in a gallery of pictures and stone carvings. As in the Toy Shoppe, the light source illuminated the room the moment they entered the building. Only the museum lights were long, bent metal shapes protruding from the ceiling, focusing their beam on the thick and lavish wood frames that hugged the art pieces to the wall. The rest of the museum fell into a hush of shadows, with the exception of a bright light that highlighted a huge stone carving that completely filled the center of the room. It depicted a man sitting with his hands on his knees, looking thoughtfully upon the pictures on the wall. A sign that read 'SILENCE' hung across its chest. The thought of putting all one's art in just one room intrigued Muk, but that thought quickly vanished when he heard the distinct and solid 'click' the double doors made immediately behind him.

"Trap?" speculated Delphinea, drawing an arrow and raising her bow. Muk pushed against the doors, but noticed too late that there were no handles. He nodded to the others and drew his sword. It was only then that it became obvious to the trio that the room had no other doorway or exit.

"They *must* have gone this way!" said a puzzled Nommie, tugging on the end of his orange beard.

"Behind paintings?" Delphinea guessed aloud. But few of the paintings on the wall hung low enough to crawl through or looked large enough to be an escape route. Oblio may have had time to jump up and skirt through one of them, but it was highly unlikely that the gangly Princess or the stocky Dwarf would have been able to manage it ~ especially, as Nommie had alluded to earlier ~ with Edmund in hot pursuit.

"There we go," Nommie exclaimed, pointing to several platinum coins scattered near the far wall.

"Curious," added Muk, eyeing the coins and nodding to an unfamiliar dagger, discarded near the foot of an urn. As he picked up the coins and the dagger, a flood of possibilities began to filter through his head. "Del, why don't you and Nommie stand back by the door."

"Uh oh…this sounds like another plan about to hatch," offered the Gnome.

"There be danger?" But Muk didn't answer Delphinea's

question. He was searching the room with his eyes…the ceiling…the walls. All the while he was absent-mindedly flipping the dagger in the air and catching it by the handle. After careful consideration, he pocketed the dagger and tossed the platinum coin in the direction of the urn. It hit the stone floor noisily and spun to a stop.

Muk was expecting something, but even he was astounded when the art-gazing stone figure in the center of the room rose and took a giant step toward the coin. The weight of solid stone foot upon floor shook the room.

"Whoa…" Muk said aloud, quickly chucking one of the precious platinum coins just ahead of the stone figure. Without hesitation, a heavy rock foot lifted and reached out to crush the sound into the floor without mercy.

Where the moveable art figure had once been sitting, there now gaped a large hole in the floor. Both Nommie and Delphinea crept slowly to the center of the room and peered into the dark recess. Sitting on the edge of the exit, the Gnome handed the teddy bear to Delphinea and motioned 'thumbs up'. He produced a gold coin from his pack and immediately rolled it into the opposite corner away from Muk. The hulk of rock took several long strides and quickly stamped out the noise.

As quietly as possible, Muk scooted to the exit and slipped safely into the hole in the floor. Dropping a short distance, he found himself standing in a cold, stone walkway that branched both left and right. Nommie and Delphinea had weapons drawn and were patiently awaiting his directions when a loud 'thunk' sealed off the opening above them. It was the backside of the stone caricature. Apparently, once silence was restored to the Art Museum, the stone figure was to resume its sitting position over the escape route.

"How did they figure that out?" insisted Muk, "and all the while being chased by a mad man?"

"More interesting…where do you poke to get back into that room from this side?" chuckled the Gnome.

"I don't even want to think about it," Muk replied with a grin.

Chapter Thirty Seven

"We Must Be In Haste,"

...Delphinea reminded them. Muk sensed the immediacy as well. He knew that Oblio, Moralee and the Princess were one step ahead of their pursuer, but probably also running scared. There was no way of knowing the extent of the power of Edmund's ring. But Muk knew about power and the look he had seen on the Lord Governor's face. It told him that Edmund was capable of anything and that there were no lengths to which he might go, to get what he wanted. Muk was pondering Edmund's true intentions when Nommie spoke.

"Left or right?"

Muk's first impulse was to recommend the route with the coolest breeze, any direction that wasn't a stuffy passageway or an enclosed room, but upon leaning into the left hand corridor, he just shouted "Here!" Drawing his sword he stormed ahead, not even bothering to stop and collect the gold coin that lay in the shadows. Twenty paces further, they came to a tunnel entrance leading up to a familiar looking, arched wooden door. 'I wonder,' Muk thought, motioning for the others to follow. There was no handle or keyhole in the door. He pushed against it, but it did not give.

"Goblin push!" Delphinea suggested as she pressed her outstretched fingers against the stone wall, imitating what she had earlier seen Peevis do. But the door remained unmoving.

"But that's it!" Muk smiled, seeing her disappointment. Gently he reached over and parted her middle fingers and squeezed her thumb in. "Goblins have six fingers," he whispered, and formed her hand into the shape of a 'V'. The next push against the wall was answered by a heavy, rolling sound from the room within.

"Brilliant!" breathed Nommie in triumph.

There was an awkward moment between Delphinea slipping her fingers from under Muk's hand and the trio bursting into the eight-sided room. Putting the embarrassment aside, they found themselves standing before the marble statue of the wizard, just as they had upon their first visit. But the room was empty. Immediately, Muk checked the doors. They were standing in the doorway between the Sand Room to the right and the Crypt Room to the left with the fruit stain still 'x-d' on its door.

"Now where?" muttered Nommie.

"There!" exclaimed Muk, pointing to the red cloth lying in front of the Sand Room door. Muk quickly closed the door and started to turn the marble statue one more turn, but stopped. A concerned frown crossed his face. He was confused. Why would Oblio lead them down the path of a dead end. The answer was obvious, she wouldn't. But she might lead someone else down that path.

"The coin is a diversion!" he muttered, turning to face the possibilities of the other six doors. Calming the need to rush ahead, Muk held a hand up in concentration. The three of them were ready to charge in any direction ~ but which one? It was Delphinea who found the clue.

"Platinum!" she said excitedly, pointing to a spot behind Muk. He chided himself for not having noticed the bright, shiny coin near the door to the small closet.

"But that doesn't make any sense at all..." Muk began to say, 'or does it?' he thought.

"Weapons!" directed Muk and, with his free hand, he waved Nommie to position the statue two turns to the left. Solid marble ground to a halt. Muk gave a mighty tug on the handle. The door opened ~ a crossbow, a sword and a hunter's arrow all aimed at the interior.

It was Moralee who stood beneath the arch, mirroring them...both hands held tight upon her sword and frozen in a pose ready to strike. There was a collective sigh of relief between them all until the Princess peeped her head over Moralee's shoulder and announced to the room..."Please come help!" she cried, "Oblio is hurt!"

Chapter Thirty Eight

She Was Breathing

...and opened her eyes to the call of her name. "Oblio, you can hear me?" asked Delphinea softly, having lifted her gently and carried her into the light of the eight-sided room. Oblio started to speak, but gave her a nod instead.

"Was that a 'dark curtain' you charmed outside the Great Hall?" Muk was quick to ask.

"Did it work?" she responded weakly, resting her hand on Muk's arm and squeezing lightly, happy in knowing that he was alive and still with them.

"It be dark," laughed Delphinea, allowing Oblio a weak smile. The girls sat her up, but she hadn't yet the energy to stand on her own.

"It took all my strength," she apologized.

"How did you find the time to figure out the Art Gallery?" Muk wanted to know.

"Can't..." was all anyone heard. The rest was drowned out by a loud 'SLAM'. The door behind them shut with a vengeance and the marble statue began to rotate on its own. Immediately, the five of them put a hand or shoulder to the cold marble and forced the statue in the opposite direction.

"Here!" Muk shouted to the others, pointing their efforts toward the dark spot on the wall...all that was left of the fruit-stained 'X'.

"You can't keep me out!" yelled Edmund's muffled voice from other side of the Sand Room Door. "I know all the secrets of the dungeon."

"So come on in!" Nommie challenged back, opening the door to the Crypt Room and motioning everyone to go through.

"I think I will," came the answer, and a moment later there was a resounding thwack against the door.

"Pick axe!" Moralee muttered and both Nommie and Muk looked at one another with concern.

"We carry her...and make for 'The Keep'," Muk said, but it sounded like it was both a question and a suggestion.

"Right!" Nommie answered and he stood facing them from the open doorway. "Moralee and I will lead. Delphinea, you carry Oblio, and Mairi you follow right behind. Muk..." he continued, patting him on the back, "you guard our retreat. And you..." Nommie leaned over and added to Theodore, "you stay this close to me," showing him a margin of distance between his two fingers.

As the sound of brute metal against wood echoed around them, Moralee rushed the group through the Crypt

Room and into the room of skeletons, her sword held high. Muk was the last to leave and just as he turned to run, the attack upon the door suddenly stopped. But he wasn't taking any chances. With his attention focused on the eight-sided room, he backed into the room where the battle with the skeletons had taken place. Only then did he quickly turn and sprint for the last remaining door. A moment later, he was greeted by his friends and the cool air of the long, dark entryway. But there was to be no relief until Moralee helped him force the wooden bar down with a solid 'Clunk'!

What was once a long measured journey of apprehension was now their salvation. It was as if they were staring into the mouth of freedom and each of them felt the growing excitement with each step. Still in formation, Oblio draped in Delphinea's arms and Muk bringing up the rear, they stepped around the wall remains of the room that had held Quimby's diamonds. Hope ushered them forward. Somewhere just ahead, Muk knew they would come to the gate guarded by the Ork, but it wasn't to be.

"I've been waiting for you!" It was the last voice in the world anyone wanted to hear. Edmund's dark shape loomed before them, his ringed finger pointing at them accusingly.

In less than a heartbeat, Moralee lunged forward to protect the others with her sword. But her selfless act was held frozen, her deadly blow stuck in mid-air. Mairi gave out a pitiful cry and Nommie's crossbow was nearly wrenched from his hands as it discharged on its own, the arrow harmlessly slamming against the wall and disappearing down the dark corridor behind them. The rest of them were caught in mid step, unable to continue forward or backward. The corridor echoed with a hideous laugh.

"Ha haaa! Caught in the act, I see. Let's see..." Edmund sneered, "let's take a closer look at the band of infamous adventure seekers. A Dwarf...and a female one at that. I bet you wish you were back in your hovel right now, tending fire and taking care of babies," he teased.

"And a Gnome...how quaint. A bit old for playing games, aren't we, grampa?" A growl came from the shadows near Nommie's feet. Apparently, Theodore was unaffected by the power of the ring and was warning him to stay a good distance from his master. Edmund's boot shot out and sent the stuffed bear dashing against the stone wall. "Well...well, I guess what my ring doesn't rule, my boots can!" he laughed again even more hideously. He held his hand up to the faint torchlight and admired the incredible beauty of the unearthly ring. "Of course, it's not as though I ever had a choice in the matter," he grimaced. But he didn't dwell on the thought, as his one good eye came to rest upon the helpless Oblio, still draped across Delphinea's arms.

"So this is your Magician. Your *spell* thrower. Impressive. But still...no match for the powers of my ring. After this encounter, I very much doubt you will even be able to *spell* your name," he cackled.

"Are we missing a Halfling thief, or are my spies as stupid as the last Dwarf off the barge? I don't recall them telling me about you…young lady."

Edmund ran a finger across Delphinea's cheek. "Perhaps the Halfling ran into a strange spell and transformed himself into a forest freak. That would be in keeping with this bizarre place, now, wouldn't it?"

"And you, my dear Princess," the former Lord Governor scolded, grabbing Mairi's arm and pushing her up against the wall. "Don't worry, the spell will wear off soon and you and I can resume our discussion on the whereabouts of the dungeon's wealthy secrets."

"But we mustn't ignore the last to join our little group…the Knight! What? No shining armour? Thinking you could just prance into *my* Realm? Whisk off with *my* Princess and live happily ever after? Hmm…" he paused with a wicked grin on his face. "No…I think not. Not without paying the price."

"Go!" he commanded and the troupe suddenly found themselves forced through the doorway from which their captor had apparently sprung. "Not you," Edmund scowled, hand around Mairi's throat. "You and I have unfinished business."

Chapter Thirty Nine

Stepping Into The Unknown

...and descending a flight of steps in complete darkness was frightening, even for Muk. But not knowing where you were going, and your body unable to stop, was decidedly worse.

"Oh, here...take this with you," shouted Edmund from the top of the stairs. It was Theodore, wiggling upside down with his tiny spear in hand and trying in vain to pierce the hand that gripped him. And lastly, it was the toy bear that was flung down the steps, bouncing topsy-turvy and coming to a sudden stop at their feet.

"And I do hope you enjoy my friends," Edmund continued to shout down the stairwell. "They have so longed to meet you!" he added, and with a wicked laugh, the door above them slammed shut. The realization of imprisonment echoed around them. It was a hopeless sound, but it did not have the same sense of permanence as the sound that followed, as a bolt was thrown down hard from the other side of the door.

The affirmation of lost hope was a cold and empty

feeling, but at least it was a feeling. The moment the group was able to move their limbs on their own, they realized at once that the spell had been lifted.

"Bastard!" swore Moralee, backing into a column that partially crumbled upon touch. It took their eyes a short while to adjust to the light in their new surroundings ~ or better said ~ the lack of light. The room was dark, but faint shafts of light found their way into the room from the ceiling. They had been sealed into a cold, empty room that smelled of dust and something musty, something acrid. The room was longer than it was wide and the ceiling looked as fragile as the columns down the center of the room ~ cracked and crumbling to the touch. Several of the columns had fallen, spreading across the floor and most probably the explanation for the gaps of light emitting from above. However, the condition of the roof over their heads and the visibly fragile columns that remained were overshadowed by the fact that the entire room was draped thick with cobwebs.

<hr />

"Uh oh," Sam muttered, covering his eyes. They were on the knoll. With breakfast and the dish chores done, the boys were waiting for Mr. Wittlesey and a list of outdoor chores for the afternoon.

"Don't worry," Pat McKirdy said, scooting across the grass to sit nearer with a fist in the air, "I've got my invisible sword!" The boys all laughed, but turned immediately back to Eff, waiting anxiously for him to continue.

Moralee swung at a curtain of webs. Something heavy dropped with them to the stone floor. It was something's dinner, long since eaten. The picked-clean bones glistened in the faint-light and the skull sported an evil grin.

"Let's be moving!" Delphinea whispered, "I cannot be here."

Moralee swung again, clearing a path through the maze of webs and dust. The hum of her sword and their shuffling footsteps were the only sounds that broke the room's cold silence, until they had traveled half the length of the room, when another sound caught their ears. It was the scurry of tiny legs. Many tiny legs, from overhead. Suddenly, what little light filtered into the room from above, was interrupted with busy shadows of hundreds of very large spiders, all frantic to find their way into the room.

"Go, go, go!" urged Delphinea, but Moralee was already slashing a path through the webbing as fast as she could swing her sword.

"Yes...that way!" Oblio instructed, as the cluster of bodies began pushing through the dark and to the right, much faster than their feet were willing to shuffle into the darkness. The sight of a mass curtain of spiders the size of Theodore dropping silently to the floor from the ceiling was unnerving, but when Delphinea had panicked, the space between them had become a shoving match. Worse than any nightmare was the horrible click, click, click of spider legs as they hit the stone floor and rushed forward to find their next meal. Moralee was now flailing her sword so quickly at the hairy, black bodies that she did not at first realize she had hit a piece of stone column.

Nommie noticed the horde of black bodies stop almost instantly when Moralee's sword first struck stone, causing a shower of sparks. He quickly released his last arrow into the dark unknown and threw his crossbow hard over the stone floor. The brief illuminating sparks revealed a sea of red eyes forming a half circle around them.

"They don't like the sparks!" shouted Nommie.

"Good, but how do we get out of here?" answered Muk, slashing his sword against the wall and floor, anything that would provide a spark of light. He thought he was doing a pretty good job at holding the oncoming mass at bay, until he spied a black clump of fuzzy legs hanging just above his head. "Hulic Hilt!" he cried, swinging madly at the darkness above him, pushing Delphinea even tighter into a corner.

"Door! Door!" shouted Delphinea, realizing that her frantic fingers had rubbed from a smooth stone surface onto cold metal.

"Does it open?" Moralee yelled, afraid to turn her back on the black horde. With Oblio still in her arms, it took Delphinea a moment to run her hands completely across the cool steel.

"Not be handle!" was all she could confirm.

"Stars above," mumbled Muk, reaching into his pocket and praying for a keyhole. He scraped the key over and over in the same place along the metal door, before realizing he was panicking and then tried the opposite side of the door. He was immediately rewarded with a small knob of metal. Feeling it with his hands, he slipped the key in and turned the lock. The door swung in, but not all the way. It scraped against higher ground, but the space between the door and the room was wide enough for him to squeeze through.

"Hand me Oblio!" Muk insisted and slowly, one by one, with an air of immediacy, they all squeezed through and made good their escape. Moralee breathed a huge sigh of relief when she finally closed the metal door behind her.

"We're not done yet," Muk announced. He said this as he led them up a steep incline in the pitch black. The passageway was cold and exceedingly narrow, but the thought of spiders left behind was a huge relief. When Muk turned an elbow bend to the left, he added in a whisper, "We need to be very quiet and regroup in the next room."

Nobody had a clue to his reasoning, but it became clear immediately upon entering the room with the collapsed rock wall. There were voices shouting in the hallway. It was Edmund and the Princess. It was time for action. Another quick decision. Muk looked to Nommie, but the Gnome was waiting on Muk to hatch another idea.

"We must leave Oblio here," he said to Delphinea, who then gently placed the Elf on the sand.

"We must strike Edmund quickly!" Moralee reminded them in an angry whisper.

"I've only a sword and a shield left," bemoaned Nommie.

"My aim is true enough," declared Delphinea.

"Nommie...all you're going to need is your pack," Muk said, taking the shield out of his hands and handing the Gnome his open pack. Nommie gave him an odd look, but nodded. "Either our weapons will defeat him..." promised Muk, "or his greed will." They all watched closely as Muk lifted the dagger he found on the Art Gallery floor and, with pronounced animation, dropped it into the open pack. Nommie didn't get a chance to nod his understanding, however, because the shouting in the hall ended with Mairi's loud scream.

Chapter Forty

Hurdling The Pile Of Stones

...in the doorway, Muk, Nommie, Moralee and Delphinea rushed down the hall toward the commotion. Astonishingly enough, they took Edmund by surprise. They could see him clearly. He had one hand around the Princess's throat and a wall torch held high in the other. Either Muk or Moralee could have struck quickly with their swords, but Delphinea had held a deadly bead on him since entering the hallway. She could have ended his life on the spot, if it weren't for the fact that he was holding Mairi over the same hole in the floor that Quimby had encountered.

"Stop!" yelled Muk. The shock of seeing any one of the troupe again swept across Edmund's face. It was almost laughable, had it not been for the seriousness of the situation. Edmund's hand slipped from around her neck to around her waist and now he held her in front of him like a shield. They had successfully surprised the former Lord Governor, but had lost the opportunity to recapture the Princess.

"Well...well, it looks as though only your Magician stayed for supper. How sad," said Edmund, his one unpatched eye surveying the group with an air of superiority. "Frankly, I thought my friends were hungrier than that," he added with a high-pitched cackle.

"Let her be and we'll let you live," Muk assured him.

"Negotiations! How nice...I'm touched," smiled Edmund.

"We'll even give you all the gold," promised Muk.

"Yes...tell me about that. Just what part of the Dungeon coughed up the gold...and did I not spy some platinum?"

"I thought you said you knew everything about the Dungeon?" queried Nommie.

"Oh...I don't think you want to try upsetting me," smirked Edmund. "Just one quick move like this..." He made a move to spin Mairi around behind him and into the black pit. He then pointed his ring finger at them menacingly. "And then of course...the lot of you would follow...willingly," he sneered. "The gold! Where did you get it?!" he shouted.

"Don't tell him!" Muk commanded and immediately Edmund's finger shot out, forcing Muk face first to the floor, sprawled before the Governor's feet.

"The gold!" he demanded.

"It be the Dragon's doing," offered Delphinea.

"And the rest of the gold...?" baited Edmund.

"We hid it in the courtyard," offered Muk, still pressed to the floor with an unseen force.

"Ah...and the *dagger!*" gnarled Edmund, with a heavy emphasis on the word 'dagger'.

"Don't tell..." Muk cried out as Edmund pointed sharply at him, pushing him even harder to the stone floor. "Aggh..." was all he could utter, a moan that sounded as if it were being squeezed out of him.

"Yes, well...it's supposed to do magic or something," explained Nommie, lifting a dagger out of his pack and sliding it across the stone floor.

Releasing the Princess, Edmund cautiously picked up the dagger. His malicious expression changed to absolute delight, until he turned it over slowly in his hand. His face darkened suddenly and a boiling anger began to pulse in his veins. "This is my dagger..." he said in a low growl. "How dare you play games with me," he snapped. Edmund visibly began to shake with rage and he aimed a threatening finger directly at the Gnome.

Seemingly from nowhere came a little glint of light. Edmund looked down to see a tiny little spear stuck in his leg just below the knee.

"You..." fumed Edmund in both surprise and pain, looking up to find the toy teddy bear standing alone against the wall. Theodore had skirted the group in the dark and launched his spear well into the same leg that earlier had booted him. Oblivious to the others, Edmund adjusted his ring and stabbed his finger at the defenseless stuffed animal, but only remembered then that his ring could do it no harm.

Theodore's sudden attack gave Muk all the time he needed. No longer forced to the floor by an unseen power, he grabbed Mairi around the ankle with his left hand and forced the dragon's dagger down hard with his right. The stab had been so forceful that the dagger pierced clear through Edmund's boot and stuck into the stone floor with a wet thunk.

The expression on Edmund's face as he realized the meaning of the second attack upon him was one of unbelievable shock. For a brief moment, there was comprehension and then he was gone. He didn't cry out or fly away or fall into the pit. He just vanished. His black ring, however, did not disappear with him. Muk watched as it landed on the stone floor near him and wobbled along the edge of the open abyss. With one hand secure upon the Princess, he lunged for the ring as it came dangerously close to tipping into the bottomless pit. But just as he was about to snatch it from the dark unknown, a sandaled foot gently pressed his hand to the floor.

"I'm sorry Muk, it wasn't meant for you," Oblio said, as they all watched the ring drop silently over the edge. Muk looked up in surprise. Oblio was standing over him and smiling. And then he heard the others laughing... Moralee, Nommie and Delphinea.

"You can let go of me now," Mairi had said for the third time. She was standing over the open pit, aptly secure in Moralee's tight grasp. Muk's left hand had a deathly tight grip on her ankle and she could not move.

"Oh," he said sheepishly, as he crawled to his knees and then stood on the edge of the pit, staring into its darkness.

"It would have changed you," Oblio reassured him. Muk was at a loss for words. He had always believed that the good or bad in a person made the difference, but now he wasn't so sure. Perhaps this ring's power was stronger than one's will. He had little time to dwell on it, however, as Mairi walked up to him and kissed him on the cheek, destroying all his thoughts.

"Thank you!" she said.

"Whoa..." mouthed Walter, his glasses all askew.

"I told you..." shouted Charlie, "it's Muk and Mairi!"

Chief had just opened his mouth to inject his two-cents worth, but at that moment, Mr. Wittlesey rounded the corner with a wheelbarrow full of rakes, hoes and shovels. The discussion was going to have to be put on hold, and Eff, for one, could hardly wait.

Chapter Forty One

The Length Of The Entryhall

...seemed much shorter than they remembered. It might have been Muk's imagination, but he was fairly certain that they had all walked a little left of center when passing the door leading to the spider room. Before reaching the gate, Nommie stopped under the last torch light to dig into his pack. He was searching for the key to the Troll gate. It was then he remembered that he had allowed Quimby to carry it for safe keeping.

"Snag!" he mumbled, "we might have a problem getting out."

"Swords!" answered Moralee, who had led the group up the walkway and was now peering around the corner into the Troll's cabin. With swords drawn, Nommie and Muk rushed up to aid Moralee, only to be surprised to find the gate wide open.

"Something's amiss," whispered Muk, as they proceeded with caution past the key keeper's dwelling. The Troll, humming as before, was too busy washing pots and pans to notice them. They were even more alarmed when they crossed the courtyard to find the far gate open as well.

"What meaning is this?" Delphinea asked, stopping at the bottom of the stairwell.

"Edmund's army must be up there just waiting his return," frowned Moralee.

"That would surely put a damper on our return," added Nommie.

"There is another option..." Muk grimaced.

"Uh oh," the Gnome replied, but leaned forward with interest.

"Okay, well...we know that there is at least one exit to the docks and I suspect one to the mountainside as well. The largest obstacle was the Lord Governor, and with him now gone, it would be easier to forge our way through the goblin camp or go looking for an alternate way out."

"Oblio be weak," Delphinea reminded them.

"No! We go up," insisted Moralee. "And then...if we find resistance..." But she never finished her thought. Loud voices were slowly approaching.

"There's no telling when..." came an unfamiliar voice from the darkness.

"Or if they ever do!" countered a second voice.

"The betting booth has them heavily favoured to return," said the first voice. "I can't count the number of people who bet everything."

"Bet everything on what?" Muk inquired, leaning his

sword into the throat of one of the guards of 'The Keep'. Nommie had his sword trained on the stomach of the other.

'Everything…everything…!" choked the first guard, staring at the clump of shadows before him.

"We have orders to bring you up!" exclaimed the second guard. His expression was open-mouthed and he seemed not to notice the point of the sword pressed against him.

"For what reason?" demanded Moralee, adding her sword to the mix.

"For what reason!" swallowed the first guard. "Believe us," he breathed heavily, "you're all heroes!"

"There is no treachery here. Come up and see for yourselves!" added the second guard, pointing the way.

Nervous energy overwhelmed the guards as *they* tripped over each other on the way back up the stairwell. Part of it was relief ~ after a long and tiring vigil awaiting them at the gate. But the greatest elation was growing with every step, realizing that 'THEY' were leading the parade of heroes up into the light from the depths of the dungeon.

Stepping into the sunlight was blinding and disorienting, but the scene that greeted them was entirely beyond belief. Throngs of people were milling around the dungeon courtyard in wait of an outcome. They were faces of strangers. None of them were mercenary guards or Edmund's henchmen. Nor did the faces belong to the handful of townspeople known to them. The moment the guards forced the crowd to step back and allow them the room to exit, scores of others rushed forward, shouting the news that the group had returned. Loud cries of joy erupted, as a whole courtyard of people burst forth, pushing and straining, desperate to see for themselves. Strangers all as they squeezed in around them, reaching out to touch them, to see for themselves that they were real.

The heroes were suddenly penned in on all sides by all the excitement and found it extremely difficult to move at all. Nommie was all but swallowed up by a group of well-wishers and hoisted to their shoulders. Moralee sheltered Oblio with her body and began pushing back. Muk grabbed hold of Mairi's hand and he and Delphinea flanked the Princess, trying their best to keep the crowd at arm's length.

"Where's the Halfling? My money was on the Halfling!" someone shouted amid the pats on the back and the cries of congratulations.

"Oblio! Oblio!" cried a child, sitting on her father's shoulders, lovingly holding a straw doll with long, white yarn-hair and a yellow cloth for a dress. And still another wall of well-wishers advanced, calling their names. Nearly half of them were holding straw dolls with their likenesses...even Quimby's.

"Your name! Your name!" screamed an old, haggard woman as she attempted to make her way through the crowd. The people around her thought the old 'Doll Lady' something of a joke and laughed as she battered her way through them with her cane.

"Your name, Deary!" she huffed, reaching up to touch Delphinea's long burgundy hair.

"Delphinea," grinned the Elf, not being able to make sense of any of the confusion. The old woman turned immediately and flailed her cane back in the direction of her vending booth. They were barely into the courtyard and still the crowd kept pushing forward to witness the historic event.

"I could try and explain some of this..." Muk shouted to Delphinea above the crowd, but then realized that he had no explanation at all.

On the balconies above them, throngs of people cheered where there had been no faces before. The Vischan banners that had hung in the courtyard only days before had all been replaced by signs of welcome and celebration.

In the distance, Muk finally recognized some familiar faces. It was the Innkeeper and his wife and a man he remembered from the pub. They were being pushed ahead of a thickening crowd, who upon hearing the news had pulled them from their duties in the Inn to be reunited with their daughter. Still hand in hand with Mairi, Muk smiled at them and tried to navigate her through the zealous crowd toward them. But his smile was brief, when out of the bright sunlight came a solid shove, knocking him unceremoniously to the ground. Swiftly, Delphinea and Moralee stepped forward. The crowd quickly parted as Moralee unsheathed her sword to the ready and it hummed through the air in defiance. A tense moment of dead calm rained upon the festive crowd.

"Marcus!" cried the Princess, who, stepping over Muk, threw herself into his arms. Marcus lifted her high into the air and the crowd began to cheer once again. A roar of joy and delight resounded throughout 'The Keep' as news of the blissful reunion spread. Thankfully, the crowd's attention followed the path of the two lovebirds, as Muk stood and brushed himself off.

"You have done us a great service!" exclaimed the Prior, motioning the five of them to follow him away from the tearful reunion. "You have restored our community like never before," he praised. "Come, come!" he said, leading them along a less populated path between the Tavern and the Priory.

"Where did all these people come from?" Muk asked.

"Hah!" cried the Prior, "you think there is a lot of commotion *in* 'The Keep'. Come! Look…see!" The prior kept pushing people to either side as he led them to the Priory. Once on the steps, he motioned for them to turn around ~ in order to get the full view of the entrance to 'The Keep'.

The heavy gates were forced open by carts and booths

pressed against them. Vendors barked their news and craftsfolk displayed their wares and everywhere children were running amuck. The Guards posted at the gate were trying in vain to keep the entrance open and clear of people. But what Muk and the others saw that was truly beyond imagination was just beyond the gates.

An entire city had sprung up out of the desolation and relative poverty they witnessed just days before. In the center of the village, freshly hewn, was an A frame building that ran the entire length of the outer village. It stood two stories high. The top level was covered in flags and banners, laundry and curtains, enough room to house and sleep the multitude before them. The lower level and, indeed, all of the outer area clear to the walls, was not just a crowd of activity, it was a virtual sea of humanity! Tents, booths, stalls, wagon carts, shops, trades and crafts, both local and far reaching in allegiance, Dwarven, Elfin, Gnomish…even Gyptish ~ all side by side in apparent harmony and celebration!

"It be unbelievable!" uttered Delphinea, exactly as the others would have described it.

Chapter Forty Two

There Are Times In Life

...when it becomes necessary to sit down and make some sense of all you know...or at least, what you think you know. For Eff, becoming ten was only the beginning. Of course, he could point to the unlikely arrival of the Pageleaf for having forever and completely changed his life ~ that and the feeling of purpose that the strange paper had instilled within him and the boys in general. The story, after all, had become as important to them as it was to him ~ maybe even more so. It was surprising then, as Eff looked silently off into the swamp, how things were allowed to change so quickly. He wasn't the only one sitting in shock. All of the boys were immersed in some bleak cloud of thought, brought on by the events that had transpired not minutes before.

The long day of bulb planting and raking of leaves had turned into a challenging game of basketball. McNaught and his team were a basket away from defeating Mr. Wittlesey's team. The Headmaster was always very serious when it came to picking his team and the score was seldom ever close. The fact that the next shot might be the winning basket for the underdog had all the boys glued to the basketball court, cheering and hoping to watch history in the making.

The court itself was what remained of the foundation of an old building long since collapsed and carted off. A post and backboard had been planted many years before when the Home was used as an army barracks, and the playing surface was squarer than it was rectangular. It also had its hazards. Remnants of a brick hearth and chimney had left a patch of raised masonry and it was there that McNaught lost control of the dribble. Mr. Wittlesey's team rejoiced in the turnover, and, on the inbound, McNaught simply grabbed the ball from the Headmaster and flung it far out into the swamp.

Eff remembered the morning of the Solar Eclipse and the way that the whole world seemed to come to a complete standstill. On this afternoon, the sun was still shining, but dead silence hovered over the court, and for the longest time, nothing was said. Not even from a wide-eyed Mr. Wittlesey. McNaught turned and stomped off in the direction of the kitchen. The Headmaster looked around slowly at each of the boys and pointed to the court, before following McNaught's heated trail. It was only then that the truth began to trickle down.

"He only has two days left before Clary." It was Freddy

who spoke, his head bowed. Sweat poured off his body. His height was one of the factors for the McNaught team lead.

"Father Griffin picks him up early Monday morning," Chief added, plopping down on the raised masonry to rest.

"Why don't we know this?" asked the twins.

"Mr. Wittlesey doesn't want to frighten anyone about going to Clary," Tommy sang in a sing-song sort of way. Clary was the Institution that took in all the boys in the State once they turned thirteen. It was clear that the majority of the boys were unaware of this by the expressions on their faces. Eff continued to stare off into the swamp, long after most of the boys had shuffled silently back into the Home. He was searching for a better understanding of life and jumped up when he finally saw his thoughts straddling the edge of discovery.

"Frank, how do you celebrate a person?"

"You mean their birthday?" answered Frank with a smile. Somehow he had known that Eff would be paying him a visit. There was an extra bowl of potatoes waiting on the counter and a peeler right beside it.

"No…more like a Prince who just saved the Princess, except the Princess really loved somebody else. You still have to reward him, don't you?" Frank shook his head. He hadn't seen that question coming.

"It sounds complicated."

"Yeah...it is, but do you celebrate the good..." began Eff.

"...without thinking about the disappointment?" Frank finished, hitting the nail directly on the head.

"Exactly!" Eff smiled, looking to Frank for the rest of the answer. Now Frank knew he was in trouble. One of the reasons that he enjoyed working alone in the kitchen was that the appliances and the pots and the pans never asked questions. He was uncomfortable giving advice. But of all the kids in the orphanage, Eff was the one he most hated to disappoint. He took a long breath and sighed.

"Welll," he finally said, "I suppose some kind of badge would be in order. Like the Boy Scouts, or a book I once read about a red badge of courage."

"Oh, this Prince has lots of that," Eff confirmed, thinking about the courage.

"Then I suppose you could go read up on 'King Arthur and the Knights of the Round Table'. Those Knights helped all sorts of people in need. Helped Princesses, fought dragons..."

"Fought dragons?" exclaimed Eff breathlessly.

"Well, yeah, I think so...but a good place to start would be in the Library."

Eff hopped off the stool and ran out of the kitchen.

"Hey," Frank hollered after him, "you gonna be alright?" The boy's bright face reappeared around the corner.

"Of course," he beamed, "I've just been enlightened!"

At bed time, the boys were noticeably quiet when the hall light went out. McNaught had sought out the infirmary directly after supper. Apparently he had decided to spend the night there. So the thinking among the boys was that the story should be put on hold until *all* were present.

"I was thinking…" Eff began to whisper.

"No story!" rasped Tommy.

"We know that!" Mike countered and the room fell back into a hush.

"What I mean is," Eff began again, "I think we should give McNaught something special. Like the heroes and the treasure from the dungeon."

"Oh, wait," sniggered Tommy. "I think I have some gold right here under my mattress."

"Shut up, you moron!" Pat hissed.

"What did you have in mind?" Chief inquired.

"Well…Frank said something about a badge of honor."

"We could color him a picture," offered Sam.

"I don't think paper and crayons will help," Freddy said solemnly.

"No…we all have to give him something. Like Muk and Nommie and Oblio and Moralee and Delphinea. A reward ~ something extra special from all of us."

"We could give him the basketball, if we could find it," Alex chimed in.

"Don't go giving away the basketball just cuz you don't like to play!" Pat scolded him.

"Besides," Mike pointed out, "where he threw it ~ I'm not sure we're ever going to see that ball again."

"Why don't we just tell him," Tommy muttered, half asleep.

"That's real dumb," Charlie groaned.

"No…wait! That's exactly what we should do!" cheered Eff.

"We should?" Tommy said with surprise.

Chapter Forty Three

It Was A Peaceful Evening

...and although it was late Somber, a fragrant warmth from the East was in the air. The sun had set on a calm windless day and there was a clear, pale orange sky above. The area in and out of 'The Keep' remained festive, but the real celebration was just about to begin. The Inn had become the focal point. The Innkeeper and his wife happily toiled away in the kitchen, complete with the help of a league of volunteers. They were preparing a meal fit for a King, or rather, as much food as they possibly could in a very short amount of time.

The guards of 'The Keep', under the Levi's command, went directly to work arranging the Inn's sitting room as a stage. The outer heavy-weather windows had been removed and the shuttered windows been folded in and fastened down, leaving an open view to the sitting room from the courtyard. The fire in the hearth had been allowed to burn to embers, so as to give light but not to interrupt the speeches. Five chairs had been set up directly into the largest of the windows, facing out, so that all those unable to find room inside ~ and that number was easily in the hundreds ~ could hear the most celebrated event in recent memory…'The Journey Within The Dungeon'.

While the Levi had seen to the preparations inside the Inn, the Lord Governor's former Butler had seen to the Guests' every need. Since the fortunate return from the dungeon, he had energetically re-introduced himself as Barnard and had become their own personal assistant. Because the Inn was already crammed to capacity, Barnard embraced them into his charge and gave them a tour of 'The Keeps' inner villa. He ceremoniously gave them each a key to a large suite that overlooked the busy courtyard. There, he and his staff waited on them…bathing and dressing them for the evening's festivities. So relieved was the Butler to hear the news of the Lord Governor's misfortunes that he was only too happy to impart the history of the last few days.

The mercenaries, grumbling excessively over the throngs of people arriving daily, had departed, coming up with the excuse to go looking elsewhere for the Lord Governor. Mr. Boggs, it seems, disappeared into the night. But not before he filled the trading post merchandise into a wagon and escaped to places unknown. The empty trading post was now a large communal living area ~ open to the public ~ for a small price.

Upon sunset, Barnard triumphantly led them to the Inn, where two of the stuffed chairs had been pushed together and a plank thrown over the armrests to create a tabletop, which was covered with a variety of vegetables, meats, fruits, nuts and cheeses. It was truly a banquet for the returning heroes, as none of them could remember their last full meal. Already, there was only standing room in the Inn, as the exploded population of 'The Keep' pushed and shoved to find sitting room in the courtyard. The Levi was just pointing out the placements of chairs and the timetable of events, when the Dwarven street urchins broke away from their parents and stormed the front porch of the Inn.

"We waited so long!" Milly rejoiced, as the children suddenly mobbed them. Muk looked down to find Freda, the littlest of the Dwarven children. She was looking up at him, her face tear-stained.

"Thay thay thay...thed...thed...u...u...u...nether coming back!" she cried, burying her head in his robe.

"Sweety, I came back just for you," whispered Muk as he lifted her into his arms.

The other Dwarven children were being waved and shouted off the porch, but they stubbornly refused to leave. Once they sat down, however, and everyone saw that they still had a clear view of the open window, order was restored. Freda, still clinging tightly around Muk's neck, also chose not to give up her perch. Casually, Muk took up one of the chairs and sat with the little Dwarf draped around him, as if it were an everyday occurrence.

When everyone had settled into place, Barnard faced the courtyard and raised his hands for silence. "This is a story for telling," he shouted over the crowd, "not for questions or undue noise!" He glared at the Dwarven children sitting at his feet, but he needn't have worried for they were silently glued to every word. A hush ensued. It was Oblio who stood and spoke first.

"I am Oblio, a shaman from the Plains of Fawr Lafant. I was drinking from the running waters of the Val, when I received a calling. Gnomish traders at the port of Wynn told of a kindred soul, stolen in the night. It is there I happened upon my friend, Nommie." She nodded and took a seat.

"I am Albion Gaeyl Penrun, known to my friends as 'Nommie'," began the Gnome, bowing to Oblio. "I come from the Kingdom of Marioneth, although most of Somber has found me trading for lavender and herbs in the Midplains. While navigating the Val downstream, I came under attack and my flatboat capsized. In need of warmth and drink, I floundered into an Inn at the nearest port. And it was there that a most fortunate convergence took place; a nearly drowned Gnome looking for a room with bath met up with a Shaman Elf looking to find directions to a place known as 'The Keep'. We traded stories and, intrigued by this Elf's sense of duty and thought of adventure, I invited myself along. That very afternoon, while I was purchasing dry clothes, I chanced upon a game of Rouss. It was here that I met Quimby, who haled no place in particular as home, but was proud to introduce himself as 'The Luckiest Halfling Thief Alive'. But, as it turned out, he was wrong. He lost in three straight sets and, having gambled without any means, ended up owing me allegiance."

At this point, Nommie took a moment to face the other four before continuing on with his story. "Quimby was undoubtedly the grumpiest person I ever met, but I truly think that the fortnight that we all shared together was the happiest time of his life." There was a long pause ~ not so much as a whisper or a cough.

"On the following day, a long, winding trail over the Gathires brought us in sight of 'The Keep'. In our stupor of wildflower scent and panoramic beauty, we were surprised from behind by a troop of armed mercenaries on horseback, charging downhill as if chased by dragon fear." Quietly, Nommie sat and Moralee stood, coughed and began to speak.

"My name is Morah of Leith. The Gathires are my home. I was sitting on the edge of my home, contemplating whether or not to enter 'The Keep'. Having heard rumors of racism and oppression, naturally I was pondering the wisdom of entering alone. It was just then that a wild pack of animals on horseback attempted to run down three innocent travelers. I appealed to the nature of the horses and lives were not lost. I was..." Moralee stopped briefly, "honored by being allowed into their company."

Moralee sat as quickly as she had stood, which caught Muk by surprise. He had been listening with such interest, he hadn't yet thought about how he would explain himself. He stood to a darkening courtyard.

"I was in the area..." Muk said to a sea of faces, shining in the glow of intermittent candlelight. His statement was received with laughter, coupled with a few, "Ahhh's" and "so cute". He looked down into two blurry eyes. Freda, still in his arms and with thumb in mouth, was fighting a losing battle with sleep. He turned to Oblio and Delphinea for some help with the child, desperation in his eyes, but they apparently mistook his look as not knowing where to start ~ what exactly he should tell them.

"Tell them the truth...*Pan!*" Oblio insisted.

"Yes, the truth be good," encouraged Delphinea.

All at once, a sudden shock of embarrassment and relief ran through Muk's veins. He wheeled quickly to face the crowd, which at this point, was easier than facing his friends. But as he turned away, he couldn't help but read their expressions. Oblio and Delphinea were knowing and anxious and Nommie supported a sly grin. It was Moralee's expression that hurt the most. She was the only one caught unaware, her eyebrows bent in confusion. Apologies would be forthcoming. He smiled. He knew that some sort of Dwarven retribution would be in order.

"Well, I *was* in the area..." Muk professed, taking a deep breath, hoping for some enlightenment to wash over him. And then he felt it. It stemmed from a nagging regret. It had been a missed opportunity during his Mirthday party to identify himself and speak freely, to thank his Uncles, to acknowledge his friends. It was a situation much like now, with friendly faces gazing intently before him and his new family proudly sitting beside. Had it truly taken him nearly a year of travel to find the courage to speak unafraid?

"I am Pan Reuschal Kammuk!" declared Muk to a buzz of excited whispers. "My friends call me Muk!" he said proudly, but he chose not to turn and acknowledge their faces. "I am heir to the Realm of Valrhun and for nearly a year have I been on a journey, to discover the beauty of the terrain, the warmth of the people and customs...and something I least expected to find along the way...lasting friendship. We lost a brave warrior in our friend Quimby, but we found the gem that was stolen from your midst and have banished Edmund, the former Lord Governor, in lieu of kidnapping and attempted murder, to a place where I doubt he will ever bother you again."

Muk's last words were welcomed with cheers and applause. In fact, all five of the returning heroes had forgotten that Edmund's demise was not yet common knowledge. Muk took advantage of the momentary celebration to sit back down. Moralee found partial retribution with a solid

'I didn't know that' punch, but it did not awaken the slumbering Freda.

"I be Delphinea, beckoned from the Forests of Valjhune to protect Muk and the good of the Realm." Delphinea sat, followed by polite clapping.

"Now that you have met all the players," Nommie affirmed, waving to the others, "let me impart upon you the exact details of the happenings that transpired in the last seven days." As the tale moved from the Troll cabin, to Delphinea's *sudden* arrival, to the skeletal war, Muk was certain that Nommie must once have been a great orator, or perhaps could yet become one, as the story, with a few minor embellishments, was as grand a tale as he had ever heard.

"...that was an army of Goblins," Moralee once corrected him.

"It was a vast sea of Goblins the size of Hob-goblins!" he continued as if not interrupted. And on he went. Once or twice Muk wanted to point out a mistake or two in Nommie's valiant attempt to retell their tale, but decided upon silence instead. So he leaned back in his all too comfortable chair, with a slumbering Freda in his lap and closed his eyes to visions of their glorious journey.

Chapter Forty Four

Muk Awoke

...to the sound of clapping and cheering. Moralee was beside him and beckoning him to stand. Apparently, he had missed part of the story, because when he eventually pulled the sleeping child up to rest on his shoulder and stood, everyone including his exalted warrior friends were applauding him. "What did I miss?" he muttered.

"Oh...you know Nommie," was Oblio's reply, as they slowly moved through the crowded sitting room full of thank you's and handshakes.

"I know him alright...but what did he say?" Oblio just laughed and followed Moralee who was pressing her way through the congratulatory mob toward the much cooler air out on the porch. It wasn't any less crowded outside, but the air was cool and sweet. The Heaven's two moons were heavy and bright and their positions in the sky left no doubt that a good seven days had actually elapsed, but Muk couldn't figure out in his head how that could be so.

The Gnome led them off the porch and really seemed to be enjoying his new-found fame, but the others, trailing behind, were overwhelmed by the attention, especially Moralee, who found the custom of complete strangers reaching out to greet her or touch her, most uncomfortable.

Muk was just beginning to wonder if he was going to have to adopt little Freda, when two beaming Dwarves approached him. The father had her quizzical expression and the mother the flaming red hair.

"She is a delight!" Muk commended them, as he handed the sleeping child over to her mother. The praise might have been too much of a shock, for it left the smiling couple at a loss for words.

Just beyond 'The Keep's' heavy gates, the group was pulled in separate ways by their admirers. Even into the late evening, the activity on both sides of the street of the marketplace was as brisk as the cool night air.

"Muk!" hollered Nommie, waving from the porch of the former mercenary outpost. "This man wants a gold piece!" he added, handing Muk a pint of ale and gesturing for another.

"All I have on me is platinum," Muk apologized.

"Platinum?" cried the vendor. "You mean to say that the stories you told were true?" he added in amazement.

"Every word of it!" Muk said convincingly, flipping him the rarest of coins. He clanked Nommie's mug in celebration and they both laughed at the frothy spillover.

"Well, ah…I…haven't the change," the vendor stammered.

"Pour three more and keep the change!" declared Moralee, as the three girls stepped up to join them.

"I sure could do that!" the vendor agreed instantly.

"Hey…that's my money you're spending!" Muk pouted in jest.

"Hero always pay," Delphinea reminded him with a gracious hug. In the daylight, they might have seen the red in his face, but Muk was hoping that the darkness of night had covered it well.

"Well…next time then, I'm telling the story!" Muk professed to another solid clunk of mugs.

"To the next adventure," proclaimed Nommie.

"To the truth!" Moralee demanded of Muk, nearly knocking his drink out of his grasp. Immediately, they all began to laugh.

"To the night air!" Muk added, laughing as hard as he had in a long, long time.

Chapter Forty Five

A Heroes Celebration

...faded from the Pageleaf just as the dinner bell sounded. Mr. Wittlesey hovered just inside the entryway as the boys happily shuffled in from the knoll. He was surprised to find them subdued and well behaved as they ascended the stairs to wash up. By the time supper was served, the Headmaster's suspicions were beginning to ruin his appetite. Something was definitely up, but he had no clue as to what. Frank also took notice of the good-natured chatter and the uncharacteristically pleasant way the boys handed the food plates from table to table. They both were astounded when Eff rose from the table and climbed one step higher upon the bench.

"I believe it is a Gnome and Dwarven tradition," he began with his milk glass held high, "to raise our drinks in a toast!"

On cue, the boys all stood up sharply. Frank and Mr. Wittlesey hesitated, then imitated the others warily. Eff nodded to Walter, then had to elbow him.

"Yes…it is…uh," began Walter, who had to stop to turn

the piece of paper with his speech on it, right side up. "It is here-and-now decreed, that henceforth every boy who leaves The Rafferty Home for Boys is to be Knighted."

Mr. Wittlesey blinked in disbelief and Frank smiled. Chief was next to read and, raising his right hand, he turned to face McNaught.

"Do you...James Travis McNaught, swear to uphold the honour of 'Rafferty' in all you do from this day forward?" he demanded.

For a brief second, it appeared that McNaught might burst into tears.

And then it was Freckles Freddy Pohl's turn.

"And..." Freddy added, raising *his* right hand, "to help and honour every 'Rafferty' brother to follow?"

All eyes were glued to the oldest of the orphans. From the look on McNaught's face, it was plain to see that the toast and the honour had taken him by surprise. But the embarrassing moment passed quickly and he boldly stood with chin up and glass held high. The spontaneous words that followed were to forever echo through the halls of the Rafferty Home for Boys.

"By the honour of *this* 'Rafferty Knight'...I do swear!"

Finis

The Journey Trilogy
The Enlightened Journey of Eff C'effsky / Book One
The Circuitous Journey of Friendship / Book Two
The Unforeseen Journey Home / Book Three

The Royal Family Trilogy
The High King / Book Four
Queen of the Realm / Book Five
The Prince of the City / Book Six

Beyond The Walls Trilogy
The Whole of the Realm / Book Seven
Beyond the Realm / Book Eight
The Journey Home / Book Nine

Author Bio

Peter Dueber lives in Cannon Beach, a small resort community on the Oregon Coast. His quiet moments include writing poetry and tales of fantasy as well as enjoying long walks on the beach. Fortunately, his work allows him close observation of all the characters that surround him ~ family, friends and strangers alike.

CPSIA information can be obtained
at www.ICGtesting.com
Printed in the USA
FSOW02n1650241016
26513FS